SILENCE WAS FAR
FROM GOLDEN

It was bad enough that Rebecca Stanwood had to hide her true identity when she assumed the role of a humbled housemaid. Even worse, she had to pretend not to have the power of speech lest her tongue betrayed her.

Thus when her employer, Oliver Ransford, found her where she should not have been, she could not explain herself. Nor could she even call for help if he did what she had learned aristocratic gentlemen were wont to do with females at their mercy.

Swiftly she had to decide: Was it better to be stripped of her disguise—or stripped of something far more precious . . . ?

D0695739

APRIL KIHLSTROM was born in Buffalo, New York, and graduated from Cornell University with an M.S. in Operations Research. She lives with her husband and her two children in New Jersey.

Dangerous Masquerade

by

April Kihlstrom

A SIGNET BOOK

SIGNET
Published by the Penguin Group
Penguin Books USA Inc., 375 Hudson Street,
New York, New York, 10014, U.S.A.
Penguin Books Ltd, 27 Wrights Lane, London W8 5TZ, England
Penguin Books Australia Ltd, Ringwood, Victoria, Australia
Penguin Books Canada Ltd, 10 Alcorn Avenue, Toronto, Ontario, Canada M4V 3B2
Penguin Books (N.Z.) Ltd, 182-190 Wairau Road,
Auckland 10, New Zealand

Penguin Books Ltd, Registered Offices:
Harmondsworth, Middlesex, England

First published by Signet, an imprint of New American Library,
a division of Penguin Books USA Inc.

First Printing, April, 1992

10 9 8 7 6 5 4 3 2 1

1

The light was dim in the shabby drawing room of the hired house located in a far from distinguished part of town. None of the occupants of the room, however, troubled to light any candles. Indeed, it is most unlikely they even noticed the inconvenience, having long since grown accustomed to it. Rebecca Stanwood faced her stepbrother, Andrew Pierce, from across the room. Beside him stood Lord Templeton, a circumstance that could not please Miss Stanwood, and had she not felt it to be a useless gesture, she would have asked his lordship to leave.

The contrast between Miss Stanwood and Mr. Pierce was so marked that had one not been told, it would have been impossible to guess that they were related. And, indeed, the relationship was simply that of two people whose parents had married: her father and his mother. Miss Stanwood and Mr. Pierce were both dressed with propriety, but it could not be said that a brown coat of Bath cloth, biscuit-colored pantaloons, and poorly polished Hessians enhanced Andrew's dark complexion or stocky figure nearly so well as Rebecca's dress of blue figured muslin complemented her petite, fair prettiness. Both were cast in the shade by the exquisite evening wear of Lord Templeton, who wore a modishly cut coat of black superfine, impeccable knee breeches, an intricately tied cravat, and the finest of white linen shirts. Were it not for the lines of dissipation that already creased his youthful face, there would have been nothing to cavil at in Lord Templeton's appearance. But at seven and twenty, he had the face of a man years older, and a mouth that habitually formed a most unpleasant smile. Rebecca did not like him.

It could be seen even in the dim light that Miss Stanwood was very pale, but her voice was steady as she said, "Why did you not tell me sooner, Andrew, the trouble we were in?"

Flushed, Pierce turned away. Even an untrained eye would have realized that he had already been drinking heavily though it was not yet dusk. Over his shoulder he told her, "I did not know the full sum of it myself, Rebecca, until I sat down today to total up the figures."

"But you have discussed this with Lord Templeton?" Rebecca hazarded evenly.

Lord Templeton bowed at the mention of his name, a quizzical smile on his dissolute face. Still, he did not speak, a forbearance for which Rebecca was grateful. It was left to Pierce to answer, and after a moment he said defensively, "Yes, I did speak with Lord Templeton on the matter." He turned back to face his stepsister as he explained, "I'd lost track of how much we owe. Our debts must be paid somehow!"

There was a note of desperation in his voice, but Rebecca's was almost placid as she replied, sitting now on one of the upholstered chairs, "Do you know, Andrew, I think perhaps we should go back to America. It is quite evident that neither Papa's family nor my mama's mean to acknowledge me, and however much he may have wished me to be reconciled with them, Papa would have been the first to say we ought to face facts when they are inescapable."

Still Lord Templeton remained silently in the background. Pierce came and sat in a chair opposite Rebecca. He took one of her hands in his as he said bitterly, "We cannot go back to America, Rebecca. We don't have the money. What I've been trying to tell you is that we are rolled up! The house is paid for through the end of the quarter, and the servants have their wages that long as well, but I cannot pay a tenth of the bills in the desk nor any of what I owe Templeton."

"This is absurd," Rebecca said impatiently. "Papa's lawyer gave you a very generous letter of credit to draw on to pay our bills while we are in England. Surely we cannot have exhausted it already?"

"Oh, yes, we have," Andrew countered grimly. "You have no notion how the expenses have mounted up."

"Nor what it costs to move in the circles to which Lord Templeton has taken you?" Rebecca asked.

Pierce flushed. "It doesn't signify how the funds were spent," he answered curtly. "What matters is that there are debts of honor to be paid and I have not the money to do so."

Rebecca directed a measured look at Lord Templeton before she replied coolly, "And I collect you owe most of them to Lord Templeton. Well, perhaps Lord Templeton misunderstood when you explained our circumstances to him. Surely he would be willing to wait until you can arrange for funds to be sent from America."

Again Templeton bowed in her direction before he said, very gently but with an edge of steel in his voice, "I regret, dear lady, but I am most impatient to be repaid. One way or another."

Pierce glanced warningly at Templeton. "You mistake the matter, Rebecca!" he told his stepsister sharply. "Lord Templeton understands our situation perfectly. It is he who advised me to add up my bills and consider whether there were any way out of dun territory. As for asking him to wait, you must know that it is customary to pay one's gambling debts without delay."

"Could you not borrow from someone else?" Rebecca asked. "Just until your mama or Papa's lawyer could send us more funds?"

"I've already tried the cents-per-centers," Andrew retorted impatiently. "Weeks ago when I first started losing at cards. They won't lend money to a mere provincial who has nothing to offer as collateral."

"What are we to do, then?" Rebecca asked quietly. "Are you telling me it must be debtor's prison for the pair of us?"

Pierce hesitated. He took a turn about the room before he replied angrily. "It's not entirely my fault, you know. You had an entire summer to look about you and find a husband. Lord, when I think of the blunt I dropped on clothing for you, I cannot understand why you wasted your chances. If you had only contrived to marry well—"

Abruptly Rebecca cut him short. "You forget, Andrew, that we could not succeed in gaining the entrée to where I might meet an eligible bridegroom."

"You met gentlemen here and you wasted those chances, playing the grand lady as though you were too proud for them," he retorted darkly.

Rebecca looked down at her hands, then at her stepbrother. Her face was grim with dislike as she said, her voice low but determined, "You are a fool if you think any of those gentlemen meant marriage by me. Nor even if they had, would I have consented to marriage with any of them."

Again Pierce sat down facing his stepsister. He took her hands in his. "Listen, Rebecca. I don't say I want you to marry just to oblige me, I only say that it would have been the end of all our troubles if you had."

Rebecca pulled her hands free and eyed her stepbrother with suspicion. Her voice was calm, however, as she asked, "What, then, do you want of me, Andrew?"

"Just to be a little nicer to my friends," he replied, avoiding her eyes. "Take Lord Templeton, for example. Just be nice to him when he calls." When Rebecca did not at once reply, Pierce pressed his advantage. "Templeton's not really such a bad sort, when you get to know him. Just give him a chance. He wants to please you. Why, he told me he means to take you to a party in Medmenham, tonight, where all sorts of members of the Quality will attend."

"Medmenham?" Rebecca repeated the name with a frown. "Where is that?" she asked suspiciously.

"Lord, I don't know. What does it signify? You'll find out when you get there," Pierce replied impatiently as he avoided her eyes.

"When I get there," she repeated again. "What do you mean? Aren't you coming?" she asked.

Templeton judged it time to intervene and he stepped forward from where he had been leaning against the wall, listening. "My dear Miss Stanwood, of course your stepbrother is to come. Indeed, you both will be honored guests at this affair, I promise you."

Still she looked obstinate. Pierce turned to Templeton and said shortly, "Will you wait in the hall for a moment, Templeton? I wish to speak with my stepsister alone."

Templeton bowed and withdrew. When he was gone, Pierce returned to the matter at hand. "Please, Rebecca, go with us tonight. And be nice to Templeton."

"Why?" Rebecca asked gently. "What difference can it make?"

Pierce looked at his stepsister consideringly and said, "You heard him: Templeton doesn't wish to wait to be paid what I owe him. But he will wait if he thinks you might be open to his suit." He paused and then added off-handedly, "Indeed, I have reason to believe Templeton will cease to press me to pay my gambling vowels and even give me a generous loan if only you will go to Medmenham with him tonight. What a dust up you are making over such a very simple request."

Rebecca went very cold. "What is at Medmenham?" she asked, quietly but implacably.

Pierce hesitated, then shrugged. "Lord, I don't know and I don't care," he told her mendaciously. "But this much I do know: you'll go upstairs and dress, in something white and pretty, or I'll drag you upstairs and dress you myself! The situation is too desperate for me to listen to any missish excuses."

Stiffly, Rebecca got to her feet. It was of no use to argue with Andrew when he was as drunk, as she realized him to be. Though they had never been close and she had long recognized that he was mildly jealous of her, it was only since coming to London that his jealousy had flared into active

April Kihlstrom

resentment. Indeed, there were days when she felt she no longer knew her stepbrother. But she did recognize the malevolent influence he had fallen under and acted accordingly. "I'll go upstairs and change," she said quietly. "What time do we leave for Medmenham?"

"That's a good girl," Pierce said enthusiastically. "Templeton didn't say, but you'd best be ready as quickly as possible."

Rebecca didn't reply but merely went out of the drawing room, holding her skirts aside to let Templeton pass her into the room. She ought, of course, to have immediately gone upstairs. Instead, she pressed her ear against the door in hopes of hearing something useful. The voices were a trifle muffled but the door was of a poor quality wood and she found she could hear surprisingly well. The crack of laughter that greeted some sally Templeton made was unmistakable. So, too, were Andrew's next words. "Do you really mean it? Am I really to be allowed to join the Hellfire Club tonight?"

Templeton's voice was calmer and quieter but Rebecca could still understand his reply. "With your sister as the price of entry, I guarantee you, Andrew, you will not be denied."

"What will happen to her afterwards?" Andrew asked, his voice a little less certain now.

There was a long silence and Rebecca had to strain to hear the answer when it finally came. "You will not be troubled by her again," Templeton said softly, "of that I promise you."

It was enough. Rebecca fled upstairs. Even had she never heard of the Hellfire Club, the name alone would have been sufficient to terrify her. But she had heard of it, in this very house. At first there had been half-understood jests among some of the gentlemen who frequented this house. Then, as the hour had grown later and the men had thought Rebecca safely abed, talk had grown more explicit. But Rebecca had crept down to listen at the door, not trusting her stepbrother's guests. While she might not know the precise nature of the place, Rebecca knew too much to go to Medmenham. To do so would not only place her virtue but possibly her life at risk.

Upstairs, the maid who waited on Rebecca had already laid out a white gown for her to wear. "Mr. Pierce said you was to look your best, Miss," she explained quickly.

"I see." Rebecca advanced into the room and closed the door behind her. Calmly she walked over to her dressing table and sat down facing the girl. "Betty, what do you think of Lord Templeton?" she asked thoughtfully.

The name exerted a strange effect upon the maid. Betty shivered and crossed herself, then said fearfully, "Mr. Dobbs, he says I'm to stay out of his lordship's way," she said, naming the butler who oversaw the running of the house Andrew had hired. "He says it's a fair shame Mr. Pierce has taken up with him and some of them others what comes here. Calls them kin to Satan, he does."

Rebecca was silent a long moment, so long that she frightened the girl. "Are you all right, Miss?" Betty asked anxiously.

"No, I'm not," Rebecca replied finally. "I find I must go away if I am to escape Lord Templeton's unwelcome attentions, for my stepbrother is too drunk and too much in Templeton's power to try to stop them. So you must help me."

"How, Miss?" the girl asked doubtfully.

"I'm not sure yet. If I run away, Andrew and Lord Templeton are sure to follow," Rebecca said, thinking aloud. "And where can I go? I have no friends in England. Nor much money. And who would hide me from my own stepbrother?"

"It's a pity you're not a servant," the girl said hesitantly. "No one notices us."

Rebecca turned her head to look at the girl, her eyes opening very wide. For a long time she didn't speak, turning the idea over in her head. It was mad, of course, to think of disguising herself as a servant. One simply didn't do such things. How could she get away with it? And yet, why not? Discovery would mean social ruin, if Rebecca had ever had any social status here to protect, but she did not. And it would be far better than to accompany Templeton to Medmenham. She must protect herself. The more she considered the notion of taking the part of a servant, the more it seemed to Rebecca that it would solve many of her problems. The money she had saved, unknown to Andrew, was not enough to pay her passage home. She could write to her father's partner or to her stepmother to send her more, but what was she to do until then? When they had first arrived in London, she and Andrew had stayed at a fashionable hotel and Rebecca still cringed as she recalled the bill Andrew had been called upon to pay. That was why he had decided it would be more prudent to hire a house for the rest of their stay. She could never afford to stay in such a hotel now. But in a more modest establishment, perhaps one meant for those who came to London to become servants, that she might be able to afford. At least for one night. If she took employment as a servant, surely Rebecca would be housed and fed and need have no further charges on her purse. And surely it would be easier to obtain a post as a maid than as a governess for, even cloistered as she had been, Rebecca was well aware that without references she could not hope to obtain any such post. Nor did a look in the mirror do aught but confirm her belief that any potential mistress would consider her too pretty to serve as a governess in any fashionable home even if she possessed the requisite skills to do so. What mistress would hire a girl who spoke as she did, her accent marking her an American? But as a maid, surely a mistress would not count her youth against her. Or care how she spoke. Nor could anything be easier than to write herself a reference. For while Miss Stanwood of Boston could not hope to pretend to provide a reference for a governess, she could and did employ maids.

At last, after Rebecca had turned the thought about in every conceivable way, she said to Betty, "Do you think you could find me clothes like yours to wear?"

The girl bobbed a curtsy. "Yes, Miss. Mary, what left unexpectedly, wore just your size. Up and left everything, she did. Mr. Dobbs said we was to keep it in case she returned, but Mary told me there was a gentleman what promised her parties and fancy dresses and she weren't never coming back."

"Then bring me her dress. Do you think you can do that without being seen?" Rebecca asked anxiously.

"I'll manage," the girl vowed, "but you never mean you're going to do it?"

"I haven't much choice," Rebecca said bitterly. Her voice changed as she added briskly, "But I don't want you to get in trouble. I'll take the white dress Mr. Pierce wanted me to wear, as well as the stockings, gloves and such that go with it, and carry all of that in my small traveling bag, the one under my bed. That way he'll think I left wearing that dress and never guess how you helped me. Do you know of any inn where I might stay for the night? And where I might go to find employment tomorrow?"

The girl hesitated. She was able to give Rebecca the names of a number of reputable agencies where she might try her luck on the morrow in finding a job, but was at a loss as to advise her where to stay. "For me mum and dad lives in Lunnon so I never had need of such," she explained.

"Never mind," Rebecca assured the girl, "I shall find something."

"How will you get out of the house unseen?" Betty asked doubtfully, after a moment.

Rebecca smiled wryly. "Surely you must know as well as I that at this hour our porter spends more of his time in the kitchen flirting with the cook, or down in the wine cellar, than at his post," she said. "And if you do not, Andrew does. Depend upon it, he will never suspect that I escaped dressed as a servant unless someone tells him."

"Well, I won't," the girl avowed fervently. "There's not many belowstairs like Mr. Pierce half as well as we likes you!"

Rebecca was startled and touched by the girl's partisanship. "Thank you," she said. "I shan't forget it. But we must hurry. I must be away before I am asked for downstairs."

Hastily Rebecca wrote out a reference for one Phoebe Finley, taking care to use her best hand. The money she had saved out of a nagging sense of prudence, when Andrew would have had her spend it on herself, went into her plainest reticule. Then Rebecca bundled up the dress as well as the stockings, gloves, petticoats, and pearl necklace and earrings she would have worn with it into the traveling bag. As for a cloak, her own would have to do. None of the servants would have one to spare, even if she dared ask for it. But her own was worn enough that anyone seeing it might guess a kind mistress had discarded it as too shabby and given it to her maid. Then Rebecca brushed her hair out in as plain a style as she could manage, tying it back with a sober colored ribbon. By the time her maid returned with the clothes, Rebecca was ready and it was a matter of moments to change her dress for the simpler one Mary had worn. It did not fit her exactly, but that was only to be expected and did not trouble Rebecca. Over the dress went the cloak and, finally, from under her pillow she drew out a pistol. At the sight of it, Betty gasped. "Oh, Miss," she said, "wherever did you get that wicked looking thing?"

Rebecca stared at the silver-handled object, and it was a long moment before she answered. "I bought it, some weeks ago," she said at last, "when I knew that the day might come when I would have to defend my honor in this house."

"Is it loaded?" Betty asked.

"Yes," Rebecca replied calmly.

She slipped it into the pocket of her cloak and then, with Betty to spy out if the coast was clear, Rebecca made her way downstairs as silently as possible. She had a moment's tremor as she passed the drawing room door, for here was her greatest danger. But as she had expected, the sounds from within the room made it clear that both Andrew and Lord Templeton were dipping freely into the brandy.

Down in the front hall, it was necessary to wait until Betty made sure the porter was not at his post. But that took only a moment and then, in a flash, Rebecca was out the front door, ignoring the startled looks of a passerby who clearly wondered what a servant was doing here instead of at the back of the house.

2

Oliver Ransford had a singularly sweet countenance. This, along with his moderate height, slender build, and fair coloring, often led people to underestimate him. It was a mistake few made twice, for he had a lively intelligence, a wicked way with a small sword, could culp nine wafers out of ten at Manton's, and possessed what devotees of the Fancy called a punishing right. At six and twenty he was the possessor of one of the largest fortunes in England, and if he did not hold a title, it was not because his ancestors could not have had one had they so desired. But the Ransfords had always been content to be simply Ransfords, and had looked as high as they wished when they chose to marry. Indeed, Oliver Ransford's own mother, the Lady Sarah Ransford, was the daughter of a duke. It was said that he had inherited much of his sweetness from her.

At the moment, on a rather chilly September night, he was walking in the small garden at the back of his townhouse pondering his future. It had begun to rain, but Oliver Ransford did not regard it, for he was too preoccupied with his own thoughts. That he was bored could not be denied. Gambling at White's, tying his neckcloth in new and intricate ways, embarking upon outrageous pranks, none of these had held his attention for long. Politics might have interested him, but lacking a peerage, Ransford had no seat in the House of Lords and no desire for a seat in the House of Commons. The past five months had seen his estates put in good enough train that very little effort would be required to keep them that way. Science interested him, but not to the point of carrying out experiments of his own and there were already, in his opinion, far too many people trying to decipher the Rosetta Stone. Commerce did not interest Ransford, and the diplomatic corps had no need of his talents. What, then, was he to do? It was his mother's opinion that what he required was a wife and then to begin to set up his own nursery. She had not said so, of course. Lady Sarah was both too kind and too shrewd to attempt to interfere in such a way, but Ransford was aware of how she felt. He would have liked to oblige her, but when he looked about, none of the eligible young ladies he saw held the slightest interest for him. They were all of them too alike, or so it seemed. If the truth be known, Ransford was rather too straight-laced for his times, though one would scarcely have called him a prude. He had had his opera dancers and kicked up larks with the other young men of his generation, and enjoyed doing so as well. But it could not be denied that he had an odd, upright streak in his nature that kept him from throwing himself whole-heartedly into any of these pursuits. A part of him was forever considering the consequences, particularly to others, of what he had done.

As Ransford was walking, lost in thought, he stumbled over something on the unlit path. There was a gasp nearby, and he found himself looking for the source of that gasp. Hidden behind a bench, he found a furtive figure crouched far back into the shrubbery. With some anger, Ransford grasped the person by the arm and yanked. "A thief, are you?" he demanded impatiently. "Well you've made a mistake, coming here! I'll hand you over to the authorities and we'll see how you like—"

Abruptly Ranford's voice cut off as he pulled the figure to its feet and realized to his astonishment that he held a woman who was clutching a small traveling bag. She was young, not above three and twenty, he thought, and very pale. Blond curls peeped out from the hood of her shabby cloak and dark, wide eyes stared up at him, terrified. She was, he thought, beautiful. "Are you all right?" he asked, wanting to allay that terror in her eyes.

Rebecca stared up at the gentleman who held her. He was not overly tall, and yet he was taller than she and far stronger. It was impossible to pull free even if she had wanted to, and Rebecca was far from sure that she wanted to break free. And yet she could not tell him who she was. What if he felt it was his duty to return her to her stepbrother's care? And even if he did not, she had no reason to feel safe in his power, for while his face was regarding her kindly at the moment, she could not forget the implacable anger with which he had seized her. Terrified, Rebecca dared not speak. The moment she did so, her accent would give her away as an American. Then, if Andrew came searching for her, this man would be able to tell him she had been here, dressed as a servant. And if he knew that, how long would it take Andrew or Lord Templeton to run her to ground? Perhaps if she said nothing, this gentleman would simply let her go. It had been a mistake to seek refuge in his garden, but the man following her had been growing too pointed in his remarks and she had been able to think of nothing else to do. Who would have thought anyone would be mad enough to take a turn about the garden on a night as chilly and wet as this?

Still the girl did not answer and Ransford's gentle voice prodded her. "Are you all right?" he repeated. "You're shivering. Come into the house where you can be warm and tell me what the trouble is." The girl shook her head, clearly frightened, and Ransford made his voice more gentle than ever as he said, "How came you to be here, alone, without even your maid to attend you?"

With a wry twist to her lips, Rebecca let her cloak fall back so that the gentleman holding her had a glimpse of her simple homespun gown. That he was surprised was evident, for his grasp slackened for a moment and his mouth opened in astonishment. Then it closed with a snap and his voice turned stern as he demanded, "Who are you and what are you doing here?"

When Rebecca still didn't answer, he began to pull her toward the house where he might get a better look at the girl. His first impression had been an indefinable one that she might be Quality. The second, just now, was that she could not be. When he reached the light thrown by the torches by the house, however, her cloak fell open again and he saw the dress she wore more clearly. Ransford, like most gentlemen, had never paid any great attention to the clothes worn by his servants, but he still could recognize this dress as something of the same sort. "Are you someone's maidservant?" he murmured in surprise.

The girl in his grasp nodded vigorously, and a little of the color came back into her cheeks.

"Whose?" he demanded.

But the girl did not answer. She only regarded him with the same wide, dark eyes as before. Ransford was puzzled. He didn't think the girl a half-wit, though that was the first explanation which came to mind. A moment later he asked, looking hard at her face. "Can you talk?"

She shook her head, then bowed it before he could catch more than the flash of something in her eyes. Thinking she might be ashamed of her handicap, Ransford took her chin in his hand and tilted it up so that she was again looking at him. Immediately she jerked her chin free and tried to break his grasp on her. But it was implacable. "No," he said, sternly. She froze in evident fear and he could feel her tremble in his hold. "I don't mean to hurt you," he went on in the same voice as before, "but neither do I mean to simply let you go. Why were you in my garden? Were you trying to steal something?"

At that her chin came up on its own accord and Ransford found himself confronted by two flashing eyes as the girl shook her head angrily. "So you were not here to steal," he said thoughtfully. "What, then? Running away from something? Hiding?" The face before him took on a half-frightened, half-melancholy look and Ransford pressed his advantage. "Were you running from your employer?" he asked.

Again she shook her head emphatically. Again Ransford paused to think. "Were you hiding from someone on the street? Someone who accosted you?" he asked.

She nodded, her eyes meeting his. "Where do you live?" he asked. "Won't your employer be missing you by now?"

And again there was that half-frightened, half-melancholy look and a quick shake of her head. "Have you a long way to go or does your employer live nearby?" he asked with concern.

Had he not had such sharp eyes, Ransford might have missed the momentary stillness, the infinitesimal hesitation before she nodded. "Liar!" he told her bluntly. That made her jump and look up at him and then swiftly away. "You haven't any job, just now, have you?" he said impatiently. "Or any place to go, either," he added bluntly.

This time her hesitation was more apparent. Abruptly Ransford made up his mind. "I have need of a kitchen maid," he said in clipped tones. "You'll do. You'd best start tonight."

The girl looked at him, fear and suspicion in her eyes. For a long moment Ransford thought she would refuse, and he waited for her to make up her mind.

Rebecca, if the truth be told, found herself in something of a quandry. She was accustomed to making decisions quickly and easily, but tonight she found she could not. It was madness, perhaps, to trust this gentleman and to take a position in his household. She knew nothing about him. But that was the point, was it not? To take a position in a household where she and her stepbrother were unknown? At least this gentleman had shown no disposition to take advantage of her situation. Certainly she must be on her guard, but for now it was a position and she had need of one. Even saving the cost of one night's lodging would be a help when it came time to purchase her passage home. That was what decided Rebecca. That and a pair of kind, blue eyes that gazed at her and made her pulse flutter. Which was, of course, absurd and a reason not to take a position in his household. But somehow Rebecca found herself nodding and allowing herself to be led inside where the gentleman presented her to the housekeeper.

"Mrs. Marsh, I've just hired this girl," Rebecca's captor said, drawing her forward into the light of the kitchen candles.

"In what position, Mr. Ransford?" Mrs. Marsh asked, bewildered.

Ransford waved his free hand carelessly. "In whatever position you find her most useful, of course," he said, frowning slightly.

"Has she references?" Mrs. Marsh asked suspiciously.

Ransford looked at Rebecca. "Have you any references?" he asked her, with some amusement.

To his surprise, she nodded and drew out the letter she had written for herself some few hours earlier. Ransford took it with another sharp look at her. Rebecca schooled herself to let her face give away nothing. Ransford read the letter in silence then gave it back to her. "Apparently this girl, Phoebe, worked for a lady who had had to economize and therefore released Phoebe from her services," Ransford said to Mrs. Marsh.

Mrs. Marsh sniffed. "I don't like it, sir," she said emphatically.

Ransford regarded his housekeeper with gentle, laughing eyes. His voice was firm, however, as he said, "Nevertheless you will accept my wishes in this matter, Mrs. Marsh. This girl is to be given employment on my staff."

"Yes, Mr. Ransford," Mrs. Marsh said, marked disapproval still evident in her voice. She turned to Rebecca and said briskly, "Well, my girl, what talents do you have?"

Rebecca looked at Ransford and he was quick to see the pleading look in her eyes. "I collect the girl cannot speak," he told Mrs. Marsh. "But I am sure that if you put her to work wherever she is needed, you will find her satisfactory."

Mrs. Marsh meant to keep a harsh tone with the girl, but at these words and Rebecca's emphatic nodding of her head, Mrs. Marsh found she was not proof against the wide, dark eyes any more than Ransford had been. "Can't talk? Poor thing! Well, I should think we can find something for her to do. There's always an extra hand needed in the kitchen or to dust the parlors. Can you do that, girl?"

Again Rebecca nodded emphatically and Mrs. Marsh softened further. "Well, there's no harm in taking her on, I suppose, sir," Mrs. Marsh said grudgingly. "Though mind, if I find she can't do the work, I shall be forced to ask permission to dismiss her," Mrs. Marsh warned Ransford.

He bowed to her. "Of course, Mrs. Marsh," he said, not in the least deceived by her stern tone. Ransford looked down at Rebecca who smiled shyly up at him, as though to thank him, and realized for the first time what a sweet face she had. "I'll leave you with my housekeeper, now," he told her kindly. "She'll show you how to go on. Your wages will be ten guineas a year, half to be paid after six months. Is that satisfactory?"

Only ten guineas? And none to be paid for six months? With luck she would be gone by then, Rebecca thought. Still, it was a place to stay and she would have her food. Andrew would never think to search for her here. Since it would clearly not do to look either surprised or dismayed, Rebecca made herself curtsy and nod as though perfectly satisfied with what the gentleman had said.

Rebecca did not want him to leave. And yet, she could not help but feel safer when his intelligent eyes were no longer on her. Instead she had the housekeeper looking her over. "Well, you'd best hang your cloak over there, and put your bag down under it. You can take them upstairs later," Mrs. Marsh said briskly when Ransford was gone.

Rebecca put her cloak on a peg by the servants' door and then turned and waited until the housekeeper looked at her from head to toe. Her hair was dressed plainly enough, and her dress was a common working dress, but when Mrs. Marsh's eyes reached Rebecca's feet, they narrowed and she spoke sharply as she said, "Hold out your foot, girl!"

With some misgiving, Rebecca did so. The dainty shoes
she wore were her own, for it had not occurred to her to
wear any others. But it was not the shoes that excited Mrs.
Marsh's greatest disapproval. "Silk stockings!" she
exclaimed, as though appalled. Her next words furthered that
impression. "Well, Phoebe, my girl, it's plain to me,
whatever Mr. Ransford might think, why you lost your last
place! And you needn't be thinking you'll get away with that
sort of thing here. Not in my house, you won't. Cast your
eyes up at Mr. Ransford and you'll find yourself in the street
in a minute, for I can't and won't abide such behavior. No,
nor you hadn't better let Lady Sarah, as is Mr. Ransford's
mother, see you wearing silk stockings neither, or you'll find
yourself in the street even faster. You'll wear plain worsted
stockings like a good Christian girl or seek another place!"

Rebecca regarded Mrs. Marsh unhappily. Without
meaning to, she let her shoulders slump. Where was she to
find worsted stockings? It had been a monumental error not
to think of such a thing before she left home, but there had
been no time. And now it looked as though her error would
cost her this place.

In that fear, however, Rebecca had reckoned without Mr.
Ransford's influence. In her experience, gentlemen never
took any interest in domestic matters and Rebecca assumed
that having placed her on his staff, Mr. Ransford would no
doubt have forgotten her by morning. Mrs. Marsh knew
otherwise and that was what stayed her from dismissing the
girl on the spot. Mr. Ransford would remember the girl and
want to know how she was getting on. If Mrs. Marsh dismissed her, she'd best have a good reason. One better than
that the girl wore the wrong kind of stockings. But she would
not abide silk stockings on the girl. Why it would scandalize
the entire staff if she did so, and not a one of them would
believe the girl to be an innocent, even if she was one. Which
Mrs. Marsh took leave to doubt. But Mr. Ransford had
plainly taken one of his fancies to the girl and that meant
she'd best step warily.

"I suppose you haven't any plain worsted stockings?" Mrs. Marsh asked sourly, correctly interpreting the expression on Rebecca's face. Rebecca shook her head. "Well, I'll give you a pair and you can pay me back out of your wages," she grumbled. "But only one pair, mind. And it'll be your job to keep them well darned and make them last."

Rebecca nodded gratefully. She dared not tell Mrs. Marsh she could afford to pay for them, for it was evident the woman thought her penniless. Rebecca dared do nothing that would draw attention to her differences from the other servants. Nor did she dare speak, for she could not sound like them and they would know at once she was an impostor.

Mrs. Marsh noted, with approval, the girl's modestly downcast eyes. Perhaps she was mistaken and the stockings were the gift of a kind mistress who had decided she did not want them after all. Time must tell. For now, there was work to be done and it would be best to begin with the girl as she meant to go on. "Do as you're told and we'll get along fine," Mrs. Marsh said grudgingly. "And don't be thinking you'll be a proper parlormaid or any such windfall; we've a full staff already. You'll be a maid of all sorts, wherever you're needed. Later, if one of my other girls leaves, well, then we'll see. You'll begin by scrubbing those flagstones," she told Rebecca. "The chef spilled some of the sauce he were making for dinner. You'll find what you need over there. When you're done, there's dunamany pots to clean as well. There's silver sand and vinegar for that over here."

3

Andrew Pierce gave his stepsister rather more than an hour and a half to get ready for the expedition to Medmenham. When she had still not appeared in the drawing room by then and Lord Templeton had begun to show signs of impatience, he went upstairs to fetch her. To his consternation, however, Andrew found his stepsister's room empty. A swift look around served to assure him that the dress he had had her maid lay out earlier in the day was gone. And the dress she had been wearing lay across the bed. Puzzled, he rang the bell pull to summon the maid. A few minutes later the girl appeared and curtsied to him. "Where is your mistress?" he asked with a frown.

"I dunno," the girl said with wide, innocent eyes. "She dressed some time ago and went downstairs."

"Downstairs?" Pierce echoed incredulously. "To the drawing room?"

"I dunno," the girl repeated. "Just downstairs."

"She dressed, you said?" Pierce asked, looking around again to be sure the white gown was indeed gone.

"Oh, yes, sir," Betty said promptly. "The white gown, it was. The one you told me to lay out for her."

It was perhaps fortunate for the maid that Pierce was so thoroughly under the hatches or he might have noticed the look of intense satisfaction that attended this reply. Still befuddled, Pierce swiftly went out and began to make a rapid inspection of every room on the floor.

When that search failed to turn up any sign of his step-

sister, Pierce proceeded to try all the rooms on the other
floors of the house. But Rebecca was nowhere to be found
and none of the servants could recall having seen her. Since
they did not trouble to hide their amusement at his
discomfort, Pierce damned their eyes and went back upstairs
to the drawing room to tell Lord Templeton that his stepsister had disappeared. At the sight of Templeton's expectant
gaze and memory of all the gambling vowels that were held,
however, Andrew's courage failed him and instead he said,
"Sorry to be so long, Templeton, but the thing is, m'stepsister's feeling a trifle under the weather. She won't be able
to go with us to Medmenham tonight."

Lord Templeton considered. Andrew Pierce had arrived
in London some months earlier in company with his stepsister, Miss Rebecca Stanwood. A chance encounter with
Pierce on the steps of Lord Stanwood's townhouse had led
to their acquaintance. Templeton had recognized at a glance
a kindred spirit, albeit one that had not heretofore received
any encouragement to blossom. Templeton had been at pains
to provide that encouragement, taking Andrew under his
wing and introducing him to the worst of the *ton*. Andrew
met high-spirited blades who combined greater or lesser
degrees of fortune with a propensity for the excitement of
gambling, boxing the watch, attending cock fights and prize
fights in the worst parts of town, and a taste for depravity
in all its forms. With such encouragement Pierce's own
tastes, in this regard, had grown and become more and more
flagrant as Templeton introduced him to worse and worse
corners of town. Templeton had done so not just for the
amusement of dragging Pierce down to his own level, but
because he had decided, upon his first meeting with Rebecca
Stanwood, to possess her. Had she shown any signs of
succumbing to his charm, he would have made her his
mistress. Indeed, as a step toward doing so he had privately
encouraged the Stanwoods' suspicions of her claim of kinship
and their belief that she was an impostor. But Miss Stanwood
had disdained, openly, the attentions of Lord Templeton. And

the same instincts which had told him, infallibly, that Andrew Pierce was a kindred soul, had also told him that Miss Stanwood was not, that she would settle for nothing short of marriage. Fortunately for his reputation, she had been so unswerving in this disdain of him that he had never been tempted to see if she would be agreeable to an honorable proposal from him. Two weeks past, Templeton had hit upon the notion of bringing Miss Stanwood to a gathering in Medmenham of the Hellfire Club. Not only would he then be able to possess her, but so would every other fellow present. Oh, yes, Lord Templeton would have his revenge for every gesture of her disdain of him. To that end, he had set about arranging matters so that not only was Pierce directly in debt to him, but so that he held the vouchers others had won from Pierce as well. That was in the nature of insurance. He wanted to be certain that Pierce would not, at the last moment, draw back from some vestige of decency Templeton had not yet had time to purge. Was that, he wondered, what was afoot right now?

Templeton stared at Pierce in disbelief and his face was marked by a pronounced sneer as he said, at last, "You appear to forget your circumstances, Andrew. I suggest you counsel Miss Stanwood to overcome her headache and come with us to Medmenham, after all. Surely you can convince her of the wisdom of doing so. Particularly when you have such excellent reasons to, er, fortify you. Unless, of course, you no longer wish to be a member of the Hellfire Club? Or perhaps you wish to repose in a debtor's prison for a while?"

Pierce's cravat appeared to have been tied too tightly, for he gave it a tug. "You mistake the matter," he said quickly. "Rebecca is truly ill."

"Indeed?" Templeton looked down at his impeccably manicured hand a moment before he said, "Do you know, it is a most lowering reflection to realize that I have been so mistaken in your character. I would have sworn that you cherished no foolish scruples and that your love of the unusual, shall we say, was almost as great as my own. A pity. Ah, well. I thought we had an understanding, but if you choose to renege that is your affair.''

This last part was said with a delicate shrug and Pierce shuddered. As Templeton turned to go, Pierce held out a hand to stop him. "Wait!" he cried.

"Yes?" Templeton said, pausing and arching an eyebrow.

Pierce flung himself into a chair and ran a hand through his hair. "She's not here. Rebecca's run away. I discovered it when I went upstairs just now, to find out what was taking her so long to come down.''

For a moment it seemed as though Templeton were frozen in place. But at last he spoke. "Where? When?" he demanded harshly. "And why didn't you say so at once?"

Flat despair filled Pierce's voice as he replied, "I didn't want to tell you because, well, because I hoped I could find her before you need know about it.''

"It would seem the lady does not appreciate my company,'' Templeton said smoothly, and a silent laugh shook his shoulders.

"That doesn't seem to discourage you," Pierce said sharply.

"No, it doesn't," Templeton agreed. "It adds, shall we say, spice to the situation. Or it shall when we find her."

Hope dawned again in Pierce's eyes. "Do you mean to help me look?" he asked.

"Oh, assuredly, I shall help you look for Miss Stanwood," Templeton agreed grimly. "And for that reason I repeat my questions. When did Miss Stanwood leave and where might she have gone?"

Pierce spread his hands helplessly. "Rebecca must have left sometime after she went upstairs, for she did go upstairs. And her maid says she did dress in the white gown I chose for her to wear tonight. But the maid has no idea where she could have gone after that.''

Templeton's dark eyes snapped together in distinct annoyance. "It appears Miss Stanwoold did not approve of the treat in store for her. A white dress, you say? An evening dress? That at least is encouraging, for while she might pass unremarked tonight, by tomorrow morning she must stand out. Unless she packed a bag?"

Pierce frowned. "I didn't think to look. But the maid said nothing of the sort and I should think she would have noticed if anything had been missing from Rebecca's dressing table."

"She appears to have fled in some haste, then," Templeton said with a smile that made even Andrew Pierce uneasy. "Good. It means that she has not thought things through. Rest assured that I shall find her. But are you quite certain you have no idea where she could have gone?"

There was a hint of menace in his lordship's voice and Pierce made haste to answer, "On my honor, I do not! Rebecca has made no friends here and the Stanwoods have made it quite plain that they will have nothing to do with her. Nor will her mother's family. She hasn't any money to speak of. At most she could have enough for a hotel for a night or two. But even if she does, would a proper hotel take her in, arriving as she must without proper baggage or a maid to attend her?" he asked.

Templeton shrugged. "I shall know soon enough," he said. "It is a place to start, at any rate. Or, rather, the second place to look. Frankly, I think we should begin here. Have you questioned the servants? Could she be hiding in the house?"

"I've talked to the servants—they know nothing," Pierce said sullenly.

"Then how did she leave? If she went out the back, they must have seen her," Templeton said with a frown, "and if she went out the front door she must have been seen by the porter."

Pierce snorted. "It's plain you don't know my porter. He spends more time drunk than at his post. As for Rebecca still being in the house, that's absurd. What would she gain by that?"

"She might have hoped to avoid accompanying me to

Medmenham tonight," Templeton pointed out dryly. "In any event, I really must insist we search the house, Pierce."

"Oh, very well," Pierce replied, still sullen, "though I tell you I have already done so. At least, I've searched everywhere except in the servants' garret." He got to his feet somewhat unsteadily. "Where do you want to start?"

"The kitchen, of course," Templeton said with raised eyebrows. "And from there we shall work our way upwards. Then if Miss Stanwood is in the house and seeks to escape us, we shall have cut off her route to the door." As Andrew still hesitated, Templeton became impatient. "Lead on, Pierce. If we find her quickly enough, there is still time to reach Medmenham in order to make your stepsister the center of tonight's festivities."

With more alacrity now, Pierce did so. It soon became evident that Templeton meant to be chillingly efficient about the search. He began in the housekeeper's rooms, much to the poor woman's indignation. He proceeded through the kitchen and storerooms and up the stairs to each floor in turn, checking every room on each floor. Nor did Templeton hesitate to negotiate the steep, uncarpeted steps that went up to the attic where the rest of the servants had their quarters. Then it was back down to the kitchen, by way of the servants' staircase, to line them all up and demand who might know where Miss Stanwood had gone.

Templeton regarded them all silently for several long moments, frustration evident on his aquiline face. At last he spoke, his voice sharp enough to make several of the servants jump. "Who was the last one of you to see Miss Stanwood this evening?"

At first no one answered. Finally one of the maidservants said, timidly, "I s'pose it must have been me, m'lord."

"When did you see her?"

"It was when I went up with some fresh hot water. A couple of hours ago, it must have been. I laid out the white dress Mr. Pierce said she was to wear, and I helped her into it. Then she sent me away. Said she wanted to sit and think a while before dinner,'' Betty said quickly, as though frightened of Templeton.

As well she might have been, Pierce thought, pitying the poor girl. Templeton turned his full stare on her. "Indeed?" he said, his voice soft as silk. "And she said nothing of plans to go out?"

The girl seemed to shrink away from him as she replied, "N-no, m'lord. Why would she?"

That served to check Templeton. "Why, indeed?" he said as though to himself. Templeton looked over the assembled servants speculatively, then shrugged. "Bah!" he said. "They're of no use to me. Come, Andrew, a word with you upstairs."

In silence, Pierce followed Templeton back to the drawing room where he watched as his lordship paced about the room for several minutes. The clock on the mantel chimed the hour and Templeton started. "We are late," he said, and swore. Abruptly he came to a decision and turned to Pierce. "Your stepsister cannot have taken much with her, nor any money, either. You did say you held the purse strings, did you not?" he asked in the same silky voice that had frightened the maid belowstairs.

Pierce pulled himself together. "Yes, of course. I told you that before," he said. "I only gave Rebecca pin money. Enough to deck herself out respectably. She can't have had much of that left, judging by the bills in my desk. London is devilish expense, you know."

"I quite agree," Templeton said smoothly. "That is what encourages me to hope that by tomorrow or the next day Miss Stanwood will have returned to your loving bosom. When she does you will instantly apprise me of it. If, that is," he added, "you do not wish to find yourself taken in charge for failing to settle your outstanding accounts. You would not, I assure you, like debtor's prison. It is a most uncomfortable place unless you have the funds to bribe the bailiffs to make matters more pleasant for you, and you, quite patently, do not. The cells are infested with rats, you know."

Pierce shivered. "I'll let you know at once," he promised fervently. Then, as timidly as the maid had done before him, he added, "Do you think I ought to enquire at the various hotels if Rebecca has gone there?"

Templeton lifted an eyebrow. "I shall do that," he said, a gleam in his eyes. "I can, I assure you, do so discreetly. And enquire at the smaller lodging places as well. If Miss Stanwood has taken refuge in any of them, I shall find her."

"And bring her back here?" Pierce asked anxiously.

Templeton bowed in reply. "I shall take my leave of you. It is too late for us to go to Medmenham tonight, unless fortune favors me, but I think, yes I think, I shall begin my search at once. Much better to leave it to me, Andrew. I know London, you see, far better than you do."

Pierce watched him go, and found himself almost sympathetic with Rebecca's desire to escape the house. That would not, however, have stopped him from handing her over to Templeton if she had walked back in just then. The image of finding himself clapped in irons, in a debtor's cell, weighed heavily on his mind, as did Templeton's reminder that such places were invariably infested with rats.

4

Rebecca woke with a start. She had been having the same nightmare, all over again. Templeton had found her and dragged her out of the servants' hall to confront her in front of Mr. Ransford. And Mr. Ransford had stared at her with a mixture of disappointment and condemnation in his eyes, making no effort to stop Templeton from taking her away.

She shivered in the cold morning air. It was still dark outside but Rebecca knew, from the sounds in the street, that it was already time to rise and begin her work, however tired she might be. She dressed in the dark, Mrs. Marsh having decided that the poor mute girl had no need of candles until she rose to the position of regular housemaid; if she ever did, which Mrs. Marsh took leave to doubt. Whatever Phoebe's previous mistress might have written, Mrs. Marsh knew an untrained girl when she saw one. Had Mr. Ransford not taken such a fancy to the girl, Mrs. Marsh might have suggested that he look into the matter and see if her references had been stolen or forged. As it was, however, Mrs. Marsh wished to do nothing which would draw his attention to the girl. The one time she had ventured to complain that Phoebe was clumsy, Mr. Ransford had asked to see the girl and talked to her, asking if everything was all right! So Mrs. Marsh had learned to answer that Phoebe was doing just fine and Mr. Ransford would nod and appear to forget the girl. No, Mrs. Marsh knew her duty. She had no intention of drawing the girl to his notice again, however many false references she might suspect her of having produced.

Phoebe, that is to say Rebecca, was well aware of the trend
of Mrs. Marsh's thoughts and it frightened her a little that
Mr. Ransford showed such a great interest in her welfare.
Rebecca had no illusions as to how vulnerable a maidservant
could be to a persistent master. She was both amused and
relieved by Mrs. Marsh's efforts to shield her from Mr.
Ransford. At the same time she knew it would be foolish
to depend too greatly upon his interest to save her from being
dismissed from her post if she proved either lazy or totally
incompetent. Therefore, Rebecca made no effort to evade
any of the tasks put to her and used her quick intelligence
to observe other servants and follow their lead in how to
comport herself and how to carry out her work. Thus far,
such efforts had kept her from being thrown back out into
the streets.

There was a soft rap at her door and Rebecca finished
dressing hastily. It was a luxury, she knew, for her to have
a room to herself, however narrow and cold and dark it might
be. None of the other underservants had such a privilege,
and she owed it to her feigned muteness. The other servants
were not cruel to Phoebe, they simply refused, one and all,
to share a room with her—a circumstance for which Rebecca
was profoundly grateful.

'' 'Urry,'' the housemaid named Mary said as Rebecca
appeared in her doorway. ''Mrs. Marsh will be ever so upset
the kitchen fire's not been lit yet. And we've got to open
all the shutters before Mr. Eames sees we haven't done
them.''

Rebecca nodded, wondering if she would be set to scrubbing the flagstones again. A moment later she discovered
her fears were well founded as Mary said, a touch of spite
in her voice, ''I'll do the dusting and see to the upper floors.
Mrs. Marsh says you can't be trusted not to wake Mr.
Ransford. You can scrub the floors. And mind this time you
don't put on your cloak when you do the front steps. It don't
look right.''

Rebecca nodded meekly, trying not to think of how red

and sore her hands would be by spring, or how cold it would be with no fire lit in her room, or how the wind would cut right through her dress as she scrubbed the front steps in the mornings. It seemed a lifetime away that she had woken to a fire roaring in her bedroom fireplace every cold morning and hot tea or chocolate beside her bed. The slightest thought informed her that matters would only get worse as winter came and the water in her cracked pitcher froze overnight. Still it was better to be here, Rebecca told herself, than in the clutches of Lord Templeton and the members of the Hellfire Club. Sometimes that was all that kept her going.

Several hours later Mrs. Marsh watched Rebecca put away the scrub brush, hearthstone, and bucket. "All right, you may eat your breakfast now," she told Rebecca grudgingly. "Mind, as soon as you've eaten, you're to empty the servants' basins and chamber pots and put fresh water in the pitchers. But not Mr. Ransford's."

These last words were spoken with an ominous frown and Rebecca made haste to nod her head that she understood. Nothing would bring her to invade his bedroom, not even if she was certain he was gone from the house, and she knew very well that this morning he was not. Meanwhile, Rebecca had no intention of missing breakfast, even if the food wasn't what she was accustomed to. It was, she thought with amusement, an absurd irony that she, like the scullery maid, Katie, had to eat in the kitchen instead of with the others in the servants' hall because their manners were not deemed good enough. Which was less from any true regard for such matters, she reflected gloomily, than from a desire to find one more way of putting them in their place.

In any event, Rebecca was rather pleased than not to eat with Katie in the kitchen, for there was less risk that way. Not that she would have been allowed to speak at the servants' table, even were she not supposed to be mute, but there would have been sharp eyes on her and someone might have noticed that her manners were too dainty for the part she played. Katie, however, was uneasy with Rebecca and made sure to keep her eyes on her plate so that Rebecca could concentrate on relaxing. Had she known how closely her employer noted her progress, Rebecca would have found that a far more difficult task.

Indeed, as it was, Mr. Ransford occupied more of Rebecca's thoughts than she wished. Try as she might to keep her mind on her work, Rebecca found herself picturing his clear blue eyes and fair curls. She found herself remembering the implacable grip of his hand on her arm and wondered how kind he would be if he discovered her deception. But that was unlikely. However benevolent an interest he might take in an unknown maidservant, he would never look closely enough to see the woman behind the role. Betty had been right when she said that no one noticed servants. Even the gentleman who had leered at her and tried to get her to accept his improper offer had not looked closely enough to realize that he had met her in her stepbrother's house. He had only seen a servant girl out on her own and apparently thrown out of her work. A girl who might be vulnerable to his improper advances. He had proposed to buy her a pretty gown and give her a fine meal, not understanding when she spurned what he obviously considered a most generous offer. And then he had pursued her when she fled in the dark, not knowing where to go.

Until Mr. Ransford had offered her this position, Rebecca had not known what she would do. One look at the sort of place that housed would-be servants new to London persuaded her that she would do better to spend more of her savings on a night's lodging at a small but respectable inn. What she had not counted on was that the inn would refuse her custom, saying that they did not cater to servants. It did not matter that Rebecca had the silver to pay for her lodgings, it was a matter, the innkeeper's wife had explained haughtily, of looking to the reputation of the establishment.

So it was that when Mr. Ransford had offered her a post in his household, Rebecca had had little choice but to accept.

That she was grateful for his kindness, however, did not stop her from being wary. Those few hours, wandering the streets of London in the gathering darkness had sufficed to make her realize how vulnerable a servant really was. And she had no intention of allowing anything to place her in that position again.

Meanwhile, there were a great many things Rebecca had to do. The most important was to find a way to write a letter home. Though she could not write to her stepmother without betraying Andrew or risking that her stepmother might tell him where to find her, Rebecca had another friend back in Boston whom she might ask to help her return home. She had always been on excellent terms with her father's partner, Mr. Johnston, and she did not think he would fail her now. That she would not have the funds to return to Boston without such help had become increasingly clear to Rebecca. Her wages would not be sufficient even if she did not mind waiting six months to be paid. Rebecca might, of course, have tried to pawn her pearls had she not realized that for a servant to appear in a jewelry shop and offer to sell such a fine necklace and earrings would be to almost certainly find herself clapped up in prison on suspicion of theft. No, it must be a letter back home to Boston.

The difficulty was in finding the opportunity to write her letter and send it off. Since she was to be mute, she could not ask to borrow pen and paper, nor would she have her afternoon off for another two weeks, so she couldn't leave the house to buy some. Late in the morning, fortune favored Rebecca, however, and she found the time to slip into Ransford's library unobserved. Mrs. Marsh had told her to clean out the grates of several nearby rooms, and after she had done so, Rebecca decided to risk entering the library as well. Her first thought, as she looked about the room, the door safely closed behind her, was that it suited Mr. Ransford perfectly. Dark wood shelves held an immense collection of books and solid, well-upholstered furniture was placed near the fireplace to encourage reading. A massive

desk stood near this cluster of chairs and it was evident that
Mr. Ransford used it often. Rebecca set down her cleaning
tools next to the fireplace, grateful to find that it did need
cleaning. If she were discovered, she would have a ready
excuse to be in here and meanwhile she could write her letter.

Rebecca ought to have moved quickly and looked about
for pen and paper. She had written the letter in her head many
times and meant to get right to the task. But the nearness
of all those books was more than she could bear. After her
mother's death, years before, she had sought solace in books
and found it there. Indeed, for some time, books had been
her best friend. To be sure, time had healed her grief and
she had looked outward again, but never had she lost her
love of books. It was a love her father had encouraged, for
he shared it as well. His library had been the envy of many
in Boston, and the sight of these books brought his
memory sharply back to Rebecca. Without meaning to, she
found herself drifting over to the shelves and touching the
spines of the finely bound volumes in Ransford's library.
How familiar the titles were, and again in spite of herself,
Rebecca reached over and pulled out the volume of Shakespeare that was so remarkably like the one her father had loved
and introduced her to, so many years ago in Boston. This
was the same edition, or very nearly so, and Rebecca found
herself on the verge of tears as she leafed through the pages.

Lost in her own thoughts, Rebecca did not hear the sound
outside the library door. Had she done so, she would have
quickly moved to the fireplace and begun to sweep out the
ashes. As it was, however, she did not notice even when,
a moment later, the door opened and Mr. Ransford entered
the room. Her back was to him and she did not notice that
he paused in surprise at the sight of her. Then quickly,
silently, he shut the library door and, with a puzzled frown,
stood watching Rebecca. His eyes did not miss the way she
stroked the cover of the book nor how hopelessly she seemed
to page through it. After a moment, he crossed the room
toward Rebecca, his footsteps muffled by the thick Brussels
carpet on the floor.

Ransford felt as though his head was all awhirl. Not only was it unthinkable that a servant should enter his library without cause, the sight of one of them entranced by holding a book was even more astonishing. And yet he was not angry. There was something about Phoebe that made it seem natural to see her with a book in her hand. Somewhere she had seen and been taught to value books. And yet she made no attempt to read this one. Indeed, it was highly improbable that she could read. Still he could not doubt that books meant a great deal to her. Who was Phoebe, he wondered. Not some drab child raised in a slum or even by ordinary working class people. That was evident in the lines of her face and the way she held herself now. Neither was she of the *ton*. The thought occurred to Ransford that perhaps she was a love child of some gentleman who had provided for her support until some time recently. If so, she was doubly to be pitied. She might have tasted of one world and found herself forced to live in the other. His voice was kind as he spoke from a point just behind her shoulder and said, "Do you like books, Phoebe?"

Rebecca jumped, there was no other word for it, and would have dropped the book had Ransford not moved so swiftly to catch it. As he did so, his hand brushed hers and she jumped again. She dared not look at him, afraid she would betray herself. She knew as well as he did how outrageous, how astonishing, her behavior must seem. But Ransford did not seem outraged. Indeed, his voice was still kind as he went on, gently asking, "Do you know how to read, Phoebe?"

Instinctively, Rebecca shook her head in denial. He must not guess, must not wonder, what she knew and why. He saw too much, that was clear. She must contrive to throw dust in his eyes. If she answered no, he might wonder what she was doing with his books, but that would be better than having him guess the truth.

Ransford turned and put the book on the shelf. "No," he said, "of course you don't. What a singularly foolish question." A tiny sigh of relief escaped Rebecca and his eyes were quick to find her face. Tilting up her chin with his hand he said, so very gently, "But you'd like to learn to read, wouldn't you, Phoebe? No one who holds a book as you did can pretend she does not love books or want to read."

It was impossible, Rebecca thought, not to want to trust this man. He was far too kind, with a way about him that made one want to tell him the truth. But she dared not. A tear started to trickle down her cheek and she jerked her chin free of his hand before he could see it, angry with herself for such weakness. Ransford mistook the matter. His hands clasped behind his back, he said coolly, "I see. As you wish. You'd best gather your things and clear out of here, then. I've work to do and don't wish to be disturbed."

Rebecca made haste to gather up her tools. Indeed, she was in such a haste, that she dropped one of the brushes and it clattered on the hearth loudly. Ransford swore under his breath and came forward to help Phoebe retrieve the brush. As he handed it to her, Ransford found himself wanting to stroke away the shattered look on her face. Without meaning to, he found himself saying gently, "It's all right, Phoebe. You needn't hurry away. Stay and finish your work, if you'd like."

But Rebecca shook her head vehemently. To her dismay, she realized that her hand was trembling. Ransford drew back again and said, coldly, "Very well, then, go."

Rebecca did so, knowing that she did not trust herself so near to him. It was impossible that she should feel this way, she told herself fiercely. Impossible that his nearness should affect her so deeply. She scarcely knew the man. For all she knew he could be worse than Lord Templeton.

Well, not Lord Templeton, she acknowledged silently. But the truth remained that she did not know Mr. Ransford. He had been kind, but why? Did he desire her? Certainly he had looked at her in a way that was more than the impersonal interest of an employer. And he would not be the first to think to have his way with a servant. No, Rebecca dared not court an interest that carried such a risk.

Intent on her thoughts, Rebecca did not see Mrs. Marsh

in the hallway to the kitchen until she almost collided with the woman. "You've taken your time about cleaning the grates," Mrs. Marsh said reprovingly. "There's work needs to be done in the pantry."

5

Lady Sarah was generally held to be one of the prettiest and liveliest brides in London when she had married Charles Ransford. A petite blonde with a trim figure and dancing blue eyes, as well as being the daughter of a duke, Lady Sarah had been considered to be the catch of the Season and Charles Ransford had caught her. Their marriage had been a remarkably felicitous one, and upon his death she had given up society for a year to mourn. Gradually she had returned, but without the gaiety that had marked her formerly. Still, at the age of almost fifty, Lady Sarah retained the power to turn heads, including that of her own son, Oliver. Just now he stood in her small but elegant drawing room which had been papered in blue and silver, his fair curls fashionably disarrayed and his fine figure encased in skintight pantaloons, a coat of superfine, and gleaming Hessians. At the moment he was staring into the fireplace, having significantly failed to hear either of the last two questions his mother had put to him. Lady Sarah rose and her purple silk morning dress seemed to float about her ankles as she moved to touch her son upon the elbow. Startled, Oliver looked down at her with a slight frown as he said, "What? Have I been woolgathering, again, Mama?"

"Yes," she told him simply.

He smiled that smile which privately Lady Sarah thought no female heart could be proof against as he took her hand and kissed it. "Forgive me, Mama."

"I shall, if you tell me it is a girl you are thinking of," she said lightly.

Oliver led his mother back to the plush sofa and sat on the chair opposite before he answered. With a wry smile he said, "It is, though not in quite the way you mean, Mama."

There was something in the way he answered that made Lady Sarah cast a critical eye over her son, for it was clear to her that he seemed to have met a check in the matter. But even a close inspection could not reveal to Lady Sarah's prejudiced eye any reason why that should be so. Oliver presented, she thought fondly, a most handsome appearance. Not the most critical observer could have found fault with the cut of his clothes, the way they moulded his fine body, or the set of his elegantly tied cravat. Nor was there any inclination in his temperament to moodiness or arrogance or sudden rages. Indeed, it was incomprehensible to Lady Sarah how any young lady could look upon Oliver and not love him. She was aware, however, that one must allow for individual preferences and prepared herself to listen to whatever Oliver had to tell her without hating the girl involved too greatly. His next words, however, shocked her profoundly.

"The girl, you see, is a servant in my household, Mama."

"But surely that is your housekeeper Mrs. Marsh's concern?" Lady Sarah said hesitantly. "In what way could a servant girl concern you?"

Again the queer smile sat on Oliver Ransford's face as he replied, "She has the most wonderful eyes I have ever seen."

"Is that all?" Lady Sarah said with a relieved laugh. "Your father was just the same. It was 1805, I think, or perhaps 1806. We had an Irish girl, then, and she had dark, fascinating eyes. At least your father thought so."

For a moment Ransford was diverted. "I think I remember her," he said. "Was her name Maureen?"

"Yes, and a heathenish name all the other servants considered it to be!" Lady Sarah confided to her son. "Your father's interest in her only set the girl apart even more from the other servants. They made her life positively miserable because of your father's attentions."

"And did it make you miserable?" Ransford ventured to ask his mother, after a moment.

She hesitated, then shook her head briskly. "Your father was too wise to indulge his fancy as he might have wished. Partly it was because he realized that it would not be fair to the girl, though I thought she encouraged him shamelessly. But it was also because he did truly love me and did not wish to hurt me that he asked me to arrange another place for the girl, and of course I did so. I wonder what became of her."

"Did you make no effort to find out?" Ransford asked, curious.

Lady Sarah shook her head. "No, for I knew that as soon as the girl was out of the house your father would forget her. And so he did."

"I still think it must have been horrid for you," Ransford said with some concern.

"Well, it was, a little," Lady Sarah acknowledged. She forced herself to smile, however, and leaned forward as she placed her hand over his. "That is why, however much encouragement she gives you, you ought to leave the girl alone, perhaps even send her away to another post. I could help you arrange one for her."

"But I'm not married," Ransford reminded his mother gently.

"Yes, but it's more than that," Lady Sarah said crossly. "It's things like how the other servants will look at her and at you. And how the world will treat her if she breeds because of your attentions," she added seriously.

"Do you think I would abandon her?" Ransford asked angrily.

"No, of course not," Lady Sarah said at once. "But don't you see? You could provide money for the girl and the child, but how could you shield her from the snubs and curses and petty cruelties that would inevitably surround both of them?"

Ransford stared at his mother, then shook his head. "All of this is nonsense," he said impatiently.

Lady Sarah gave a sigh of relief. "Well, I thought so,"

she said confidently. "I knew you had too much sense to be taken in by a brazen baggage such as I collect this girl to be."

"You are mistaken," Ransford replied in a colorless voice. He rose to his feet and crossed over to the window. Over his shoulder he said, commanding his voice with an effort, "She gives me no encouragement." He paused then smiled mischievously at his mother as he added, "You would like her, I think, if you saw her. She is modest in her demeanor, tries very hard at her work, although Mrs. Marsh tells me she is not very experienced at it, and never speaks."

"Never speaks?" Lady Sarah echoed in surprise. "Do you mean she never speaks unless spoken to? You must know that is only proper in an underservant, Oliver. What did you expect?"

"No, I mean that she never speaks," he replied curtly. "So far as I can determine, she cannot speak."

"No wonder you are concerned with her, then," Lady Sarah said at once. "The poor child! But how did you come to hire her if she cannot speak?"

Ransford turned and faced his mother. He smiled that singularly sweet smile again as he said, "I found her in my garden one night. Cowering among the bushes. Something, or more likely someone, had evidently frightened her into hiding there. She seemed to have nowhere to go and no one to turn to, so I offered her a job on my staff, much to Mrs. Marsh's disapproval," he added, a twinkle in his eyes now. "And before you scold me, let me tell you, Mama, that the girl did have a letter of reference."

Lady Sarah was silent a moment. When she did speak, she chose her words carefully. "I would not have had you turn away someone who genuinely needed your help," she said, "but are you certain she came to your garden by chance? That she did not do so to somehow entrap you?"

"Entrap me?" Ransford said, in patent bewilderment. "How could a mere servant do that?"

In spite of herself, Lady Sarah smiled. "I know. When

you say it that way, it does sound absurd. But you must admit it is a strange way to acquire a servant!"

"Oh, I'll allow that," Ransford agreed, "and that is why you see me so preoccupied about the girl. I must suppose her to have been frightened into taking shelter in my garden, and yet I cannot help but think there is more to the mystery than that."

Lady Sarah watched her son with dismay. It was plain he was touched by the girl's plight, and not for the world would she have had Oliver so hardened that he did not feel so. But it was one thing to be concerned and quite another to develop a *tendre* for a servant. It was patent that whatever Oliver might say, those wonderful eyes he had spoken of had captivated him in a way he did not yet understand, and it was that circumstance which filled Lady Sarah with the most profound misgivings. Yet to say anything to warn Oliver off would plainly only make matters worse and perhaps create a rift between them.

Ransford was not oblivious to his mother's distress. He came back across the room to her and sat again, taking one of her shapely hands in his. "Don't fret, Mama. I mean to do nothing foolish. I would neither seduce a helpless servant nor so far forget myself or my position as to think the difference in our stations was unimportant."

"I do know it," Lady Sarah assured her son gently. "Still, I wonder if it might not be a good idea for me to visit your establishment and talk with Mrs. Marsh. Perhaps she has observed something which will help us sort out the mystery surrounding your servant, for I know you too well to think you can ignore such a puzzle right under your nose."

Ransford laughed. "Well, I should be obliged to you if you could find out anything," he acknowledged.

Would you? Lady Sarah thought silently as she looked at her son's face. *Would you be obliged to me if I found out something you did not want to know about her?*

But that was a question which could not be asked aloud and Lady Sarah did not try to do so. Instead she stood up, shook out the wrinkles from her skirt, and said briskly, "Mrs. Marsh is quite accustomed to having me descend upon her unannounced to make sure they are treating you as they ought. And while in her own mistress she would find that an intolerable impertinance, she makes allowances for a doting mother, since she dotes upon you herself, Oliver."

"She does?" Ransford asked in astonishment.

Lady Sarah laughed and it could immediately be seen where Oliver Ransford had acquired his own sweet smile. "Didn't you know it?" she asked.

"No," he replied, shaking his head. "I simply knew she ran my household efficiently. She and Mr. Eames between them. Though I suppose I shouldn't be surprised since she was with you and Papa before I inherited the house and staff and has known me since I was in short pants." He paused, then added in an aggrieved voice, "I wish you had not removed from the house when Papa died. You know you were most welcome to stay."

"And you know very well that I prefer my own establishment," Lady Sarah countered gently. "We would forever chafe at one another if we were under the same roof. You would find my friends boring and I should fret over the sort of fellow bachelors you are forever entertaining and the wild parties you and they would prefer."

In spite of himself Ransford laughed. "Now, Mama, when have I ever held orgies at my house? If I had, you know that Mrs. Marsh would instantly apprise you of the fact the next time you came to call," he told her, his eyes twinkling. "I know what it is, whatever flimsy story you choose to tell instead. You think you would find my friends boring, Mama. And you hope that living in your own establishment as you are, I won't come to hear of all the *beaux* you are collecting! Major Collingsworth, indeed! As though he weren't twenty years older than you and far too disreputable."

"Yes, but so charming," Lady Sarah countered, her own eyes laughing. "And he knows the most interesting people. Come, dear, don't scold. You must know that after your father died, it was far too painful for me to remain in that house with all those memories.''

"I wondered if that was it," Ransford said quietly. "Do you still miss him?"

"Yes," Lady Sarah said simply. "But I don't mean to repine. Most days I go on very well. Now let us agree it is best for both of us to have our own establishments and forget the matter.''

"Whatever you wish, Mama," Ransford replied, genuine affection in his voice. "But you do mean to help me solve my mystery, don't you?"

"Of course," she retorted, a gleam of mischief in her eyes. "You know I cannot resist a mystery any better than you can yourself, Oliver. When shall I descend upon your poor household and pry what information I can out of your staff?"

"Whenever you wish," Ransford replied carelessly.

Lady Sarah tilted her head slightly to look at her son. "Considering how absentminded this girl with the wonderful eyes is making you, I think I had best do it soon," she retorted playfully. "I've a number of appointments today and tomorrow, including a visit to my dressmaker this afternoon. But I could drop by the day after tomorrow, perhaps in the morning. I shall talk with Mrs. Marsh while your servants are trying to rouse and dress you, hours earlier than you are accustomed to rising.''

Ransford only laughed. "Shall I give you a ride to your dressmaker?" he asked. "My carriage is waiting outside."

"That would be lovely," Lady Sarah said warmly. "Just give me a moment to get my pelisse.''

As they rode in Ransford's carriage a short time later, Lady Sarah hesitantly spoke about a matter that had been in her mind for some time. Until now she had never spoken of it aloud, for she knew her son too well to suppose he would take her efforts kindly. But now she could not help herself as she said, "Oliver, have you ever thought about taking a bride?"

Ransford tried to turn off the matter as a joke. "Why do

you ask, Mama? Are you afraid I am getting too far along in years and might die without an heir? I am only six and twenty, you know.''

"I know to the day when you were born," Lady Sarah answered tartly, "and I do not think you are getting old." She paused and her voice softened as she went on, "If you were a different sort of son, I might think it early for you to think of choosing a bride. If you were immature, or prone to wildness that needed time to burn out, or were finding great pleasure in the chase of bits of muslin, I might not say a word. But you are none of those things. Indeed, I have often thought you grew up far too fast.''

"I see," Ransford replied evenly. "You still have not told me, however, why you must press me to think of a wife."

"Because I think you are lonely," his mother answered frankly. "Lonely and bored and in need of distraction, which a wife would give you. A good wife, at any rate," she added thoughtfully.

"What?" Ransford replied playfully. "I should have thought that a bad wife would be far more distracting than a good one! She would lead me a merry dance and I should constantly be having to prevent her from disgracing me. Surely that would combat my boredom, as you call it, more completely?''

Lady Sarah looked at her son reprovingly. "I said I wanted you to be distracted, not unhappy," she told him coolly. "Not a flighty young thing, not for you. Rather I would have you marry a young woman old enough to know her own mind and challenge yours. Someone who could bring you comfort as well as distraction.''

Ransford repressed a sigh. His voice was noticeably taut, however, as he said, "Who is she, Mama?"

Lady Sarah looked down at her hands. "Who is who?" she asked carelessly, as she played with the tassle of her reticule.

"The young woman you wish to match me with," Ransford replied, not troubling to suppress the sigh this time.

His mother turned troubled eyes to her son. "I don't mean

to vex you, truly I don't," she said. "But I did happen to meet the sweetest young lady who is all of those things I said. Her mind is well formed, she is accomplished with water colors, the pianoforte, and can sing as well. She is almost twenty, but I assure you she has not wanted for offers and you would think her quite pretty."

Ransford looked down at his mother. He could, at that moment, cheerfully have strangled her. And yet he could not doubt that she only wanted what was best for him. "The name of this paragon?" he asked, relenting at last.

Lady Sarah gave a tiny crow of delight. "Her name is Amanda Wetherford and you can meet her if you join me at the theater tonight," she said in a rush.

"I see," Ransford said repressively again.

"Oh, do give over that high-handed tone with me," Lady Sarah said impatiently. "I am your mother and I won't stand for it. Obviously I've put your back up. You think I'm meddling and resent it. Well, that is perfectly natural. But, indeed, I didn't invite Miss Wetherford to go to the theater with me because I meant to have you meet her. I invited Miss Wetherford because I am her godmother. Her mother, Meredith, and I used to be best friends and when she solicited my kindness for Amanda, I couldn't refuse."

"If she is your goddaughter and has been out, or so I presume if she is twenty, for some time, why am I only now hearing about her?" Ransford asked, in some confusion.

"Because Meredith married Sir Geoffrey Wetherford, a gentleman from North Umberland, and I have not seen her since she went there to live after her wedding. I agreed to be the girl's godmother when she was born, but other than sending presents at the appropriate time, there has been nothing very much for me to do for her, until now," Lady Sarah explained, meeting her son's eyes this time. "Amanda was brought out, but only in the north. She did not find a husband, though Meredith tells me she had quite a few offers. That is why Meredith decided to bring her to London this Season. They have spent this summer in Brighton and just returned to London a week ago. Which you would have known had you been here in the spring instead of taking refuge in the country then.''

This last was said in a tone of aggrieved frustration and Ransford found himself trying to explain. ''I have no patience, Mama, for the sort of folderol that goes on during the Season. I dislike being figured as a matrimonial prize solely on the merits of my fortune. Any young lady I am introduced to is certain to either be overcome with the most annoying shyness or unbecoming boldness in an effort to capture me. I cannot have a comfortable conversation with any female unless she is already married, for otherwise she either agrees with everything I say or contradicts me in an effort, again, to capture my attention. I have borne it for several years, but this Season I found I could not,'' Ransford said, the words tumbling out as his own frustration found vent.

Lady Sarah listened sympathetically, then patted her son's hand. ''I do understand, Oliver,'' she said. ''And if you don't wish to meet Amanda, well, I have not told her to expect you to join us, anyway. It is vexatious to be viewed as a figure of prey, I suppose, but one day you will meet someone who does not see you that way. Someone you can feel a *tendre* for. That is what I would like for you, above all things,'' Lady Sarah said sincerely.

Ransford kissed his mother's hand. ''If I could find someone like that, I would marry her out of hand.''

''How gallant,'' Lady Sarah said dryly. ''I should feel more comforted, however, if I could think you meant it, rather than finding it a convenient excuse not to look about you for a wife.''

''Well, I am grateful we have reached your dressmaker's establishment,'' Ransford countered as the carriage came to a halt.

When he had safely seen his mother inside, Ransford gave his coachman orders to wait upon Lady Sarah's pleasure, saying that he had decided to walk.

6

In the end, Oliver Ransford decided not to disappoint his mother. To be sure, he had no wish to encourage Miss Wetherford in whatever daydreams his mother and Lady Wetherford might have concocted between them, but he knew to a nicety how to be polite while making it clear to the young lady that he had no true interest in her. He had, after all, had a great deal of practice in that respect.

Ransford presented himself at his mother's box at the theater fully half an hour before the production was to begin. He knew Lady Sarah too well to think she would forgo the pleasure of seeing who was and was not present, or the pleasure of presenting Miss Wetherford to any acquaintances who might prove beneficial to the girl, though if she had been in London for the Season she must have already met almost everyone there was to meet. Ransford was not mistaken in supposing, however, that his mother would be pleased to see him arrive early as well. The moment he entered Lady Sarah's box, she rose to her feet to greet him.

"Oliver, dearest! I'm so glad you could come, after all. I must make you known to the daughter of a dear friend of mine. Amanda, make your curtsy to my son, Mr. Oliver Ransford. Oliver, this is my goddaughter, Miss Amanda Wetherford."

Ransford found himself looking directly into the speculative eyes of Miss Amanda Wetherford, a smile hovering on her lips as she said, a trifle breathlessly, "Good evening, Mr. Ransford."

Oliver found Miss Wetherford rather pretty, with a good deal of countenance, a fine figure, and the nicety of taste to know that somewhat bolder colors suited her more than the pastels of a girl in her first Season. However he had found Miss Wetherford, Ransford would have exerted himself to be pleasant. As it was, he found himself agreeably surprised and did not regret the impulse that had led him to gratify his mother by appearing here tonight.

As Lady Sarah had promised, Miss Wetherford was something out of the common way. It was not simply the brown eyes and dark curls falling from a knot on top of her head so that they framed her face, or the rich amber gown made by one of London's finest *modistes*. Miss Wetherford was able to converse on a number of topics, all of which were likey to be of interest to Oliver. So amiable was Miss Wetherford, in fact, that the unwelcome suspicion began to occur to him that someone had coached her remarkably well concerning his tastes. Driven by a mischievous sense of humor, he started to take positions contrary to his usual opinions just to see what she would do. To do her credit, Miss Wetherford accepted this about face without a tremor of surprise. Unfortunately she was perfectly willing to adapt her opinions to suit his, and by the time the curtain rose, Oliver was conscious of a sense of annoyance in his breast.

Lady Sarah watched her son conversing with Miss Wetherford with undisguised satisfaction. Under other circumstances, Lady Sarah would have been inclined to take Oliver to task for being so rude as to ignore other acquaintances who waved to her box. But these were not other circumstances. Oliver actually appeared to be interested in a young lady his mother had drawn to his attention, and she was not about to disdain her good fortune.

Indeed, a far ruder interaction was about to take place in the pit of the theater during the first intermission. It was sufficiently disruptive to draw the attention of quite a few members of the audience, including Lady Sarah. Miss Wetherford was conversing with two young gentlemen who had come to Lady Sarah's box to speak with her so that Lady Sarah was able to touch her son's elbow. "I see Lord Templeton has a new acquaintance. The fellow who is arguing with the man behind. Have you met him yet?"

Ransford looked where his mother pointed and shook his head. "No, I have not. I've heard of him, though. A provincial from the colonies, I collect, and one of Templeton's more disreputable protégés."

"He claims that his stepfather was one of the Stanwoods of Stanwood Hall," Lady Sarah said dryly.

"A respectable family," Ransford said with some surprise.

"But the Stanwood who went to the colonies wasn't," Lady Sarah countered thoughtfully. "It all happened about the time you were born, Oliver. He was the youngest son and ripe for all sorts of mischief and scandal. Finally it became too much for his family and he was sent out of the country. He was supposed to go to India and went to America instead, but not before running off with a girl just out of the schoolroom. Her name was Felicity Harcourt and I knew her fairly well. It was not, precisely, a *mésalliance,* but the two families were not on very good terms and Stanwood's abduction of Felicity did not mend matters."

"And this is the stepson?" Ransford asked. "Why is he here in England? If anyone has told me, I must suppose I was not paying much attention."

"Well, there is also said to be a stepsister," Lady Sarah replied cautiously. "Stanwood's daughter, supposedly. The Stanwoods, however, refuse to acknowledge her. One must suppose the Harcourts refuse to acknowledge her as well. They never forgave Felicity, you know, for running off with young Stanwood."

"I suppose the daughter is unpresentable?" Ransford hazarded idly.

"No one really knows," Lady Sarah answered with a twinkle in her eyes. "It is one thing for her stepbrother to go out and about; you know how careless men may be about such things. It would be quite another for an unpresented young girl to do so. And if the Stanwoods of Stanwood Hall refuse to acknowledge her, no one will like to offend them by inviting her to their parties or sponsoring her.''

Oliver bent his shrewd gaze on his mother as he said, ''Mama, why are you so interested in some provincial nobody?''

Lady Sarah glanced at her protégé to make sure that Miss Wetherford's attention was engaged elsewhere, then lowered her voice and told Oliver, ''Sally Jersey overheard Templeton talking about the girl. Sally thinks she ran away from her stepbrother and that Templeton is spitting mad.''

''Carlisle Templeton?'' Ransford said with a frown. ''Why should he care?''

''Apparently he had an eye on the girl,'' Lady Sarah replied innocently.

''Marriage?'' Ransford asked in surprise. ''I don't believe it. Templeton is too proud to marry a nobody. Unless he had hopes of getting the Stanwoods to acknowledge her?''

''On the contrary,'' Lady Sarah said smoothly. ''I'm told he quietly advised the Stanwoods against recognizing her. That he assured them she was a fraud.''

''What could be his game then?'' Ransford said, more to himself than his mother.

''Sally Jersey thought, perhaps, that he wished to make the girl his mistress,'' Lady Sarah replied seriously. ''It is hard to believe, but if so I applaud the girl for having the courage to run away rather than submit. But I am astonished, Oliver, that you have heard none of this! If it were true, I should have thought you would be telling me that bets had been laid at White's as to the odds of his success in seducing the girl, not that I should be the one to give you the news.''

''Remember, I've been out of town for most of the summer. But ten to one, it's all a hum anyway,'' Ransford answered impatiently. ''It sounds like one to me. Even if I could believe such a thing about Templeton, what about the stepbrother? Surely he would have acted to prevent such an occurrence? Even if the girl is a provincial nobody, he could not wish to see such a thing happen to her.''

"That is why I was hoping you might know something," Lady Sarah confided. "It all seems absurd to me, as well, and I was hoping you might, if you had met the stepbrother, have some notion of the truth.''

"Well, I don't," Ransford replied shortly. "Nor do I greatly care. But," he added, softening a trifle, "if I were to give you my opinion, it would be that *if* the tale is true, which I doubt, then the reason I have not heard of it is that Templeton is acting with great discretion. Which won't do him a bit of good if Lady Jersey is determined to spread the story.'' He paused, eyed his mother's dissatisfied countenance, sighed, and then shrugged. "Very well, Mama. I am giving a card party tomorrow night, and since I've already invited Templeton, it would be a simple matter to suggest he bring this stepbrother along and I can see what sort of fellow he is.''

"What a splendid notion, Oliver," Lady Sarah said meekly.

Ransford was not deceived. With a pretense of wrath he said, "As if you didn't hope I would do so, all along, Mama! Well, if the fellow can't behave himself better than he is tonight, I shall greatly regret inviting him to my house."

"You must do as you wish, Oliver," was Lady Sarah's innocent reply.

As they watched, it became evident that Templeton and his friend intended to leave the floor of the theater and Ransford decided to make his invitation at once. In truth, he was grateful to have an excuse to escape the box. Miss Wetherford's admirers had been dismissed by her with consumate skill and she was about to turn her fawning attentions back to him.

An exquisite sense of discretion had prompted Templeton to persuade Pierce to take a turn in the corridor until the play should resume. He was in no better frame of mind than Pierce, but he had no wish to inform the world of his ill temper as Pierce seemed perfectly willing to do. With poor grace, Pierce followed Templeton outside where, after a few minutes, they encountered Ransford. Templeton greeted Ransford with pleasure but introduced Andrew Pierce with some reluctance, for he placed no dependence on how the American would behave. In spite of his lordship's amiable greeting, it was apparent to Ransford that something had occurred to put Templeton out of temper, and he did not believe it was the contretemps in the pit. Ransford began to wonder if perhaps the rumor about the American's stepsister were, in some part, true. He talked lightly for several minutes and then said, as though struck by inspiration, "Templeton, why don't you bring your friend to my card party tomorrow night?"

Templeton hesitated, but Andrew Pierce seemed eager to accept. After a moment, Templeton shrugged and said, "Why not?"

There was an edge to the words and Ransford added, with an engaging smile, "I have not long been back from the country, you see, and I depend on you to tell me the latest *on-dits*. Being away makes one feel quite out of touch, and no one ever knows as much as you do."

That amused Templeton. "You missed the Season," he observed with a sly smile. "Fleeing the matchmaking mamas were you?"

"Something of the sort," Ransford agreed ruefully.

"But I notice Lady Sarah has a young lady with her tonight," Templeton went on. "Apparently you didn't run far enough, long enough."

Ransford laughed. "Very true. But Miss Wetherford is my mother's goddaughter and I must have met her sooner or later," he retorted good-naturedly. "Tonight is my first encounter with her."

"And your last?" Templeton suggested with a faint smile.

Ransford assumed a dignified air. "Oh, if she remains in London then I make no doubt I shall encounter her here or there or somewhere," he said carelessly.

Abruptly Templeton abandoned the sport and turned to more important matters. "I hope you still have some of that burgundy left that you had last time I was at your house, Oliver," he said hopefully.

Ransford smiled. "I think I might find a bottle or two in my wine cellar," he admitted. "I look forward to having your opinion on a new port I've found, however."

"I look forward to trying it," Templeton replied easily. "And to persuading you to give me your secret for obtaining such treasures."

Again Ransford laughed. He made some light comment to Pierce and then took his leave of them. He returned to Lady Sarah's box shortly before the curtain was due to rise. "Well, you have your wish," he told her dryly. "Templeton will bring his friend to my card party tomorrow night, and I shall see what I can ferret out of the fellow about his stepsister."

Lady Sarah was conscious of a twinge of remorse for prodding him into inviting the fellow. "Do you dislike having him come to your party, dearest?" she asked, a tiny worried frown on her forehead.

Ransford was amused. "Rest easy, Mama," he told her reassuringly. "One more guest will not trouble me. Or Eames. I shall simply tell him to lay another cover at dinner, that's all. It won't be the first time, I assure you. And while I must confess my first impression of the fellow was not promising, I may well discover myself to be mistaken."

Lady Sarah turned to Miss Wetherford and said, "You see, Amanda, how amiable Oliver is?"

Miss Wetherford turned wide, brown eyes on Ransford as she said, admiringly, "Indeed, I cannot imagine a more amiable son."

Oliver replied suitably, but to his relief the curtain was finally rising and he began making plans to escape the box directly the next intermission began. He would not be so rude as to leave the theater altogether, but with careful planning he need spend no more time conversing with Miss

Wetherford. He glanced over at his mother and wondered how she could have been so henwitted as to suppose that Miss Wetherford would suit him. Had he been of a less amiable nature he might have been angry at her. As it was he was simply resigned to her good intentions. Such amiability, however, did not extend to pretending an interest in Miss Wetherford that he did not feel. To do her justice, Lady Sarah would not have wished him to do so. She had already realized that, in spite of a promising start, he was not taken with her protégé, and with a suppressed sigh she had resigned herself to his evident imperviousness to Miss Wetherford's charms. If only he would discover a suitable girl on his own!

Oliver Ransford paused in the doorway of his library. It was late and he was tired, but something bothered him. In some indefinable way, he felt that something was wrong with the room. Nothing had been moved, so far as he could tell, and it was definitely empty of anyone save himself, but Ransford would have sworn that someone had been in here, and not very long ago.

To be sure, he told himself impatiently, the servants must come in here several times a day: to clean the grate, dust the shelves, lay a fire in the fireplace ready to be kindled. But he had the impression that someone had been here just moments ago. Abruptly Ransford realized that there was a faint trace of smoke in the air, and when he moved swiftly to feel the wicks of the candles that stood unlit on his desk and the mantlepiece, he found them warm. So someone had been in here! For what purpose? Absurd to think any of the servants could have been looking for books to read, or that they would have dared even if they had wanted to do so. Absurd were it not for the fact that Ransford had discovered the girl, Phoebe, in here holding a copy of Shakespeare and staring at it just yesterday. Could she have been in here again?

Ransford frowned again. He was becoming absurdly

fanciful of late. The girl had been quite chastened at the sight of him and it was ridiculous to think she would risk such a thing again. Phoebe. Oliver found himself dwelling on the thought of the girl and all the incongruities about her. Worse, he found himself imagining that she could talk and was confiding in him the circumstances of her appearance in his garden and why the book of Shakespeare had attracted her so much, even the circumstances of her birth and childhood.

Impatiently, Ransford shook his head. Was he in his dotage to be daydreaming over a servant? There were men who trifled with their servants, he knew, but he was not one of them. He had always thought it infamous of someone to take advantage of girls who they must know would find it difficult to refuse their advances.

Perhaps his mother was right, Oliver thought with a humorous glint to his eyes, to hint that he ought to be thinking about taking a wife. Certainly he was old enough, and while he had had his share of *chère-amies,* the amusement involved in such liaisons was losing its edge. What had his mother said? That he seemed bored and lonely and in need of distraction?

Ransford poured himself a glass of wine from the decanter that always stood filled on his desk, and then sat in his favorite chair near the fireplace. In spite of the early autumn chill, the fire had not been lit since no one had expected him to sit here tonight. Nor did Ransford light the fire, now, himself. It was enough to sit in his favorite chair and sip his favorite wine. And ponder what was amiss in his life. Not a great deal, he concluded after several minutes, only perhaps, as his mother had said, boredom and a touch of loneliness. But Amanda Wetherford was not the answer. Nor were any of the other young ladies he had met over the past several Seasons. Well, perhaps tomorrow's card party would help ease his malaise.

As Ransford sat in his library pondering these questions, Rebecca crept silently down the hallway to the back stairs which led up to her attic room. It had been foolish beyond permission to risk entering the library again tonight, and madness to trust servant's gossip as to when Mr. Ransford would return. He had almost caught her, and would have done so had she taken three more minutes to write her letter. The library was at the back of the house and she had not heard his return. It was only good fortune that she had extinguished the candles and left the room precisely as he came up the front stairs. That had given her time to seek refuge in an antechamber until Ransford had entered the library and closed the door. Now she fled to the servants' stairs, sure that once she reached them she would be safe. Unfortunately Rebecca had reckoned without the second parlormaid's toothache. Indeed, since she took her meals in the kitchen with Katie, Rebecca had not even known the parlormaid was suffering from such a plaint. As it was, when Rebecca opened the door to the staircase, she encountered Mrs. Marsh on her way down from the girl's room where the housekeeper had just seen her back into bed after giving her a composer laced with laudenum. Hastily Rebecca stepped inside, onto the landing of the staircase, and pulled the door closed behind her. She did not notice that it failed to latch and, indeed, swung partway open again.

At the same time, Rebecca's other hand went instinctively to the pocket where her letter was hidden. Mrs. Marsh's eyes looked, for a moment, as though they would start from their sockets. "Well, I never!" she gasped. "Wandering about the house at this hour. Where have you been, my girl, and what have you been doing?"

Rebecca started to back away as Mrs. Marsh advanced down the stairs toward her. But Mrs. Marsh was quicker. In a flash she had Rebecca's wrist in a firm grasp. "You'll come downstairs to see Mr. Eames with me, my girl," the implacable housekeeper told Rebecca. "He'll know what we ought to do with you."

She started to pull Rebecca toward the stairs that led down to the kitchen when suddenly the door to the hallway was pulled all the way open. Both women froze in astonishment. Mr. Ransford stood in the doorway, not looking best pleased. "Trouble, Mrs. Marsh?" he drawled as his eyes rested on Rebecca's frightened face.

7

Abruptly Mrs. Marsh found her tongue. "You wouldn't
credit it, Mr. Ransford, but I found Phoebe coming up the
stairs just now. Aye, and through that very door!"

Her voice died away as she realized what she had said.
Sly as boots, Phoebe was, but it didn't look like the master
was going to complain. Not if they'd both been together,
which was what it very much looked like to her. Assignations
were something Mrs. Marsh didn't hold with, and until now,
she'd have vowed and declared that Mr. Ransford didn't hold
with them, neither. But if Phoebe hadn't been with him, then
why had they both come through the very same door?

Ransford had a tolerable notion what his housekeeper was
thinking for she had a very expressive countenance. At the
moment it reflected profound disapproval, and he found
himself silently cursing Phoebe for placing him in such an
insufferable position. The only consolation was that he was
now fairly certain that she had found the intruder to his
library. What he was to do with her was another question
entirely. One could hardly question a girl who could not talk.
Particularly not with Mrs. Marsh hovering about. And yet
he could scarcely send the housekeeper to bed without the
woman drawing her own mistaken conclusions as to what
was afoot.

A grim twitch played about his mouth and Rebecca found
herself wondering if she could pull free of Mrs. Marsh's hand
and run up the stairs to her room. She might have tried to
do so if she could have placed any dependence on Mr.

Ransford not following her. But it was far more likely, she reflected, that he would follow her and drag her back downstairs and that humiliation would be far worse than this.

It was certainly bad enough. In an icy voice Ransford said, "Mrs. Marsh, will you be good enough to bring Phoebe into the library? I have some questions I wish to put to her there."

"But, sir, you'll never get answers from her, unable to talk as she is," Mrs. Marsh protested in a bewildered voice.

"I think she will find a way to reply to them," was Ransford's grim reply. "In any event, I intend to pose them and would prefer not to waste any further time standing here, discussing the matter."

"Yes, Mr. Ransford," Mrs. Marsh said, distinctly cowed. Then, sharply, she said to Rebecca, "Come along, now, Phoebe. Mr. Ransford wants to ask you some questions."

Meekly Rebecca did as she was bid. Her face was pale but otherwise did not betray the consternation she felt. She could only suppose that his words and his evident anger meant that he had discovered some trace of her presence in his library. Which would not be wonderful, she told herself acidly, considering that the candles must have still been warm when he relit them. She could only hope that he had not also noticed the faint impressions her writing had lelft on his blotting paper. She consoled herself with the thought that there was no reason he should have noticed and that if he did he would only suppose they were his own. She did wish, however, that Mrs. Marsh would loosen the grip she had on Rebecca's wrist, for she very much feared that in the morning she was going to have bruises there.

Her wish was granted, but there her comfort ended. The light in the library was far better than that given off by Mrs. Marsh's candle. For the first time both she and Mr. Ransford had a clear view of Rebecca's countenance. To Mrs. Marsh's relief, there was nothing of the lover in the way Mr. Ransford ordered Phoebe to stand where the light threw her face into sharp relief. Having done so, he did not at once speak. Instead, he studied Phoebe's face, noting both her pallor and her quiet composure, trying to understand the girl. Without a doubt she understood the trouble she was in, but she was not trembling as one might have expected. To be sure, she could not know that he had guessed she had been in his library, but to be found wandering the house at such an hour would be quite enough to justify her dismissal, if he so chose. But that was the rub. Did he choose to dismiss her? Not, he was honest enough to admit to himself, without knowing more of what was behind those speaking eyes. Abruptly Ransford came to a decision. "You may leave Phoebe with me, Mrs. Marsh. I wish to speak with her alone." Mrs. Marsh regarded him mutinously, her arms crossed upon her chest in disapproval. He smiled at her and said lightly, "I shan't take advantage of her, you know."

"Shoe's on the other foot, I'm thinking," Mrs. Marsh said with a sniff. "It's what ideas she has in her head, I'm worried about."

"Nevertheless, you will oblige me in this," Ransford said gently but implacably.

He crossed the room and held open the door for her. Mrs. Marsh had no choice but to curtsy and withdraw. Ransford watched her go, then turned back to face Phoebe, who still stood in the light of the candles, pale but composed. She was, he thought, quite beautiful, and he had no trouble understanding why Mrs. Marsh was so concerned about the girl and what his intentions might be toward her. Had she been of his own class— Ruthlessly Ransford cut the thought short. She was not of his class and it was pointless to pretend otherwise. Instead he walked back to Rebecca and looked down at her face. His voice was brisk as he said, "I shall save us both time, Phoebe, by telling you that I already know you were in here tonight. I found the candles still warm when I entered," he explained dryly. A troubled look crossed Rebecca's face and he was quick to pounce on it. "Yes, you do know what I am talking about, and you must know that I should have a perfect right to dismiss you for it."

Instinctively, Rebecca's chin tilted up as she nodded. To

her surprise, Ransford said, "I shan't dismiss you, however. Instead, I intend to arrange for you to learn to read."

Rebecca stared at him in amazement, her mind whirling with conjecture. Ransford waited a moment, then he went on, "It has been in my mind since I found you in here, holding a book. You stared at it with such longing that however much you denied the wish to learn to read, then, I cannot believe it to be the truth."

What would he want in return? Rebecca wondered silently, cynically. And yet she was touched. If she had in truth been a mute servant, unable to read and longing for books, then Mr. Ransford's offer would have been generous beyond belief. As it was, her difficulty was to know how to tread. What should she indicate? That she knew how to read already? That she did not want to read? Or let him have someone try to teach her? Rebecca bit her lower lit, undecided. Which was the greatest risk?

Ransford, watching her, was puzzled. What ailed the girl? Why didn't she jump at the chance? Surely she wanted to read? He began to speak his thoughts aloud. "Are you afraid of me? Will it reassure you if I tell you I do not mean to teach you myself? That someone else shall do the trick? Or, are you worried about the other servants, Phoebe?" he asked gently. "You need not be. I shan't let them trouble you over this. Or is it that you are afraid you cannot learn? I think you can, you know, or I should not have suggested it. In spite of your silence, I think there is a fine mind behind those eyes. In any event, why should you not at least try?"

It seemed he had all the answers. Still Rebecca shook her head and resolutely kept her eyes on the floor before her. She knew that if she looked at him she would be undone. Already the gentleness, the hint of kindness in his voice held her on the verge of tears. Worse, far worse, he was coming toward her and now took her hands in his. "What is it, Phoebe?" he asked as gently as before. "I know that something draws you to this room. If it is not the books, then what? The fireplace? Have you not been used to sit in rooms like this before?"

Still she dared not look at him. A betraying tear trickled down her cheek, as it had the day before, but this time he was quick to see it. "My dear Phoebe," he said, wiping it away with a finger, "will you not trust me? Will you not confide in me?"

Now Rebecca did look up at him. How could he ask her these things when he believed she could not speak? How was a mute girl to confide in him, even if she dared? It wasn't as if she didn't want to. But how could she trust him? To tell him the truth would mean her ruin. Even if he did not condemn her for her masquerade, he could not, would not, let her stay. No, nor help her get a post as servant in anyone else's house, either. Then what was she to do?

Ransford saw the withdrawal in her eyes. He took that and her continued silence for rejection. His voice became a trifle remote as he said, "Very well. You may go, Phoebe. But I do not wish to catch you in my library again without permission."

Rebecca all but fled the room in relief. Catch her in his library again? No, she would take no more such risks. The letter was written and in her pocket, and he need not fear she would trespass again. Mr. Ransford's eyes saw too much, guessed too much. She would not willingly expose herself to such a catechism again. If only she might reach her room tonight without encountering Mrs. Marsh.

That was, and Rebecca knew it, a forlorn hope. Mrs. Marsh was waiting on the landing on the servants' stairs for Rebecca to appear. Her arms were crossed over her chest and a look of marked disapproval was fixed upon her face. "So there you," she said when Rebecca appeared. "Close the door soundly. We don't want Mr. Ransford down upon us again." Rebecca did as she was bid and waited. Mrs. Marsh unleashed a tirade on her head. "So you was in Mr. Ransford's library tonight! I make no doubt you'll find yourself dismissed in the morning. And without your wages, if I've anything to say about the matter. Mr. Ransford's had a sharp disappointment in you, my girl. I knew from the start you wasn't what you seemed, and now he knows you're not to be trusted, as well. Let that be a lesson to you not to go passing yourself off as a servant in respectable houses. I don't know whether you're no better than haymarket wares or whether you're in league with footpads. But I, for one, shall be happy to see the back of you. You'll have your things packed and be ready to go, first thing in the morning, as soon as I shall have had my orders from Mr. Ransford.''

Rebecca forced herself to nod meekly and turn and start up the stairs, knowing Mrs. Marsh intended to follow and make sure that she went to her bed. What, she wondered, would the housekeeper have to say in the morning when she found Rebecca was not to be dismissed, after all?

In the library, Ransford sat thinking over his encounter with Phoebe. His eyes chanced to light on the inkstand on his desk. The cap was off and someone had evidently forgotten to replace it. It was possible, of course, Ransford thought grimly, that one of the servants had knocked it off while cleaning the desk, but he did not believe it. He looked more carefully. A faint outline of a few letters could be seen pressed into the blotter on his desk, as though someone had pressed hard while writing a letter. It was not of his doing, Ransford was certain, for it had been several days since he had written a letter and the impressions would have faded by now. Grimly, Ransford looked closer, trying to make out what the letters were. All to no point, for they were too few to make out much of anything. But his suspicions were confirmed: one or two were distinct enough for him to be certain that they were not in his handwriting.

Ransford was in a cold rage. He was a lenient employer and, he hoped, a kind and fair one. And yet for a servant to sit at his desk and use his ink and, presumably, paper, was the outside of enough. Who would dare? And why? How many of the servants could even write a letter? The only possible answer was Phoebe. She had already been caught trespassing in his library, and it was beyond belief that two separate persons would have dared do so in one day. And yet, it appeared to be an absurd notion. Phoebe could not even read, or so she had indicated. How much more unlikely it was that she could write. Ransford's eyes glittered with the knowledge that she must have lied to him. Why? Did it matter?

Ransford tried to convince himself that he might be mistaken. He tried to recall whether any of his friends had been by in the last day or so and might have paused to write a note. Perhaps while he was out one of them had called and, upon finding him absent, asked Eames to allow him to leave a message for Ransford. Yes, that made sense, except for the fact that Ransford had received no such message. Besides, the few letters he could see clearly, appeared to have a distinctively feminine flourish to them. Nor did Ransford think that his mother had come by, for the servants would surely have told him if she had. In the end, Ransford was led back inexorably to the image, however incongruous, of Phoebe sitting at his desk and calmly writing a letter. Well, it was a mystery he was not going to be able to solve tonight. But he did intend to be more careful, in the future, not to leave things around until he found out for certain who had been writing at his desk and why. A servant who dared do that might dare other impertinences as well. More importantly, it only strengthened Ransford's determination to discover the circumstances of the mystery that surrounded Phoebe. Another employer would have dismissed the girl at once. Ransford vowed, instead, to keep her under his watchful eyes.

8

Phoebe scuttled along the narrow passageway to the kitchen, bucket in hand. She had managed to clean up the spill in the entranceway just in time. Mr. Ransford was expecting guests for dinner and word had it that they were due any minute. Mrs. Marsh, holding sway belowstairs, was all atwitter with excitement. Her fury at Phoebe's continued presence in the house was forgotten in the need to be certain that everything was ready for company. And the need to pacify the French chef who was in a fury over what he declared was the incompetence of the staff.

"There you are, Phoebe. Finally! Stir the soup for Frenchy. Katie, are the vegetables all cleaned? Mr. Eames, have any of the guests arrived yet?" Mrs. Marsh asked the hapless butler as he came through the kitchen with several bottles of Mr. Ransford's finest wines.

Eames halted just long enough to reply, with a calm voice that stood in sharp contrast to Mrs. Marsh's confusion, "Not yet, Mrs. Marsh. I understand they are due within the half hour. But I don't think you need fear they will be late. They never are."

"I hope not," Mrs. Marsh said with a worried frown. "The roast is cooking faster than Frenchy expected, and we wouldn't want to see it ruined."

"I am sure Alphonse will find a way to prevent that calumny," Mr. Eames replied repressively, "even in the unlikely event that Mr. Ransford's guests should prove tardy. I, however, must see to the table at once. And the port. Lord

Templeton is to be one of the company, and last time he was here he was heard to find fault with the port. I should not like to see that happen again.''

"Good Lord, I should think not!" Mrs. Marsh said fervently. "It would be the outside of enough to have people saying Mr. Ransford sets a shabby table.''

Eames bowed to Mrs. Marsh and moved quickly toward the stairs to the dining room. There wasn't a moment to be lost. Mrs. Marsh turned back to check over the kitchen. The chef was regarding the roast with grave concern. Katie was cleaning up the last of the vegetable scraps. "Katie, go and fetch the soup tureen from that upper cupboard," Mrs. Marsh directed. "Phoebe, leave the soup and fetch down the serving platters. Is the fish all ready to go in the pan for Frenchy? Did you soak it in chamomile tea as I told you earlier today?''

Rebecca nodded as she and Katie hurried to do as they were told, grateful for the bustle of activity that precluded anyone noticing her distress. Templeton, in this house tonight! What did he know? What if he mentioned her? And what if he brought Andrew?

No! That way lay madness, Rebecca told herself sternly. She must not dwell on Templeton. He was not likely to descend to the kitchens, and under no circumstances would she be sent abovestairs to wait on the company. That task fell to Mr. Eames and the footmen. Nor was it likely that Templeton would mention her. Why should he? Or Andrew? Neither could want people to know she had run away, surely. And if either of them did mention her flight, how could Mr. Ransford possibly make the link between an American young lady, a Miss Stanwood, who had disappeared and Phoebe, his silent servant? There was, of course, the letter of recommendation she had written herself, signed by Miss Stanwood, but Mr. Ransford had scarcely glanced at it. Surely he would not remember now?

A tiny corner of her heart protested that it was not fear of discovery that had set her emotions in such a tumultuous fever, but the knowledge that Mr. Ransford was acquainted with, indeed appeared to be a friend to, Mr. Templeton. Foolishly, Rebecca had allowed herself to weave forbidden daydreams about her employer and imagined him as some sort of knight who had rescued her. She had imagined him as far more honorable than any of the other gentlemen she had met since Andrew had brought her to London. But Rebecca had had no proof of that, she only knew that he had had a kind heart and had offered her a position when she so patently needed one. But had she not had her own doubts about his intentions? Had she not found excuses to avoid him since entering his employ? Why then did she feel so devastated to have her suspicions confirmed? Why was she so stunned to find that Ransford was one of Templeton's set? That he had never set foot in the house Andrew had hired for them meant nothing. Perhaps Ransford had been out of town until the night he found her in his garden.

Still Rebecca felt the ache of disappointment and ruthlessly suppressed it. She had wanted to believe, had believed, that Ransford was different. Now she must accept that he was not. How could he be, if he was a friend to Lord Templeton?

Abruptly Mrs. Marsh's sharp voice recalled Rebecca to the present, and she hastened to take down the rest of the serving pieces that would be needed.

As Rebecca moved about the kitchen some time later, helping Mrs. Marsh, Lord Templeton greeted Mr. Eames in the foyer, handing a footman his cloak as he did so. "Good evening, Eames," he said laconically, "this is a friend of mine, from the former colonies, Mr. Andrew Pierce."

Eames, who knew Lord Templeton, bowed and greeted the newcomer with more reserve than he might otherwise have done. He had all the instincts of the best of servants, and he could not entirely like Lord Templeton.

As though aware of Eames's disapproval, Templeton gave an ironic glance to Pierce and then went on, a queer smile on his face. "I trust Ransford is in good health these days?

It seems to me that he has been from his clubs a great deal, this year. Is everything all right?''

''Mr. Ransford has been, I collect, attending to business at his various estates,'' Eames said repressively, for however many times Lord Templeton might have been a guest in this house, he was not on such terms with the family as to make it allowable for him to gossip with the servants.

Templeton was amused rather than vexed. ''You are quite right to snub me, Eames,'' he said, a twinkle in his eye that robbed the words of any offense. ''It was most improper of me to ask.''

At this handsome admission, Eames unbent a trifle and replied, ''Well, as to that, m'lord, you're not the first, I'm sure, to wonder tonight where Mr. Ransford has been these past few months.'' Then, reverting to his previous impersonal role, the butler said, very properly, ''If you will follow me? I believe you will find Mr. Ransford in the drawing room with a number of other gentlemen who have already arrived.''

Templeton followed Eames, with Pierce close behind. He found himself wondering how affable Eames, who already disapproved of him, would have been if he had known about Medmenham and the Hellfire Club.

Medmenham. That reminded Templeton of his grievance against Pierce's stepsister, Rebecca. The others in the group had not been pleased with his failure to produce her. Had he brought Miss Stanwood to Medmenham that night, it would have been a coup. The others, when it had been their turn, had produced nothing better than frightened servant girls like the one from Pierce's household named Mary. But he would have been the first to produce an innocent young lady to be sacrificed, as it were, on pleasure's altar. Instead, the tongue lashing he had received from the group's founder still stung. Rage flared briefly as Templeton considered his singular failure to find Miss Stanwood. Somehow he would and when he did, she would pay for the humiliation he had suffered on her behalf. But for now that must be forgotten.

Ransford knew nothing of his activities in the club and he must not. Friends or not, Ransford would be more than disapproving. He might actually take action to end the club, as its original incarnation had been ended some fifty years earlier. No, he must pretend to be no different than the rest of Ransford's guests. However much he might despise some of his fellow members of the *ton,* Templeton had no intention of being made an outcast. Look at Rebecca Stanwood's own father, banished from England by his family and forced to seek his fortune in America. Or look at John Wilkes. His position in Parliament had meant nothing in the end. He had also fled England. True, his offenses had been political as well as being a member of the original Hellfire Club, but Templeton was nevertheless wary. Always he kept an eye on his best interests. And that was one reason why he was here.

As Eames had warned, Lord Templeton and Andrew Pierce were not the first to arrive. Ransford turned from his other guests to greet them with a ready smile. He and Templeton were friends, as two men are who had gone to Oxford together and who had moved since birth in the same circles. Indeed, Templeton was liked by most men. He was known to be an excellent shot, a bruising rider to the hounds, a shrewd man at cards, and a charming guest. Ransford could not be oblivious, of course, to the rumors that had circulated, from time to time, concerning Templeton, but he was inclined to think they were exaggerated. To be sure, there had been that matter at Oxford. No one knew precisely what sort of trouble it was that had gotten Templeton sent down, except that the dean of students had considered it extremely serious. But since no one cared to ask Templeton, it was the sort of thing that had only enhanced his reputation among the hey-go-mad undergraduates who had remained behind and who had envied Templeton his daring for whatever it was he had done.

Certainly, without strong grounds, Ransford was not the sort of man to disdain his friends or to make a new acquaintance feel unwelcome in his house. He greeted Templeton warmly and introduced Andrew Pierce to the others. Templeton immediately jumped into the thick of things, demanding to know if the story he had heard concerning Alvanley was true. Had he really bet on a race between two cockroaches? And when had this astounding event occurred? That led to a number of other anecdotes and Templeton found himself in the center of a laughing group. Pierce, off to the side, was both flattered and surprised when Ransford addressed him kindly and said, "I understand you are from America. Have you been here long?"

Pierce flushed. "A couple of months," he replied. "Is it so evident?"

Ransford took pity on the man. "No. But you are something of a curiosity for having come from America. I won't make the error of referring to it as the colonies," he added with a smile. "But tell me, how do you like England thus far?"

"It is not very hospitable to newcomers," Pierce said bluntly. Then, as he realized how this might sound, he colored and added hastily, "Not that I have cause to complain. Lord Templeton has been kind enough to take me out and about. It is my stepsister, Rebecca Stanwood, who has found her welcome a cold one."

"Stanwood." Ransford repeated the name meditatively. "Not one of the Stanwoods of Stanwood Hall?" he asked as if surprised.

"Her father, my stepfather, was," Pierce conceded. He went on spitefully. "But they have refused to acknowledge her. As have her mother's family. And, naturally, with that refusal, there are few doors open to her."

"A pity," Ransford agreed. "Perhaps I could do something for her. If my mother were to invite your stepsister to tea and took a liking to her, she might do a great deal to help Miss Stanwood take her place in our society. Perhaps on Monday?"

Before Pierce could reply, Templeton's smooth voice

intruded to say, "A pity Miss Stanwood is indisposed. A trifling ailment, Pierce assures me, but nevertheless one likely to linger on beyond Monday."

"Oh, indeed?" Ransford asked Pierce politely.

"Yes. Some sort of—of ague," he stammered.

"Perhaps when she is recovered, then," Ransford said, kindly.

"Yes, certainly," Pierce replied woodenly. "You are very good."

"Not at all," Ransford said with a distant smile.

He gave both men a slight bow then turned to speak with some of his other guests. Ransford gave all the appearance of a host offended but too polite to say so.

When he had moved away from them, Pierce and Templeton conferred in an undertone.

"Why the devil does he want to invite Rebecca to tea with his mother?" Pierce demanded.

Templeton smiled. "Ransford has a taste for taking up lost causes, perhaps. In any event, it does not signify. She cannot go when she is not at home to receive the invitation. I suppose you have still had no word from her?"

"None. Where can she have gone?" Pierce asked, anxiety rising in his voice. "If we do not find her soon, I am done up!"

"Softly!" Templeton warned. "You do not want anyone to overhear you. Talk of something else, I advise you."

That was all very well for Templeton to say, Pierce found himself thinking aggrievedly. What difference did it make to him if Rebecca were found or not? To be sure, he wanted her and Pierce would even have said she was an obsession to him. But if Rebecca were never to be found, Templeton would shrug and look about him for another victim. Pierce, on the other hand, would be ruined if she were not found and restored to Templeton's grasp. However accommodating his lordship might be in return for Rebecca's favors, he had made it quite clear that not a penny more would be advanced to Pierce in the absence of them. It was no wonder that Pierce felt himself to be all but desperate. It was rapidly becoming clear to him that he was not going to be able to find Rebecca unless she came back to him of her own accord. And that seemed increasingly unlikely with each passing day. What if she never came back? Pierce had seen too much of the dark side of London to doubt that it was a possibility. The knowledge that Rebecca would have been in even greater danger had he succeeded in getting her to Medmenham with Lord Templeton did not weigh with Andrew for a moment. That, at least, would have served a purpose. This did not. Worse, it had caused Templeton to look askance at him, and the thought of Templeton's anger was a frightening prospect, indeed. Rebecca had no right to place him in such an impossible situation!

The appearance of two more of Ransford's guests provided, to Pierce's mind, a welcome interruption, and he turned with the others to greet the arrivals. Unfortunately for Pierce, one of the two men was Giles Stanwood, Rebecca's cousin, even if he did not choose to acknowledge the connection. Andrew flushed as he recalled his reception by Stanwood when he had gone to call upon them on Rebecca's behalf. Giles had threatened to have him thrown out in the street and called Rebecca a strumpet.

From the startled and angry expression on Stanwood's face, it was evident that he recognized Andrew as well. In a clear voice that carried, he said to Ransford, "I didn't know, Oliver, that you had taken to inviting riffraff to your parties."

Pierce turned a darker red but did not at once answer. Ransford seemed amused. To Giles he said, "I collect the pair of you have met?"

"Yes," was the curt reply that came from both men.

"I also collect that you have taken each other in profound dislike," Ransford added, the amusement in his voice even more pronounced now. "I beg, however," he went on, "that you will both strive to recall that you are guests in my house and refrain from pursuing your quarrel here."

Both men hesitated and then Stanwood bowed. There was irony in his voice as he said, "Certainly, Ransford. One of us at least, is a gentlelman."

Andrew flushed but he, too, bowed and said, "I shouldn't dream of imposing our quarrel on you, Mr. Ransford."

"Good," Oliver said, a singularly sweet smile on his face. "Someday one of you may choose to tell me what it is about, but for now, I should much prefer to sit down to dinner and then to play cards. Eames, I presume you have come to tell me dinner is served?"

Ransford's butler, who had been standing in the doorway of the room, an appalled look upon his face, hastily collected himself and said, with the proper lack of emotion in his voice, "Yes, sir, I was."

"Good. Then let us go in to dinner, gentlemen," Ransford said, a touch of gentle irony in his own voice.

Belowstairs, consternation reigned as one of the footman, hastily sent to the kitchen to procure a forgotten ladle, told the women there, "It was that close to the one gentleman, Lord Stanwood, calling out the other, a Mr. Pierce!"

"Well, who is this Mr. Pierce?" Mrs. Marsh demanded. "We've all heard of Lord Stanwood, but who is the other fellow?"

"Dunno," the footman shrugged. "An American, by his accent, I think."

"An American?" Mrs. Marsh exclaimed. "What would an American be doing here?"

"Lord Templeton brought him, they say," the footman replied. "I wasn't at the door when he came, but that's what they tell me."

"Fancy that," Mrs. Marsh said with a sigh. "An American in the house. And brought by Lord Templeton. Well, it's to be hoped this American isn't as fussy as his lordship, for I don't reckon they eat quite the same in the old colonies as they do here."

"Don't worry, Mrs. Marsh," the footman assured her. "There's no one can find fault with our chef's cooking.

Many's the guest who has praised Mr. Ransford for finding such a treasure as Alphonse.''

"Well, Mr. Eames will find fault with you if you don't hurry back upstairs with that ladle," she warned him gruffly. "Now go along with you, at once!"

As the footman disappeared down the passageway, the women in the kitchen settled down to gossip over this juicy tidbit and conjecture on the cause of the quarrel between Lord Stanwood and the American, Pierce. Alphonse held himself resolutely aloof, though no one doubted he understood every word that was said.

"It doesn't entirely surprise me," Mrs. Marsh said with a sniff of authority. "Lord Stanwood is a high stickler—a high stickler, indeed. And they say his father was just the same. He's not one to sit down to dinner with just anyone."

Mrs. Marsh paused and stared about her, daring any of the other servants to contradict her. Her eyes fell on Rebecca, who was struggling with her own sense of indignation which now outweighed her fear. How dare Lord Stanwood object to Andrew's presence in this house. He was Ransford's guest, not Stanwood's, after all. And while Andrew's parents might not have come from the ranks of lords and ladies, his mother was more of a true lady than some Rebecca had seen with a title here in London. But Phoebe could not speak, and so Rebecca was obliged to swallow her anger and remain mute. She could not hide, however, the look of rebellion on her face, a look that caused Mrs. Marsh to say, suspiciously, "What ails you, Phoebe? You look as if you're fair bursting with something to say."

That sally drew a laugh from the other servants, and Rebecca forced herself to smile what she hoped would pass for a shy smile of her own. After a moment Mrs. Marsh went on, "You don't happen to know Lord Stanwood, do you?"

Rebecca shook her head decisively. Andrew had gone alone, that first time, to call upon the Stanwoods. Perhaps that had been a mistake, but he had said he wanted to speed matters along and Rebecca had still been feeling ill from the journey. She never knew precisely what had transpired, but

Andrew had returned to tell her that the Stanwoods refused to acknowledge her or even see her. Rebecca had found that difficult to believe, but when she had gone on her own to call on the Stanwoods, the butler had refused to admit her, saying he had orders to the contrary. Her mother's family butler had done the same. Perhaps she should have returned home to America then and there, but Andrew had refused to give up. He had hoped that by striking up an acquaintance with members of the *ton,* he might find someone who could be persuaded to help plead her case to the Stanwoods of Stanwood Hall. Or to the Harcourts, though Andrew had been far less interested in them. A cynical voice inside told Rebecca that was because the Harcourts neither ranked as high nor possessed so large a fortune as the Stanwoods.

For a while, before she had taken his measure fully, Rebecca had also allowed herself to hope when Lord Templeton had offered to serve as her champion in that regard. Too late she had realized that what he offered was not championship, but a desire to have her for his own. By the time she had run away, Rebecca would not even have been surprised if someone had told her that Lord Templeton, so far from aiding her cause, had warned the Stanwoods and Harcourts not to accept her.

Mary, the housemaid, laughed. "Oh, she's afraid of her own shadow, she is. Probably afraid the gen'lemen will bring their quarrel down here."

There was general laughter at that, and Rebecca felt herself coloring. Hastily she turned away and began cleaning the pans that had cooked up the first course. "Ah, well, leave her alone," one of the other housemaids said belatedly in a kind voice behind her. "You know she can't speak to defend herself. Likely you'd be skittish too, if you were mute."

Tears unexpectedly stung Rebecca's eyes. The precariousness of her position had never weighed as heavily on her as it did now. She must, she decided, take steps to seek another situation as soon as possible.

9

It was close upon midnight when Lord Templeton made his way toward the back of the house to where Ransford's kitchen was to be found. In spite of the lateness of the hour, he did not despair of finding Ransford's servants out and about, for the very excellent dinner that had been served earlier had just been supplemented by a late supper, and the servants were certain to still be cleaning up belowstairs. An observer, noting the trimness of Lord Templeton's figure, might have been pardoned at being surprised to discover that he had a passion for food. But the truth was that however moderately he might indulge this passion, he could not bear an ill-cooked meal and had been known to go some distance out of his way to patronize a hostelry noted for its cuisine. Or for its wine. And since Ransford was noted for the cellar he kept, Templeton had been imbibing freely ever since his arrival. That accounted for his present confusion in the hallway that led to the kitchen. The difficulty was that he had momentarily forgotten why he was going there. He was not, he told himself irritably, cast away, but he had been partaking heavily of the burgundy and there was no denying that while some perverse impulse had made him form the intention of speaking to Ransford's cook, he could not remember precisely why.

The lapse, however, was only momentary for he soon recalled the sweetbreads. That was it. He needed to speak with the cook about the sweetbreads. His own cook, while excellent in other matters, had never learned the knack of preparing sweetbreads in quite this way, and Templeton wished to have Ransford's chef explain it to the fellow. Never mind that his own cook wasn't here; Templeton was certain that something could be arranged if he only spoke with Ransford's chef.

Just why it was so important to obtain directions for properly prepared sweetbreads was a matter beyond the comprehension of Ransford's other guests. Nevertheless, none of them made any effort to dissuade Lord Templeton from his self-appointed task. Indeed, it was doubtful that they could have, even if they desired to do so, since Templeton was known to be implacable once he got the bit between his teeth. In any event, most of them were sufficiently cast away themselves that the action seemed perfectly acceptable even if incomprehensible. So they had watched as he left the drawing room, a trifle unsteadily, and then returned to their card games. What was, after all, one man's eccentricity when counted against the possible gain or loss of a fortune in one night? Even Andrew Pierce was more intent on his own hand of cards than on his friend's journey to the kitchen region of the house. As for Ransford, he was indifferent. Let Templeton ask his cook for a thousand recipes if he chose.

Templeton found the kitchen. It was late, of course, and he had to curse the scullery maid twice before she would go and get the chef, who was enjoying a comfortable cose with Mr. Eames and Mrs. Marsh in the housekeeper's sitting room. As Lord Templeton waited impatiently for the fellow to appear, another maid, a clumsy creature, appeared in the doorway to the kitchen, tripped over a raised spot in the floor, and dropped the coal scuttle she had come to fill. Templeton glanced at the creature, and if his eyes narrowed at the sight of her it was only for the briefest of moments, and then his eyes passed on again.

Rebecca, for that was who it was, felt a marked degree of panic. Her first thought was that Mr. Ransford had betrayed her, the second that she must escape from here, the third that she must do her best not to let Lord Templeton see her in the light of the kitchen candles. She hastily retrieved the coal scuttle and edged toward the door that led to the coal bin. To do so she had to pass Templeton. Deciding there was nothing for it but to brazen the matter out, Rebecca moved past him as quickly as possible, her eyes modestly focussed on the floor. To her profound relief, Templeton seemed to give her scarcely a glance and let her pass without a word. At the same moment, Katie returned with the French chef, and he and Templeton entered into a spirited discussion concerning the proper preparation of sweetbreads.

By the coal bin Rebecca had to pause, her heart pounding from fear. Still, it had seemed that Templeton had not seen her or, rather, for he could not help but have seen her drop the coal scuttle, he had not detected the person beneath the servant's disguise. Out of prudence, Rebecca took more time than she needed to fill the scuttle and she was relieved to see, when she returned to the kitchen, that Lord Templeton was gone. Instead, Alphonse was holding forth on the madness of English gentlemen and the wisdom of avoiding their company whenever possible. Mrs. Marsh, who had followed to the kitchen to see who had summoned the chef, scolded Rebecca for the coal dust spilled on the floor when she had dropped the scuttle.

"I'll not keep a sloppy household, Phoebe!" Mrs. Marsh told the girl sternly. "You know where the bucket and scrub brush is, I'll be bound, and as soon as you've carried the coal in to Frenchy's grate, you can come back here and clean up the dust."

Rebecca curtsied her understanding of her instructions and hurried to carry the coal to Alphonse's room. It was impossible not to think of her own unheated room at the top of the house, under the eaves, but equally impossible to rail against what could not be changed. At least, she told herself impatiently, she appeared to have escaped Templeton's notice. And that was worth whatever discomfort her present guise required.

Rebecca would have been far less sanguine had she been

privileged to know what was in Lord Templeton's mind which was seething with conjecture, for he had recognized her. He had known that she had gone to ground with remarkable success, and for the past several days nothing had exercised his mind so thoroughly as the attempt to guess where she might be. Not by the wildest workings of his imagination had he suspected that she might have passed herself off as a servant, nor that he would find her in the house of an old friend. Did Ransford know who she was? Impossible! And yet how could he not have noticed how unlikely a servant he had hired? The moment he heard her speak he must have known something was amiss. From the gentility of her speech to the oddness that came from having been raised in the colonies, by her own mouth Miss Stanwood must have proclaimed her unsuitability for the post of a drudge.

And yet, Ransford was not the man to ignore such a mystery. Was it possible he had not heard her speak? That she had been engaged by the housekeeper and Oliver had scarcely set eyes on her since she had entered the house? Aye, that might be the ticket. Why should Oliver, after all, trouble himself over a kitchen drudge? He, Lord Templeton, certainly did not. Not unless the creature was unusually pretty and, dressed as she was with her hair all unkempt, one would not look twice at Miss Stanwood now.

Still, Templeton was uneasy. Ransford had unaccountably sharp eyes and it was hard to imagine he did not know what went on in own house. Yet if he did know and countenanced her presence under his roof, particularly as a servant, it argued that Ransford had heretofore unsuspected depths. The matter clearly demanded further study.

Not by the blink of an eye, however, did Lord Templeton's countenance betray any of this as he returned to the others. To be sure, he did not reclaim his seat beside Lord Rufford. Instead he chose a just vacated seat at the table where Ransford was playing. "Did you get the recipe for sweetbreads from my chef?" Oliver asked Lord Templeton politely.

Templeton waved a hand negligently. "I have decided," he said gently, "that I do not care so very much, after all, about sweetbreads."

That provoked a certain laughter and Templeton smiled thinly in response. "I do not commend you, however, on all your servants, Ransford," he said coolly. "You have one, in particular, who is remarkably clumsy."

"Oh?" Ransford said absently, as he regarded the cards in his hand thoughtfully.

"Yes. A little dab of a thing," Templeton said, leaning forward. "Fair hair, large eyes. She dropped a coal scuttle on the kitchen floor."

"I presume she cleaned up the resulting mess," Ransford said, with an indifferent yawn.

"I presume so," Templeton replied, an edge to his voice as he added, "I didn't remain to find out. I really would suggest you dismiss her."

"Would you?" Ransford said sweetly, finally looking up to meet Templeton's eyes. "But then, she is not your servant, is she?"

For a moment, Templeton thought he read a challenge in Ransford's clear, blue eyes. But if so, it was gone in a flash and Ransford was studying his cards again, all thought of the careless servant apparently dismissed as he hesitated over what card to play next. As for Lord Templeton, he held his own counsel. If Ransford did not know the full story of the girl he had employed—and it certainly appeared that he did not, for otherwise he would scarcely have been so casual about the matter—Templeton had no intention of enlightening him. It was precisely the sort of circumstance Ransford would be likely to interpret as a cause for chivalry. No, it would be far better to let Ransford think her a mere servant and then lure her away from the house before abducting her. That way no one would connect her disappearance with him. And by the time Templeton was done with her, Miss Rebecca Stanwood would not wish to return to her family or Oliver Ransford or anyone else who had ever known her. Indeed, Templeton thought he could turn a neat little profit by persuading her to seek refuge with a certain abbess he knew who would pay handsomely to acquire such a genteel girl for her brothel.

The thought made Templeton quiver in anticipation, but he only took another sip of wine from the glass a footman had placed at his elbow and played his own card in the game. It would not do for anyone to guess the triumph he felt at discovering Rebecca Stanwood's refuge.

That it was Rebecca Stanwood he had seen, Templeton did not doubt. He could not guess how she had come to be working here, but he had studied her sweet face often enough in the weeks before she disappeared that he could not be mistaken. At times he had accused himself of being obsessed with the chit. But once Templeton had her in his grasp, that obsession would soon be erased, along with her innocence. And he would take great pleasure in erasing that innocence as well as punishing her for the chase she had led, a chase that had until now been fruitless and caused him to be the target of raillery among some of his fellow members of the Hellfire Club.

Templeton glanced over at Ransford. It would be a challenge, and an amusing one, to steal the girl away from this house without Ransford ever knowing he had done so. And yet it was difficult to hold his tongue until it was time to leave with Andrew Pierce. They stayed until well after midnight and then decided to walk homeward together, even though their houses were in different streets.

When they were out of sight of Ransford's house, Templeton told Pierce idly, "I believe I have found your stepsister, Andrew."

"My stepsister?" Andrew echoed in drunken astonishment. "Where?"

"I'll swear I saw her in Ransford's house tonight," Templeton replied coolly.

"Why didn't you tell me?" Andrew demanded. He turned and started in the direction they had just come. "I'm going back there and get her. It's not proper for Rebecca to be in Ransford's house, and I won't allow it."

"Oh, no, you're not!" Templeton exclaimed, grabbing Pierce by the arm and stopping him. "I've reason to think Ransford has no notion who she is, and if that's so, I don't want him to learn it from us."

"Doesn't know who she is?" Andrew asked incredulously. "Why'd he take her in, then? Was he foxed? How do you even know she's there?"

"If you will continue to walk homeward with me, I shall tell you," Templeton said calmly, and waited.

After a moment Andrew grumbled, "Very well. But I want to know everything. It seems very strange to me."

"It will sound even stranger, presently," Templeton said, with a ghost of a laugh. "When I saw your stepsister, she was carrying a coal scuttle."

"What?" Andrew demanded, stopping still in the street.

Templeton gave Pierce a tug on the arm to start him moving again. "Come along," he said sharply. "I don't want to draw anyone's attention."

"There's no one's attention to draw," Andrew objected with some asperity.

"Do you want to hear about your stepsister or not?" Templeton asked impatiently. That silenced Pierce and Templeton was able to go on. "I believe your stepsister, a most enterprising young lady, has taken refuge in Ransford's house in the guise of a servant. I've no notion how she obtained the post, but you may be sure that if Ransford knew the truth of who she was, he would appoint himself her champion. He is, you see, the chivalrous sort."

"Thought he was a friend of yours," Andrew said suspiciously. "Can't be the chivalrous sort if he's a friend of yours."

Templeton kept his temper with an effort. "One cannot account for all one's friends," he replied curtly. "In any event, I don't want him to guess who she is."

"Well, then how are we to get Rebecca?" Andrew asked. "Should I go round tomorrow and tell him she's my servant and I want her back?"

Templeton shook his head. "Too clumsy. She might take

it into her head to tell him the truth and then where should we be? No, I shall have to take care of the matter. I know a couple of men who can be depended upon. They'll find a way to spirit her out of the house and no one will be the wiser.'' He paused, then added, ''I shall have to take care, however, that they know they are not to, er, damage the goods.''

It took Pierce a moment to grasp what Templeton meant, then the two men shared a wicked laugh. ''I shall leave you here,'' his lordship said, ''and go find my two men. You shall hear from me as soon as I have word about the matter.''

The men Templeton wanted were to be found at a particularly disreputable inn in a particularly disreputable part of London. Another man might have feared for his safety, but Templeton was known here and only a newcomer would have failed to get out of his way. Tonight, Templeton encountered no newcomers. He did, however, find two men who had done him certain services in the past. They were not the sort to cavil at unusual requests or ask questions Templeton did not wish to answer. Templeton found them at their usual table and sat down with them. ''You've got a job for us, my lord?'' one asked.

''I do,'' he agreed. ''A servant. A girl in a house on Grosvenor Square. I want her. I want her soon and I want her alive. You understand?'' he said. ''You are not to harm her beyond what is needed to subdue her and cause her to come with you.''

One man rubbed his chin. ''That may take a bit of force in itself, m'lord.''

Templeton nodded. His voice was silky as he replied, ''Perhaps. Perhaps not. I shall give you a letter. I'll have it sent round tomorrow night. It should convince her to come with you, and by the time she suspects the truth, you should be well clear of London and it won't matter if she screams or struggles.''

''Clear of London,'' the second man echoed. ''To Medmenham, like the others?''

"To Medmenham," Templeton agreed, "but not precisely like the others. This one is special. And if either of you touches her, you will have me to answer to."

Both men shivered at the menace in Templeton's voice.

"We won't, m'lord," the first man said fervently.

"Good," Templeton said, with a smile that chilled the two men. "You are to send me word the moment you have her."

"The Hellfire Club again, eh, m'lord?" the second man said knowingly.

Templeton's hand came down on the table with a loud smacking sound. "I do not want you to think about why I want her!" he hissed. "It might not be healthy for you to think too hard about that question. Do I make myself clear?"

"Very clear, m'lord," the first man said hastily. "Don't fear, m'lord. We'll get the girl, all right and tight. No, nor without a mark on her, if that's the way you want it. Just take a day or two to look over the place and get friendly, like, with one of the girls who works in the house. Then we'll get that letter to this particular girl, just like you said. We knows our business."

"I hope you do," Templeton replied, the menace patent in his voice. "We will all be very sorry if you don't."

Then, with a nod to both men, Templeton rose to his feet and slowly made his way out of the taproom. A sigh of relief seemed to go about the room with his departure.

10

Rebecca rose in the dark and dressed in her unheated room, shivering with the cold. She had not slept well. Even after Andrew and Lord Templeton had left the party she had not been able to stop being afraid. Now the letter she had written in Mr. Ransford's library, at such risk, seemed a mistake. In it she had told her father's business partner, Mr. Johnston, to send his answer to her plea for help to his house, in care of the servant Phoebe. But Rebecca no longer felt certain she dared risk staying here until the letter could reach Mr. Johnston and a reply return. Indeed, her one impulse was to fly the house, and she would have done so had she had any notion of where to turn. But she did not. All the evils of her situation that had faced Rebecca when she left the house Andrew had rented still faced her now.

It was thoughts such as these that had kept Rebecca awake. Unfortunately, she had found no answers other than that she must, for the moment, remain in this house. And if she was to remain in this house, she must do her work, however tired she might be. The other thing she must do, as soon as possible, was decide what to do about that letter. For the moment it lay safely under her pillow. She dared not risk carrying it about in her apron pocket, for even if no one spotted it, there was the risk that she would spill something on it as she emptied slops or scrubbed the floors.

With a sigh, Rebecca headed down the dark, uncarpeted stairs, thinking wistfully of all the books in Ransford's library. If she could find a way, she would have crept in there to read, for the volumes she had seen had seemed to beckon her and reading had always been one of the pleasures of her life. It was foolish beyond permission to even think of doing so after having been caught twice by Ransford. However kind he had been in offering to arrange for her to learn to read, he had been equally implacable in barring her from his library when she spurned that same generous offer and his request for her to trust him. But Rebecca found the thought of all those books impossible to banish from her thoughts. And it was safer than thinking about Ransford or the way he had looked at her when he offered to teach her to read, or the way he had looked at her in the hallway yesterday as though he might speak to her again, and then had changed his mind and turned away abruptly as though he could not bear the sight of her.

Lady Sarah greeted Mrs. Marsh with real affection, for she had depended upon that redoubtable lady to look after Oliver ever since Lady Sarah had moved into her own London townhouse. The trust had not been misplaced, Mrs. Marsh seeing in Ransford the son she had never had. Mrs. Marsh, for her part, had more than once been heard to say that one couldn't find a sweeter lady in London than Lady Sarah, Mr. Ransford's mother. It was always a bit unnerving, to be sure, to have her ladyship descend unannounced as she did this morning. But on the other hand, Mrs. Marsh had had, for several days, a feeling that her ladyship might do so, for nothing would be more likely if she were to get wind of the new girl. Indeed, Mrs. Marsh was not altogether averse to discussing the matter with Lady Sarah. That conversation between Mr. Ransford and Phoebe, late at night in the library, hadn't sat well with Mrs. Marsh. It hadn't sat well at all. And while Phoebe had been on her best behavior ever since, Mrs. Marsh still didn't trust the girl, not by a long shot. But what if her ladyship blamed her for the state of affairs? It wouldn't be unnatural for her ladyship to do so, Mrs. Marsh thought anxiously. So it was that she greeted

Lady Sarah's appearance with very mixed feelings, particularly when she learned that her ladyship wished to see her in the drawing room rather than in the housekeeper's parlor, where she usually came and condescended to drink a cup of tea with Mrs. Marsh.

"How are you, Mrs. Marsh?" Lady Sarah said kindly when the housekeeper stood before her in the drawing room.

"Quite well, m'lady," Mrs. Marsh answered with a curtsy.

"Please sit down," Lady Sarah said, indicating a chair placed very close to hers. "I should like to talk to you about one of my son's new servants."

That did it. Mrs. Marsh knew trouble when she heard it coming. Gingerly she seated herself in the chair indicated and said, a trifle gloomily. "Phoebe? That's who you want to talk about, isn't it? I told Mr. Ransford he shouldn't hire her. Not without talking to her former mistress. If the girl really did have a former mistress and didn't just write the letter herself. Or buy it. But I expect he felt sorry for her, not being able to talk and all as she is. Up and hired her, he did, telling me to find a place for her without even asking me if I thought it was right to do so."

Lady Sarah's voice was cool as she replied, all but interrupting Mrs. Marsh's monologue. "I believe you have mistaken my intent, Mrs. Marsh. I do not mean to criticize the girl. Not without good reason, at any rate. I simply wish to know more about her."

That stopped Mrs. Marsh. It wasn't her place to criticize Mr. Ransford or his choice in hiring, either. Carefully she said, grudgingly, "Phoebe tries to do her work. I suppose it isn't her fault she hasn't been well trained. I mean, one can see she isn't accustomed to working in a household such as this. And, of course, she can't answer back. But there is something about her that makes me uneasy and I can't change that, try as I will, even without knowing, as I do, that she was found wandering about the house the other night."

"Perhaps I better see this Phoebe for myself, Mrs.

Marsh,'' Lady Sarah said thoughtfully. ''Will you send her in?''

''Of course, m'lady,'' Mrs. Marsh said, recognizing the dismissal in Lady Sarah's voice.

A few minutes later Mrs. Marsh was calling Phoebe's name in a loud voice in the kitchen. Phoebe emerged from the cellar with a full coal scuttle in hand. Mrs. Marsh didn't bother to ask what room it was destined for, but immediately told Katie to take the scuttle wherever it was bound. Then she directed her attention to Phoebe, who had coal dust on her face, hands, and apron. ''Oh, lord, it'll never do for you to go into her ladyship looking like that,'' Mrs. Marsh moaned impatiently. ''Here, come and wash that dust off your face and hands. And take off that apron. I'll try to find you a clean one. If I can't, you'll just have to go in without one.''

Go in where? Rebecca wanted to ask, as she did as she was bid. And who was her ladyship? Mr. Ransford's mother? Rebecca could not help but remember all the times Mrs. Marsh had warned her that if Lady Sarah was to hear of her odd starts, she would find herself dismissed on the spot.

No one had bothered to tell Phoebe, of course, that Mr. Ransford's mother had come to call. Even now, as Mrs. Marsh shepherded her toward the drawing room, all she would say is that Phoebe must mind her manners and remember to curtsy to her ladyship and not— Here Mrs. Mash had caught herself. She'd been about to tell Phoebe not to answer pertly but that wasn't possible, was it? Still, there was something about the way the girl looked at one that might offend her ladyship and Mrs. Marsh made a push to explain it to the girl.

''It's not precisely that you stare, Phoebe, but you really ought to keep your eyes lowered when her ladyship addresses you. And even though you can't answer with your tongue, keep your wits about you and nod or shake your head. Her ladyship will understand,'' Mrs. Marsh advised kindly, now that the vexing responsibility of what to do with Phoebe no longer lay entirely on her shoulders.

So, somewhat bewildered and extremely wary, Rebecca entered the drawing room as a footman held the door for her. His expression, it seemed to her, was a mixture of sympathy and contempt and she could not help wondering what was in store for her or, rather, for Phoebe.

In the few moments before Rebecca lowered her eyes, she had the impression of a very pretty, petite lady with fair hair and blue eyes. The resemblance to Mr. Ransford was remarkable. The voice that spoke as she curtsied was unexpectedly kind, and Rebecca found herself warming to this unknown lady whose first words confirmed the suspicion that she faced Oliver Ransford's mother.

"Hello, my dear. I'm told your name is Phoebe. Mine is Lady Sarah. I understand you are new in this household."

Rebecca nodded, careful not to look directly at Lady Sarah. But Oliver's mother was determined to put the girl at ease. "Please sit down," she said to Rebecca gently. "I only wish to discover a little of your past history."

There was no mistaking the flicker of alarm in Phoebe's eyes at those words, and Lady Sarah did not try to hide her awareness as she said coolly, once Phoebe had taken the chair so recently occupied by Mrs. Marsh, "It will be better if you tell me the truth, you know. For I shall otherwise make it my business to learn what you have tried to conceal. And while you cannot speak, I have no doubt you can find a way to tell me what I wish to know if you choose to do so."

Rebecca looked at Lady Sarah now, anguish evident in her fine eyes, and Oliver's mother began to understand why he had been so taken with the girl. There was a lively intelligence behind those eyes, and pride and breeding as well. No more than Mrs. Marsh did Lady Sarah think Phoebe had had a long career as a servant. No, she had come to such a post very recently and had yet to learn the sort of servile behavior expected of someone in her position. Though Lady Sarah had to admit the girl had tried to pretend to such an attitude. The downcast eyes, the meek expression, the rounded shoulders with which she had first approached Lady Sarah argued that the girl was trying to fit into her post here.

It was not her fault that she did not succeed. Oliver had been right to think there was some mystery here. Lady Sarah only hoped the solution to it would not distress her son, for she had no confidence that it would redound to the girl's credit.

To say that Rebecca was dismayed would have been a grotesque understatement. That she might be unmasked had been a possibility she had faced from the first day she took this position, and Rebecca had thought herself prepared for the moment when it might happen. And yet now she discovered she was not prepared. Worse, all instinct told her to prevaricate, to pretend not to understand, to stave off the moment when Lady Sarah, and therefore Mr. Ransford, would learn the truth. Rebecca tried to brace herself for what Lady Sarah might say next. But her ladyship did not speak. Instead, after several moments of silence, Rebecca risked another look at Lady Sarah. Fine blue eyes met her own darker ones. There was a mixture of sympathy, intelligence, implacability, and determination here to be faced, and silently Rebecca reached her decision. Lady Sarah meant what she said. She would make a formidable enemy. And yet Rebecca also felt that she would make a formidable ally, as well, if she could be enlisted on Rebecca's behalf. What did she have to lose? Her position? That was already forfeit for Rebecca could think of no way to dampen Lady Sarah's suspicions. Could she betray her to Lord Templeton? Perhaps, but Rebecca could not bring herself to believe she had entirely escaped Templeton's notice the night before. Could she find her reputation in shreds if Lady Sarah spread about the tale of her masquerade? Undoubtedly, but what reputation did she have to lose? The Stanwoods refused to acknowledge her and so did the Harcourts. In the weeks she had been in London with Andrew, not one invitation had come her way save through Lord Templeton or from ladies who even Rebecca knew were not the thing. Besides, she meant to return to America, didn't she? What difference could it make there what Lady Sarah or anyone else said here?

It was perhaps fortunate that Rebecca was not better

acquainted with some of the ladies of the *ton* or she might have been even less trusting than she now was. She might have realized that there were ladies who would be as swift to oversee her ruin, and with as much pleasure, as Templeton. But perhaps even if she had known all this she would have made the same choice.

Slowly Rebecca raised her eyes until she was looking directly at Ransford's mother. Her voice was calm and composed as she said, "I have no doubt, Lady Sarah, that you will be angry with me. Please, however, hear me out before you condemn me for the choice I have made."

Lady Sarah caught her breath. When the girl looked at her like this, with such an eloquent plea for help in her eyes, Sarah understood even better why her son had taken the girl under his wing. But the audacity: to pretend to be mute when she was not! Her voice was frosty as she said, "I collect you can speak. No doubt you will tell me why you have pretended otherwise?"

"I was afraid my voice would betray me," Rebecca said simply. "My name is Rebecca Stanwood and my home was Boston. My stepbrother, Andrew Pierce, and I came to London this summer. It was my father's dying wish that I reconcile with his family. Unfortunately, I have been unable to do so."

"I knew you had a look about you that was familiar," Lady Sarah said thoughtfully. "Your grandmother, Clarissa Stanwood, has just the same eyes. How like Giles to ignore that in refusing to acknowledge your claim as a Stanwood."

"It is not entirely his fault," Rebecca said. "He has never seen me."

"What?" Lady Sarah demanded incredulously. "You did not go to see the Stanwoods? But I have heard that you presented your claim of kinship and was rejected."

"I was indisposed with a trifling ailment and Andrew thought it better not to wait. Lord Stanwood threw him out of the house and refused ever to receive me," Rebecca explained quietly. "My mother's family was no more kind when he approached them."

"What a muddle your stepbrother made of things," Lady Sarah said impatiently. "As great a muddle as he did, I suspect, with Lord Templeton."

"You know about Lord Templeton?" Rebecca asked, her voice faltering.

"A few days ago, Sally Jersey overheard Templeton quietly tell someone you were missing," Lady Sarah explained, "and while the news has not yet spread very far, it has begun to spark the most delicious gossip."

"What is being said about me?" Rebecca asked hesitantly.

"That Templeton had marked you as his prey. That he did not mean marriage. That you fled your stepbrother's house rather than submit to Templeton," Lady Sarah said, ticking off the points on her fingers. "The greatest source of conjecture was where you had fled to, and why you had fled, for one would presume that your stepbrother would have defended you."

Rebecca rose and paced the room as Lady Sarah watched patiently. "It's very difficult to say this about my stepbrother," Rebecca said, at last. "He and I were never close, but I had thought we fought no more than other brothers and sisters. Indeed, when he offered to accompany me to London, I was grateful for his support. Too late I realized that my welfare meant less to him than what my person could bring him, either as a recognized Stanwood or, if not that, then from Lord Templeton. He offered to tear up Andrew's gambling vowels and, I collect, sponsor Andrew in society if I accepted his attentions. I knew I must escape the house, but I had no notion where to go or who to turn to since the Stanwoods and the Harcourts refuse to acknowledge my existence. I didn't have the funds to hire my own house or stay in a hotel for more than a night or two. Nor did I have the funds to buy passage home again. I was also afraid Lord Templeton would find me, asking at every inn and hotel in London, if need be. Then one of the maids in the household said that it was a pity I wasn't a servant for no one ever noticed a servant. And that was when I decided to engage on this madcap escapade. Only when I left the house and tried to find a place to stay, for the first night at least, a gentleman on the street accosted me. When I said I didn't wish for his attentions, he pursued me and I ran, hiding, finally, in Mr. Ransford's garden. He found me and I pretended to be mute so that my accent would escape notice. Mr. Ransford was kind enough to offer me this post and I accepted. Unfortunately, it seems I have not been quite as successful in escaping attention as I thought to be," Rebecca concluded seriously.

"That was to be expected," Lady Sarah said dryly. "Indeed, my son told me there was some mystery about you and asked me to delve into the matter."

At once Rebecca was on her knees before Lady Sarah, her hands over one of Lady Sarah's. "You won't tell him, will you? I just want to go on being the mute maid, Phoebe."

"But why not tell Oliver?" Lady Sarah asked in a bewildered voice. "He can help you, if you let him."

These words did not comfort Rebecca, nor did she loosen her grip on Lady Sarah's hand. "Please, you must not tell him! I have seen Lord Templeton a guest in this house just last night. You may think you know your son well enough to trust him, but it is my life and honor and I cannot."

"This is all nonsense," Lady Sarah said impatiently, but she could not, she admitted silently, deny that her son and Templeton were friends. Instead, she softened at the terror evident on Rebecca's face. "Well, what am I to tell Oliver, if not the truth?" she demanded reasonably.

"Nothing. That I am merely a servant, one he need not trouble his head about," Rebecca said, rising to her feet and drawing away from Lady Sarah.

"But you wish me to leave you to remain in his household, knowing that if your identity is discovered by the *ton* it will be a scandal to his name as well as yours?" Lady Sarah asked reprovingly.

Now Rebecca turned to look directly into Lady Sarah's eyes. "I will leave this house, if you desire it," she said. "I ask only that you recommend me to some other house, some lady's house, if you think you are able to do so. I may not have been bred to it," she added with a wry smile, "but I have become a tolerable belowstairs maid in the short time I have been here."

Lady Sarah's kind heart was touched even further, for she did not doubt that Rebecca meant what she said. "Why not come and stay with me, as my guest, instead?" she suggested kindly. "I shall not ask you to carry the coals to the grates," she added, her eyes twinkling as she stared, pointedly, at Rebecca's hem, still smudged with coal dust.

For a long moment, Rebecca did not answer. She could not, for Lady Sarah's offer was a kindness she had not expected nor knew how to repay. It was also an offer every instinct told her to refuse. She could not trespass on the benevolence of someone who had no obligation toward her.

It was as if Lady Sarah could read her mind for she said gently, "It would be a favor to me. I am much alone, these days, and would find a companion a treat. Though I can well understand if you think it would be a dead bore to be cooped up with someone like me."

For the second time, Rebecca found herself on her knees before Lady Sarah. "No, how can you say so! I would find it a great pleasure to be in your company."

"Then why," Lady Sarah said logically, "are you trying to refuse me?"

Troubled, Rebecca took her time to answer. "You are very kind to me," she said at last. "But I have no claim on you. Nor have you perhaps thought how much my relatives, the Stanwoods of Stanwood Hall, would dislike it if they knew you had taken me in. Or the Harcourts."

"Do you think that would trouble me?" Lady Sarah asked coolly. "It is not for me to answer them, it is for them to answer to me as to why they have disowned their cousin from America. And make no mistake, whatever impression they might have gained from your stepbrother, they ought not to have rejected the claim without meeting you,'' Lady Sarah said sternly. ''Had they done so, they would have seen at once that you were a true Stanwood. But I do wonder, child, why your stepmother did not come with you. I collect your own mother is dead. Her name was Felicity Harcourt, was it not? As I remember it, your father married her just before leaving with her for America and her family disowned her for doing so.''

''Did you know my mother?'' Rebecca asked with some astonishment.

''We were in school together,'' Lady Sarah replied. ''I did not know her well, but I remember the scandal when she ran away with your father. What happened to her?''

''She died some years ago, in childbirth, and the child with her,'' Rebecca explained quietly. ''After her death, my father married Andrew's mother.'' Then, remembering Lady Sarah's earlier question, she said, ''My stepmama's health would not permit her to accompany me to England and, in any case, it was necessary for her to stay and put my father's affairs in order.'' Rebecca paused and looked down at her hands a moment, then back at Lady Sarah. ''You have not asked,'' she said, ''but I cannot doubt you wonder why I did not come to London before now. The answer is that I saw no need. I was happy in Boston. But as my father lay dying, he begged my stepmother to send me here, to England, to seek out my family, both families, and I did not think I could disobey his wishes. I was grateful when Andrew offered to bring me. I could not know then what his apparent kindness would cost me.''

Before Lady Sarah could reply to these revelations, the door to the drawing room opened. Still on her knees before Lady Sarah, Rebecca stared in horror as Oliver Ransford's calm voice broke the stunned silence to observe, ''Well, Mama, what have you discovered about Phoebe?''

11

Rebecca's eyes flew to Lady Sarah's, pleading for her silence. Ransford did not miss her silent plea and his eyes narrowed in patent disapproval of the tableau before him. Lady Sarah's eyebrows rose, as if in surprise, and her voice was a trifle cool as she said, "I have discovered, Oliver, that your servant, Phoebe, is just the sort of girl I have been looking for to take a post in my household."

"You cannot be serious!" Ransford exclaimed incredulously.

"Why not?" she asked, puzzled. "Mrs. Marsh tells me you have no real need of an extra girl, and she will suit my needs perfectly."

"Phoebe, will you please go to the kitchen?" Ransford told her without looking directly at the girl.

Rebecca cast another mute look of appeal to Lady Sarah who smiled and nodded encouragingly. "I shall see you again before I leave this house," Lady Sarah told her calmly. "Run along and try not to worry."

Rebecca did as she was bid, keeping her eyes on the floor as she passed Ransford who held the door open for her. She could feel his anger as clearly as if she had looked directly at his face. But he did not speak until she was out of the drawing room and the door shut again behind her. Even then Oliver did not at once say anything, but merely stared speculatively at his mother. How much had she guessed, how much had she learned about Phoebe? he wondered. Or was it merely the fear that Phoebe might entrap him that moved her?

''Well, Mama?'' he said at last. ''May I ask why you've decided to take my servant away from me?''

Lady Sarah watched her son, amused at the way he thrust his lower jaw forward just as he had when he was a child. ''I've told you, Oliver,'' she said gently. ''I do not think you truly need her and I should like to take her into my household.''

''I see.''

Lady Sarah waited a moment, and when he said nothing more she asked, ''Why are you so angry with me, Oliver?''

''Because I think you are less than honest with me,'' he retorted roundly.

''How so?'' Lady Sarah asked, spreading her hands in a pretty gesture of confusion.

''I think that you wish to remove Phoebe from my house because you are afraid I shall make a fool of myself over her, only you are too devious to say so,'' he replied bluntly.

Lady Sarah nodded her head in acknowledgement. ''I will allow that I came here with that thought in my head,'' she said honestly. ''Do you think that such an unreasonable concern for a mother?''

''I should hope you would have more trust in my good sense,'' Oliver retorted scathingly. ''Particularly as I assured you the other day that you might have.''

''Yes, but Phoebe is a taking thing,'' Lady Sarah replied with a smile. ''And you would not be the first gentleman to succumb to a servant with a pretty face. To be sure, the Earl of Berkeley was before your time, but even so, you must know the story of his eldest son and the thirty-three bastards he is supposed to have fathered, all within ten miles of Berkeley Castle. And before that there was Lady Henrietta Wentworth, who was Lord Rockingham's sister. She married her footman and went to live in Ireland on one hundred pounds a year. So don't try to flummox me into believing either that such a thing is impossible or that I should find it desirable. To be honest, Oliver, you appear to be all but obsessed with the girl.''

As his mother had been relating these stories, Ransford's lively sense of humor had begun to reassert itself and he found himself smiling. "Very well," he conceded, "I suppose I must allow that you have had reason to be worried. But do you still think so?"

"Your annoyance at the notion of Phoebe leaving your household does not reassure me," Lady Sarah told him dryly.

"At least allow that the girl is not trying to entrap me," Ransford said teasingly. "Unless you have concluded that she is?" he added uncertainly.

"If I thought that, I should not have invited her to join my household," Lady Sarah replied sensibly.

"What do you think of her, Mama?" Ransford asked, unconsciously imitating Rebecca by coming to sit on a low stool by Lady Sarah's feet and taking her hands into his. "Do you not find her a most unusual girl? The other day I found her in my library, holding a copy of Shakespeare. She denies knowing how to read, of course, but she could not hide her love of books. Then, a day later, at night, I discovered she had been in my library again. I have reason to believe she can write. Why she will not admit that she can read, I cannot understand," he said. "But I do know that she is something quite out of the common way."

"And do you have no guesses as to who or what she is?" Lady Sarah asked thoughtfully.

Ransford got up and paced about the room. "At first," he said, a puzzled frown on his brow, "I had no notion what to think. But I have begun to wonder if perhaps she might not be the daughter, born out of wedlock, of some member of the *ton*. If I am right and she can read and write, then she has been educated far better than one might expect, for it was a copy of Shakespeare that I found her holding. Scarcely easy reading! But whose daughter, or why she should have taken refuge in my garden, I cannot imagine. You have seen her, Mama. What do you think?"

Lady Sarah regarded her son calmly, understandding more, perhaps, than he knew himself. "I think her a well-behaved girl and I agree that she is something out of the common way. More than that I refuse to say until she has been in my household awhile and I know her better.''

Ransford let go of his mother's hands. ''You still mean to take her from my household, then?''

''Yes, I do,'' she replied calmly. ''I like the girl and I think I will enjoy having her about me.''

''About you?'' Ransford echoed. He shot his mother a swift, appraising glance as he said, skeptically, ''You cannot mean to make her your dresser or anything of the sort. And mute as she is, Phoebe could scarcely serve as a companion, could she? How much about you will she be, carrying coal scuttles and scrubbing floors belowstairs?''

Lady Sarah's eyes avoided Oliver's as she said, airily, ''Oh, I thought to have her about me to fetch things and run errands and such. Don't you think it will be pleasanter for her than carrying coal scuttles and scrubbing floors, as you have her doing here?'' she asked innocently.

''Oh, I think it would be far pleasanter for the girl,'' Ransford agreed grimly. ''I just wish I could understand why you are being so kind to her. I thought you were to unravel the mystery for me, and instead you are helping to make it greater.''

''I told you, I think we should suit,'' Lady Sarah replied, now meeting Ransford's gaze limpidly. ''More than that I refuse to say. It is not for you to approve or disapprove of the servants I hire.'' She paused then and added in a thoughtful voice, ''I do concede, however, that as her current employer, it is up to you to say whether you will allow Phoebe to come work for me. Would you really mind so very much, Oliver?''

Ransford could not refuse the anxious plea in his mother's eyes. ''No, of course not,'' he told her affectionately. ''If it would give you pleasure, by all means take Phoebe with you. Today, if you wish. As you have pointed out, Mrs. Marsh will manage admirably without her, and I cannot help agreeing that it will be a kinder, happier position for Phoebe herself. I cannot think she was made to carry coal scuttles or scrub floors, either.''

Lady Sarah beamed at Ransford. "Thank you, Oliver," she said. "You are the best of sons! Will you tell Mrs. Marsh or shall I?''

"Why don't you tell Mrs. Marsh," Ransford said as he headed for the drawing room door, "and I tell Phoebe?''

Lady Sarah nodded approvingly. "An excellent notion. I shall know just how to soothe any ruffled feathers Mrs. Marsh might have, and I am sure Phoebe will be comforted to know you approve of this change.''

Ransford paused in the doorway and arched a quizzing eyebrow at his mother. "I'm not entirely sure that I do," he added, then he was gone.

Lady Sarah had only a few minutes to wait before Mrs. Marsh rapped at the drawing room door and then entered with a curtsy. "Mr. Ransford said you wished to speak with me again.''

"Yes, Mrs. Marsh. Please come in. I just wanted to tell you that I have decided to take Phoebe with me. You have seen for yourself how out of place she is here,'' Lady Sarah told the housekeeper kindly.

Bewildered, Mrs. Marsh could only think to say, "I'm sure it's the wisest thing, but what will you do with her?'' As soon as she had spoken, Mrs. Marsh realized she had gone beyond the line and tried to retract her words. "That is to say, I'm pleased to hear it, your ladyship.''

Lady Sarah smiled thinly. Her mind had been filled with conjectures from the first moment she had realized that Phoebe was Rebecca Stanwood and now, with an eye to the future, she said, "Phoebe is a most unusual girl, Mrs. Marsh. I shall take her under my wing.'' Lady Sarah paused, then repeated what she had told Oliver. "As you have no doubt noticed, Mrs. Marsh, Phoebe is unsuited to scrubbing floors and carrying coal scuttles. I believe there is more to her than we both realize. I shall take her to be a companion to me, fetching my shawl and running errands and such. I am, after all, getting on in years.''

As Mrs. Marsh found it impossible to imagine Lady Sarah as getting on in years, she was not unnaturally struck dumb by this pronouncement. Lady Sarah took the opportunity to add, thinking of both Lord Templeton and the future, ''I shall depend upon you, Mrs. Marsh, to make sure that none of the servants gossip about Phoebe after she is gone. They are to talk to no one about her. No one.''

That caused Mrs. Marsh to goggle even more. At last she crossed her arms and said grimly, ''I know I'm speaking out of turn, Lady Sarah, but I'm not one as is easily hood-winked, you might say. If you don't mean to tell me what's afoot, that's fine. Just so long as you get the girl out of this house I'll be satisfied.'' She turned to go, pausing only to say, over her shoulder with the air of one divulging a dark secret, ''She had silk underwear!''

Lady Sarah managed to preserve her countenance, but as soon as the door shut behind the housekeeper, a peal of laughter escaped Oliver's mother. He reentered the room in time to hear her. Tilting his head slightly to one side, he smiled and said, quizzically, ''Well, Mother? Do you mean to tell me what is so funny?''

Lady Sarah started to oblige him when she realized that to do so would not only be indelicate but, in view of Rebecca's determination to keep Oliver ignorant of her true circumstances, distinctly imprudent. So instead of sharing the scandal of the silk underwear and Mrs. Marsh's evident suspicions, she said, ''I don't think Mrs. Marsh would approve of my doing so.''

That caused Oliver to give a laugh and retort, ''Heaven forbid I should ask you to offend Mrs. Marsh's sensibilities! I collect it is something she considers grossly improper, and for the looks she's been casting in Phoebe's direction, it concerns her.''

But Lady Sarah refused to satisfy his curiosity. Instead she asked, ''Did you tell Phoebe she is to come to work for me?''

"Yes, and I am not entirely sure she liked the notion," Ransford replied, a little troubled.

"She did not refuse?" Lady Sarah asked anxiously.

"No, she did not refuse," he agreed slowly.

"Well, it is only a natural anxiety at exchanging a position she knows for one that is new to her," Lady Sarah said with conviction. "I shall soon set her at ease. Does she come with me now or do you send her over in your carriage later?"

Ransford hesitated. "I had meant to send her over later, but from the look on Mrs. Marsh's face just now, perhaps it would be best if she left as soon as she was ready. I told her to come back in here when she had packed her things."

"I'll wait for her, then," Lady Sarah said briskly. "I shouldn't like to think Mrs. Marsh would have a chance to bully her before she left."

"No, indeed," Ransford agreed heartily. He paused and then added, "I am beginning to think you were right to take her out of this house. I had no notion Mrs. Marsh disliked her so intensely."

"Not dislike, precisely," Lady Sarah said. "I think it is just that she does not understand Phoebe and therefore is uncomfortable with her."

Ransford nodded. "You will be kind to her?" he asked.

"Mrs. Marsh?" Lady Sarah quizzed her son.

"Phoebe," Ransford retorted scathingly.

"Of course, Oliver," Lady Sarah said, abandoning the game.

A moment later there was a timid knock at the drawing room door. "Come in," Ransford said, constraint in his voice.

It was Rebecca. She carried her small traveling bag with one hand and had her cloak over her arm. She cast a frightened look at Ransford and a grateful one at Lady Sarah, who immediately rose to her feet and came toward Rebecca. "Come, my dear," she said kindly. "It is time we went home."

"I'll walk you down to your carriage, Mama," Ransford said promptly.

He did so, walking beside Phoebe who refused to look at him. But when he handed her into his mother's carriage, he held her hand until she was forced to look into his face to make him let go. "If you ever need a friend," he told her with simple sincerity, "I am here."

Rebecca dared only allow herself a quick nod of understanding before she pulled free her hand and let the footman close the carriage door. Then they were pulling away from the curb and Rebecca did not allow herself to look out the window to see if Ransford were still watching her.

Across from her, Lady Sarah smiled a quiet smile of satisfaction to herself. After allowing the girl to brood for a few minutes, she said, with dancing eyes, "Rebecca, I have directed the coachman to stop at my dressmaker before taking me home. You must have more fashionable clothes."

Rebecca looked at her, bewildered. "Your dressmaker? But I don't understand," she said. "Mr. Ransford said I was to be some sort of hired companion."

"Well, that's what I told Oliver," Lady Smith said with a mischievous smile, "since you didn't want me to tell him the truth. But I told you I meant you to be a guest in my house. Didn't you believe me? I mean to take you out and about."

"But if Lord Templeton sees me—" Rebecca began.

"Lord Templeton will not dare to trifle with you while you are under my protection," Lady Sarah said firmly.

"He will say—"

Again Lady Sarah interrupted Rebecca. "He will not dare to say anything, for he will know that if he does so, I shall tell the *ton* what he intended and make a scandal for him."

"You've already said that the *ton* knows," Rebecca pointed out doubtfully.

"I've said that the *ton* thinks so," Lady Sarah countered, "and that is a far different thing than for me to say so for certain. Many still doubt the story. Lord Templeton will not risk my confirming it. I am," she said, smiling grimly, "the daughter of a duke, and society will take my word before his, I assure you."

Rebecca shivered, not doubting Lady Sarah for a moment. Still she worried. "Won't the *ton* wonder why I am staying with you instead of with my stepbrother?" she asked.

"We shall say that I knew your mother, and for her sake I have taken you under my wing and mean to bring you out," Lady Sarah said with a wave of the hand. "The first task will be to outfit you with a proper wardrobe of clothes."

"I haven't enough money for clothes," Rebecca said quietly. "Andrew gambled away almost everything we brought. It would be better to get my clothes from the house he hired, if it could be done safely."

"It could be done," Lady Sarah assured her, "but I have no intention of doing so unless you can assure me that your clothes were bought here and not brought from America, for I do not mean you to be a dowd. I mean for you to dazzle everyone and to have them realize that you are unmistakably a Stanwood. None of them would wear an unfashionable gown, I assure you."

In spite of herself Rebecca was surprised into laughing. But she would not be deterred. "Some of my clothes were bought here, Lady Sarah. I own, however, that I would rather not warn Andrew where I am, but I am in earnest when I say that I have not the money to pay for a new wardrobe such as you envision."

"I don't mean for you to do so," Lady Sarah said blithely. "I have my own reasons for wishing to outfit you as I shall, and considering that I have just rescued you from an existence of drudgery scrubbing floors and carrying coal, I think it would be most ungrateful of you to cavil at fulfilling my whims."

Rebecca shook her head. "I don't mean to be ungrateful," she said earnestly, "but I don't wish to impose."

Lady Sarah looked at Rebecca, her eyes twinkling again

as she said, "Don't worry, my dear, I shall most assuredly tell you if you are in danger of becoming an imposition to me."

And with that Rebecca had to be satisfied, for they had reached the salon of Lady Sarah's *modiste*.

If Madame Jeanette was surprised to see Lady Sarah accompanied by an underservant, she did not say so. Nor did she do more than blink when told that this underservant was the person to be outfitted with an entire new wardrobe, everything of the best and most fashionable. Lady Sarah was shrewd enough to know, however, that if she did not tell Madame Jeanette something, that lady would not be able to keep from telling the tale of Lady Sarah's mysterious whim to someone else and soon it would be all over London. Therefore, as soon as Madame Jeanette had personally escorted Lady Sarah to a private room and before the assistant was summoned, Lady Sarah swore her to secrecy and said, "I know I can trust your discretion, Madame Jeanette. This is a young lady who has been persecuted by one of our more dissolute lords and was forced to take refuge in pretending to be a scullery maid to escape his unwanted attentions. With your help I mean to rescue her and make her the toast of London. Will you help us?"

"*Bien sûr,*" Madame Jeanette agreed, agog with curiosity. "But *mademoiselle,* who is she?"

"A young lady from America," Lady Sarah confided, "whose relatives here refuse to acknowledge her, but I mean to make them do so; and if they think she will bring them credit, they will find that they wish to do so. Which is why we need your genius."

"She shall be a diamond of the first water when I am through with her," Madame Jeanette vowed.

"But no one must know a word of this," Lady Sarah warned sternly. "If anyone discovers the story, I shall know it was from you."

"*Moi?*" Madame Jeanette said, genuinely shocked. "I am all discretion. No one shall hear her story from me. And my assistant? All discretion as well. But it is better, I think, that I wait on you today all by myself. It is well, yes?''

"It is well," Lady Sarah agreed with a sigh of relief.

12

Two mornings later, Rebecca was happily ensconced in Lady Sarah's library. It was too early for callers, and in any event, until the clothes had arrived from Madame Jeanette, she and Lady Sarah had agreed that it would be best if Rebecca stayed out of view. One simple gown had been provided by Madame Jeanette so that the servants would not see Rebecca arrive dressed as a servant, and the coachman had been warned not to say a word about the transformation that had taken place at Madame Jeanette's establishment. But as this dress had been chosen solely on the grounds that it would fit Rebecca and was ready at once, neither Lady Sarah nor Rebecca could feel entirely satisfied with her appearance. To be sure, Rebecca had the white dress which she had taken with her when she fled Andrew's household, but it was only suitable for evening wear even if she had not come to hate the sight of it.

Rebecca did not mind her temporary seclusion. Once she began to go out and about with Lady Sarah, Lord Templeton would have to be faced and, in spite of all of Lady Sarah's reassurances, Rebecca was not eager for that moment to occur. Besides, it was so cozy to curl up on a rainy day with one of the deliciously foolish novels that filled the shelves of Lady Sarah's library. The room itself was light and airy with large windows and pale pink curtains that matched both the red coloring in the rug Lady Sarah had ordered from Brussels and the paper on the wall. The furniture was comfortable and positively encouraged one to sit beside the flickering fire, fed by obliging servants to provide a warm glow to the room.

This morning was such a morning, and as Lady Sarah was busy writing letters in the drawing room, Rebecca felt no guilt over absenting herself to enjoy Mrs. Bethfrey's latest novel. So engrossed was she that she did not even hear the library door open and someone enter until a familiar, well-bred voice behind her said coolly, "So you can read. I wonder why you were so determined to have me think you could not?"

Rebecca jumped and turned to look up at Oliver Ransford, who was regarding her with an impassive expression on his face. Guiltily Rebecca tried to hide the book, but Ransford took it from her hands and said, more gently this time, "It's all right, Phoebe. I didn't mean to startle you and I certainly don't mind you reading a book. I just wish I knew why you thought you needed to hide such a skill from me."

Which meant, Rebecca thought, that Lady Sarah had not yet told her son who Phoebe was. Ransford came around and sat on the chair opposite Rebecca's determined, it seemed, to put her at ease. "My mother told me you were in here," he said, "but not what I would find you doing. Please don't be frightened. I think it's wonderful that you can read. If nothing else, it must make life less lonely for you." He paused, then added gently, "I wish you could bring yourself to trust me more, Phoebe. I've a notion there's a great deal to you that you will not let me see."

Ransford stared at Rebecca, achingly handsome in his favorite jacket of blue Bath cloth that matched his eyes, and pantaloons of biscuit hue. Rebecca wanted to tell him the truth, had meant to tell him the truth, but when she tried to speak no words came out. Instead, she was paralyzed by fear. He was a friend of Lord Templeton and he even knew Andrew now. Whatever Lady Sarah's assurances that she was safe here, Rebecca could not help feeling that if they knew where she was, Andrew and Lord Templeton might try to take her away. Later, when it became common knowledge Rebecca was a guest in Lady Sarah's house, it would be harder for them to try to harm her.

To be sure, she might be wrong to be suspicious of Oliver Ransford. If she was, Rebecca ought to tell him the truth now, for the longer she waited the worse it would be. He would not like her masquerade, but it would be better if he heard the story from Rebecca's own lips rather than from someone who would tell him he had been made a fool by her. Useless to deny, either, that she wanted to tell him the truth, to trust him and to have him see her as she really was. For what had only been a seed so long as Rebecca was in his house, now became a full grown truth: she was in love with Oliver Ransford. She loved his kindness, his quick intelligence, and much more that she could not even put into words. But her head must rule her heart, and Rebecca did not speak.

Ransford, of course, did not expect her to speak. He went on, gently, "How do you like it here, as my mother's companion? Is she kind to you?"

Rebecca nodded emphatically.

"I'm glad you're happy here," Ransford said.

Even to him the words sounded lame and he rose to his feet, holding out a hand to her. "It is time, I think, that I took you back in to see my mother. She asked me to come and fetch you, you know."

Rebecca rose and gave him her hand, trembling slightly at his touch. She was not prepared for the wellspring of longing that rose in her heart. A longing to be held by this man. A longing to be kissed. She could not break the gaze that bound her eyes to his and it seemed as if he was about to lean forward, perhaps even to kiss her on the lips, when the door to the library opened, breaking the spell.

"Here you both still are," Lady Sarah said mockingly, but the look she bent on them was kind, indeed one might say approving. "Have you had a pleasant conversation together?"

Ransford shot a warning glance at his mother, unable to

credit the insensitivity in her choice of words. Rebecca colored, pulled her hand free of Ransford's, and looked at the floor, unable to meet Lady Sarah's eyes.

"I have been asking Phoebe if she is happy here, and she indicates to me that she is," Oliver said, his voice reproving.

"I see," Lady Sarah said dryly, scarcely concealing the tremor of amusement in her voice. "Well, perhaps Phoebe will oblige me by going upstairs to fetch my shawl?"

Rebecca nodded and edged past Lady Sarah to get to the door. Still she could not meet Lady Sarah's eyes. Once outside the room she sped upstairs to fetch the shawl, but then found herself lingering before she came back down with it.

Oliver Ransford had gone and Lady Sarah was waiting for her in the drawing room. "You are quite safe," Lady Sarah told Rebecca reprovingly. "Oliver left while you were tarrying abovestairs. I collect, from what he said, that you did not tell him the truth about yourself?"

"I could not," Rebecca said quietly.

"He must find out the truth sometime and he won't like knowing you could have told him today and did not," Lady Sarah said impatiently.

"I know, and I meant to tell him," Rebecca replied, her voice low and steady. "But I found I could not do it. I know he will have to know soon enough, but when I tried, no words came out."

Lady Sarah hesitated. Then she said, a little more gently, "Would you like me to tell Oliver? He would understand why you felt you could not tell him yourself."

"No!" Rebecca exclaimed. At Lady Sarah's surprised look she went on, cautiously feeling her way. "I know you mean to be kind, and I have no doubt you would handle the matter better than I. You would know just the words to choose and what it is he would most wish to know. But I should like to tell Mr. Ransford the truth myself." Rebecca paused and began to pace about the room. "Surely there is no great hurry? So long as I tell him before the rest of the *ton* discovers the truth, there is no great harm done. And I will tell him. Before he can discover it from somewhere else.''

Now Rebecca looked at Lady Sarah, a plea in her eyes. Lady Sarah opened her mouth to refuse, then closed it again. She sighed and adjusted the shawl about her shoulders before she spoke. Finally she said, ''Very well. I don't understand it, but I shall give you the chance to tell Oliver yourself. Mind, you have only four days. Madame Jeanette has promised to have the first of your dresses and shoes and whatnot here by Thursday and I mean to present you at a small gathering on Friday night. I will not have Oliver looking the fool, which he will if he arrives to discover that everyone present knows you as Miss Rebecca Stanwood when he has known you only as Phoebe.''

''I understand,'' Rebecca said quietly. ''And I shall tell him before then, I promise.''

Lord Templeton was speaking with two men. He had arranged to meet them at an inn on the outskirts of London, an inn chosen for the impossibility of his encountering any other members of the *ton* at such a place, at such a time. It would have been obvious to anyone watching that Templeton was in a towering rage. ''What do you mean, she's not in that house?'' he demanded incredulously. ''I saw her there, myself, not three days past.''

''She may have been there three days ago, m'lord, but she's not there now,'' the first man answered patiently. ''We asked. We coaxed. We even bribed one of the girls, m'lord. I tell you she's not there.''

''There is something odd about the house, though,'' the second man said slowly.

''What?'' Templeton demanded instantly.

''I'd say they knew the girl we was asking about, they just wouldn't say what they knew,'' the man answered, refusing to be hurried.

''You mean you think she is still there?'' Templeton asked eagerly.

The second man shook his head. "I'll be bound she's not. They weren't lying about that. More it's like she's gone but they've orders not to talk about her. Strange doings for a servant girl," he added, puzzled.

That froze Templeton. He had no wish for these men to guess the truth. And yet he could not resist asking, "Do you think it likely you can persuade any of them to tell you more?"

Both men shook their heads. "Someone's put the fear of God into 'em and none'll say a word."

After several more minutes of fruitless discussion, Templeton dismissed the two men. He sat thinking at the table for some time. Finally he rose to his feet, paid the shot, and left. Perhaps Pierce had heard something. If Rebecca had left Ransford's house, maybe she had gone back to him.

Templeton strode outside, his angry impatience under careful control, to where his tiger stood guard over his lordship's carriage. Any number of curious eyes watched from nearby doorways, and more than one ragged urchin dashed forward for a closer look at the sweet goers harnessed to the phaeton. Templeton ignored them all, merely saying to his tiger, "I believe, William, it is time to go."

Relief was patent on the tiger's face as he watched Templeton climb into his carriage. As soon as Templeton was ready, he let go the horses' heads and scrambled up as the phaeton surged forward. He didn't like this part of London, nor did he like the look on his master's face. But he had had ample experience with both in the past and had been employed by Templeton too long to dare speak a word of complaint.

Andrew Pierce was in the drawing room, already started on a bottle of madeira, when Lord Templeton was announced. Pierce was instantly on his feet. "Have you got Rebecca?" he demanded. A moment later his face fell and he said, "You don't have Rebecca."

"You're drunk," Templeton said contemptuously, tossing his gloves onto a nearby table.

Pierce wagged a finger at Templeton. "Not so drunk I don't know we're in the suds. I'm in the suds, anyway. I can see by your face you haven't got Rebecca. Without Rebecca I'm all to pieces. Won't be able to join the Hellfire Club, either. I ought to go back to America, but I can't. Pockets to let, you know. Won't hear from m'mother for months. She'll send funds and I'll have to go back home. Just as if I'd never left. All because you don't have Rebecca."

"How do you know that?" Templeton asked sharply.

Pierce snorted. "Lord, I looked at your face when you came in. Looked at your face yesterday. And the day before that. I'm not so drunk I don't know something's happened. You must have lost Rebecca."

Templeton grimaced and said curtly, "You're right. I have lost your stepsister. No, don't come to blows with me! I never had her in my grasp, I only knew where to find her. She was at Ransford's house, disguised as a servant, but now she's gone from there and I don't know where to look. I had hoped she might have come here."

"Well, she hasn't," Pierce said decisively.

Templeton considered Pierce carefully. Incredible to suppose the fellow was pretending. Where to look next, that was the question. Had Ransford been so taken with the girl that he offered to set her up somewhere? It seemed unlikely, for she had been carrying coal when he last saw her. Had she been dismissed for unacceptable performance of her duties? He had urged Ransford to do so, and for all Oliver's apparent disdain of the notion perhaps it had taken root. That seemed more likely, but then why would the servants have orders not to speak of her? The third and most frightening possibility was that Ransford had discovered Rebecca's identity and was hiding her from Templeton. But surely, if that were the case, Ransford would have come to seek him out, Templeton assured himself. And even if he did not, what, after all, could Ransford do?

He needed some place quiet to think. So, with one last look at Pierce, Templeton retrieved his gloves and said, "If you do get wind of her, Andrew, let me know at once. As you yourself said, without Rebecca you are in the suds.''

Then Templeton left. He would not have been pleased had he known the direction Pierce's thoughts were taking. Andrew had begun to wonder if he should look for Rebecca himself. He would not dare oppose Templeton directly, but he could not help thinking that there might be some advantage to be had by approaching Ransford and threatening to expose Rebecca's presence in his house unless Ransford paid him off. But Andrew could only do so if Rebecca could be found. Otherwise, he only had Templeton's word she had been there, and by Templeton's own account she had flown the coop. Nor could he demand that Ransford marry her, and therefore take a hand in Andrew's welfare, if no one knew where she was. Confound the girl! Why must she make his life so difficult? Pierce wondered sourly. It was just like her to be so selfish.

From there it was a short step to remembering all his past grievances against Rebecca. Andrew Pierce had never wanted his mother to marry Edward Stanwood. But she had. And he might have become reconciled had he not seen how both his mother and his stepfather doted on his stepsister, Rebecca. She must go to a select academy while a more ordinary school was considered sufficient for him. She must take her place in society while he was to learn to work in his stepfather's business. Never mind that his stepfather himself almost never set foot in the offices managed by the partner; he, Andrew, was expected to do so. When he had asked why, the partner had brutally informed him that while Edward Stanwood might obtain business for the firm by mingling socially, Andrew hadn't the character or breeding to do so. So he was expected to report to work every day. Once Andrew had dared complain about how differently he and Rebecca were treated, and this had drawn such wrath down upon his head that he had swiftly changed tack. He had become her kind stepbrother to whom she might look for any number of treats. That this approach had brought Andrew a great deal of approval from his mother and stepfather only enraged Andrew further. He was too shrewd to say so, however, and merely bided his time until Edward Stanwood's death. That had been a blow, for instead of leaving his children well provided for, Andrew had discovered that Edward Stanwood had managed to squander the greater part of his wealth. Oh, they were not paupers, but his legacy was not what Andrew had counted on.

He might have washed his hands of his stepsister had it not been for her father's final request. Andrew had been all kindness as he offered to accompany Rebecca to England. There he might stand on a more equal footing with her, he thought. She would be his *entrée* to the *ton,* and even though her family had refused to acknowledge her, so it had been. And now if he could, he meant to use her to even greater profit. If she could again be found. But he would not waste his chances by putting Ransford on his guard. No, Andrew must wait until he or Templeton managed to get wind of Rebecca again. Then he would see. Perhaps, he thought idly, she would still end in the hands of the Hellfire Club. But if Ransford appeared tractable, she might be fortunate enough to end up his wife, instead.

13

To Lady Sarah's dismay, Rebecca made no effort to keep her promise. It was not as though she lacked the opportunity to do so. Oliver Ransford began to visit his mother every morning, causing Lady Sarah to comment dryly that she had not known she had such a dutiful son. He even made a point of seeking Phoebe out to talk with her each day before he left the house. Every time he did so was a trial for Rebecca. She consoled herself with the reflection that each day brought closer the time when she might tell him the truth.

Thursday morning, Ransford discovered Rebecca again in the library, but this time she was trying to write a letter to her stepmother. Lady Sarah had offered Rebecca the use of her own writing desk, but she had preferred the quiet of the library, which she had come to view as a sanctuary. She had known it would be difficult to write this letter, for she could not bear to distress her stepmother by telling her what Andrew had done. And yet it had been far too long since she had last written and she must say something. Rebecca did not mean to ask her stepmother's help in returning to Boston. Another letter had already been written, the first day she was here, and posted off to America to request help from her father's partner. In it Rebecca had told him frankly that she felt compelled to leave Andrew's roof and was without funds. She had also asked him to keep to himself this knowledge of her circumstances. Rebecca had known Mr. Johnston since her childhood and did not fear he would either fail her or divulge what had passed to her stepmother.

Unfortunately, she could not guess what Andrew might have said in his own letters to his mother, and that made her task all the more difficult. Several attempts had already been consigned to the fire burning in the gate. Rebecca was poring over her latest effort when the library door opened. She looked up, expecting to see Lady Sarah wanting to know if she were ready to go to the Pantheon Bazaar to look for gloves and fans and such.

It was not, however, Lady Sarah who had entered the room; it was Oliver Ransford. "So I was right," he said grimly, advancing toward her. "You were the one writing at my desk in my library."

Miserably Rebecca nodded. Ransford regarded her thoughtfully and said, "I wonder why you were not willing to let me know that you could do so, when you worked in my household. I would have been delighted and you could have told me a great deal that I would have liked to know."

Rebecca shrank back into her chair, daunted by the dilemma this placed her in. She must either tell Ransford the truth or carry this farce even farther, pretending to write notes in answer to his question. Her heart beat wildly. No more than ever did Rebecca feel ready to bring her masquerade to an end.

But she had no chance to do so. The terror Rebecca felt was evident on her face and halted Ransford in his movement toward her. He was too intelligent not to realize that she was afraid of him. Grimly, his lips pressed tightly together, he inclined his head toward the girl. "I collect my presence distresses you," he said. "And since I do not wish to distress you, I will go. But I would give a great deal to know what it is I have done to offend you or to make you so afraid of me." A tremor twitched about Oliver's mouth as he added, "I have not been used to consider myself an ogre. It is a novel experience to find that you so obviously do." He paused and then relented as he said, more gently, "I cannot doubt that you have had reason to be afraid sometime, somewhere, in your past. Please try to believe that I would never willingly add to your fear or give you cause to be afraid of me. If ever you need a friend, I am here.''

So swiftly did Ransford turn and move to leave the room that he did not see Rebecca rise to her feet and reach her hand out after him. Had she called out his name he might have paused and turned back to discover the truth, but she did not. Not, at any rate, until the door had closed behind him with a distinct slam, and then it was too late for him to hear her. Nor could Ransford see her slowly sitting down again or the tears that fell silently on the letter she had worked so hard to write to Andrew Pierce's mother.

Lady Sarah knew at once that something had gone wrong by the fierce expression on her son's face. She did not try to keep Ransford from leaving, nor did she beg him to tell her what was wrong. Rebeccas could tell her that much, she decided grimly. For now, Lady Sarah only walked her son to the front door and hugged him warmly before he left.

That brought a smile to Oliver's face, and he looked into Lady Sarah's eyes with a mixture of pain and humor to be seen in his. "I do not seem to be in favor with your companion," he told her lightly. "It is a most lowering reflection since I have always accounted myself something of a success with the ladies. But no doubt it is good for my character to receive such a setdown now and again.''

Lady Sarah was not deceived. For all of Oliver's cheerful words, she could well guess what they cost him. She clasped her son's arm a moment, then said lightly, "I hope you do not mean to despair? Whatever her present mood, my companion is likely to receive you kindly another time.''

"At your command?'' Ransford asked harshly. "I thank you, no, Mama. If she dislikes me, that is her privilege and I pray you will not try to change her mind.''

Lady Sarah hesitated. Finally she said, "Oliver, will you do me a favor?''

"What is it, Mama?'' he asked warily. "I mistrust that

look in your eye, and I refuse to commit myself until I know what scheme it is you are hatching.''

Lady Sarah turned innocent eyes up on her son. ''I only wished to ask you if you would take her out for a drive tomorrow afternoon,'' she said, in a hurt voice.

For a moment Ransford looked at his mother as if he thought she had lost her wits. Almost he voiced the thought aloud that it was absurd to ask him to take a girl, who had been no better than a scullery maid in his house less than week before, out for a drive in his curricle. But there was an earnestness about her that forbade him from doing so. Instead, with a tautness about the mouth he answered, ''If you wish. If you can prevail upon her to go,'' he could not resist adding as a parting shot.

''Oh, she'll go,'' Lady Sarah said wisely.

''I won't have you force her,'' Ransford warned. He sighed, then added, ''I wish, with all my heart, Mama, that Phoebe trusted me, but she does not. Something has happened in her life to make her look at me, and perhaps all men, with terror. I have no doubt that she would come with me, at your command, but she would not be happy to do so. And I suspect that she has had more than enough unhappiness in her life. I will not add to it.''

''Just be here to take her for a drive about two o'clock in the afternoon,'' his mother replied, ignoring the warning. ''I don't think you will regret doing so. And neither shall she. And if you are worried about the proprieties, you may have your groom stand up behind.''

Ransford started to ask his mother what precisely was in her mind, but he did not. Partly his restraint was due to filial respect, but a greater part was due to the knowledge that if his mother had made up her mind to tell him nothing, then that was precisely what he would learn from her. So he took his leave, walking briskly in the cold autumn air and thinking that he hoped his mother had a warm cloak to lend the girl if she expected him to drive Phoebe about in this weather!

Lady Sarah, meanwhile, headed to the library to discover

just what folly Rebecca had committed this time and to inform her of the treat in store for the next afternoon.

Rebecca had indulged herself in a hearty fit of tears and was now over the worst of it. At the sight of Lady Sarah, she hastily dried her face and looked enquiringly in that lady's direction.

"I collect you still could not bring yourself to tell Oliver the truth," Lady Sarah said with something of a twinkle in her eyes. "And unless I make a push to do something about it, I suspect you never will. So I've arranged for Oliver to come and take you out for a drive tomorrow afternoon in his curricle."

"But didn't he think that an odd request?" Rebecca asked, awed by Lady Sarah's audacity.

"Indeed, I think he is afraid I have lost my wits," Lady Sarah laughed openly now. "But he is too kind to say so. In any event, he did not refuse and the rest must be up to you. Our party is tomorrow night, you know, and he must be told before then."

That brought back to Rebecca the evils of her situation and she took a turn about the room before she replied. "But to tell him in an open carriage! I cannot like the idea."

"You cannot like the idea of telling Oliver anywhere," Lady Sarah retorted dryly. Still, she took pity on the girl and added, coaxingly, "Come, Rebecca, you have not thought. At least in an open curricle you have the advantage that Oliver will be fully as aware as you are of how public a situation you are in. If he is angry, as you clearly expect he will be, he will not be able to give full reign to his anger for fear of drawing attention to the pair of you. So you see, however eccentric my notion first appears, there is a great deal of sense behind it."

Now it was Rebecca's turn to laugh. "Are you never at a loss?" she asked.

Lady Sarah tilted her head to the side and said, "I don't think so."

Rebecca laughed again.

* * *

Ransford was not in the best of moods that evening at White's. And yet his luck at cards was running strong. Templeton watched for several minutes, then took the empty chair when another member of the *ton* rose from the table at which Ransford sat. Oliver acknowledged his presence with a curt nod, a singular lack of courtesy that caused Templeton's eyebrows to raise in surprise. Had he uncovered Rebecca's masquerade after all? But if it were that, then why not cut him altogether? "You seem a trifle out of sorts," Templeton commented lazily.

Ransford shrugged. Another gentleman wagged a finger and said, "If I did not know better, I should think Oliver had been unlucky in love. Is it the charmer your mother had in tow a few nights ago at the theater?" he asked.

Now Ransford smiled and replied dryly, "When and if I develop a *tendre* for someone, it will scarcely be a lady chosen by my mother for me."

"Then who is it you've fallen in love with?" a third fellow asked jovially. "Someone ineligible, perhaps?"

"Someone ineligible? Preposterous!" another fellow snorted. "Ransford is far too well aware of what is due his name to behave in such a ramshackle manner."

It could be seen that a nerve twitched in Ransford's cheek, but only for a moment before he had himself well in hand again. "Much too well aware of what is due my name," he agreed, wondering what his cronies would say if they saw him driving Phoebe about on the morrow. Then, with a touch of impatience he added, "I cannot comprehend where you, any of you, came by this absurd notion that I am in love! I very much wish you will change the subject."

"Speaking of preposterous creatures," Templeton said lightly, "I hope you got rid of that careless servant I saw at your house the other night. The one who dropped the coal scuttle."

"Oh, she proved unsuitable so she is gone," Ransford replied, equally lightly. "Why do you ask?"

"No particular reason," Templeton hastened to reply. "I simply dislike incompetence in a servant."

Ransford smiled thinly. "So do I," he said.

Templeton wanted badly to ask where this servant had gone, but he could not. Already several of the gentlemen watching the card play or sitting at the table were looking at him oddly. In any event, it was unlikely that Ransford would tell him. Well, he would find her. However Miss Stanwood had obtained her post in Ransford's house, she would not find it easy to do so elsewhere without references, and Templeton doubted Ransford had given her one. Which meant she would soon be desperate. And although Templeton preferred to find her while her value to him and the Hellfire Club was enhanced by her innocence, he was not above enjoying the notion of her downfall at hands other than his own. It was only the thought that she might escape everyone that he could not bear.

As for Ransford, it seemed odd to him for Templeton to take such a dislike to someone else's servant and wish to see that servant dismissed. Still, had it been anyone other than Phoebe, he might have simply shrugged the matter off, but as it was, he found himself wanting to take up the cudgels in her defense. Since it would have done neither himself nor her any good, Ransford restrained himself and, with an effort, forced his attention to remain on the cards in his hand. Unfortunately, it seemed that fate was determined to thwart him. The final ripples from his exchange with Templeton had scarcely faded away when Lord Alvanley stopped by the table and said to Ransford, "Well, Oliver, shall I come to your mother's soirée tomorrow night? I understand Lady Sarah has a charming guest staying with her. Or so Sally Jersey says your mother told her."

For a moment Ransford was puzzled. Then he laughed. Amusement was evident in Ransford's voice as he said, "As usual Lady Jersey has things a trifle muddled. I collect she must mean Miss Wetherford. My mother is her godmother and has taken Miss Wetherford under her wing. She is amiable, accomplished, has a fine countenance, and is, I collect, quite eligible.''

''And what he hasn't told you,'' another voice called out, ''is that you would be quite bored with the girl in ten minutes. I know. I danced with her at Almack's. Once was quite enough.''

''Perhaps,'' Alvanley agreed reluctantly. ''Pity. Sally Jersey seemed to think I ought to go. But if that's the truth, I shall go to a cockfight instead.''

''By all means go to the cockfight,'' Templeton said lazily. ''Just tell me which one and I shall be there, for you always bet on the wrong cock and I shall recoup all of last month's gambling losses in one night by betting against you.''

There was a roar of laughter at that as Alvanley indignantly refuted the charge. A third gentleman chimed in to say, ''Now you really must go to the cockfight, Alvanley, if only to defend your honor!''

''Indeed, he'd best not since he is bound to prove Templeton right,'' a fourth voice pronounced warningly.

''No, I watched Alvanley last week and he won three out of four bets,'' a fifth voice countered instantly.

As the good-natured bantering continued, Alvanley soon found himself surrounded by a crowd of gentlemen, all of whom proposed to accompany him the next night to watch the cocking and betting. Ransford rose quietly from the table where all the hands of cards had been abandoned in favor of the far more interesting discussion surrounding Alvanley. No one even noticed when he left the room.

14

Oliver Ransford arrived at his mother's door precisely as her mantle clock chimed the hour of two. Beside Lady Sarah, Rebecca waited dressed charmingly in a walking dress of soft green satin with a darker green velvet pelisse laid over the back of a nearby chair. Ransford was suitably, if a trifle soberly, attired in a dark brown jacket and pale pantaloons. He paused in the doorway of the drawing room to study Rebecca and to collect his thoughts. That Phoebe looked beautiful he could not deny. But what had possessed his mother to dress her in a gown far beyond the means of any servant? Didn't she realize the harm she could do, encouraging the girl to have ideas above her station? What if his mother tired of Phoebe, what then? What other employer would display such a conspicuous disregard of the distance between servant and mistress?

And yet, she was achingly beautiful. Had circumstances been otherwise, Oliver would have found himself wanting to take Phoebe into his arms and kiss her. Indeed, he wished to do so now and found himself cursing the promise given to take Phoebe for a drive. He had no intention of placing the girl in an intolerable position, and to be so near her and unable to give vent to his emotions would be intolerable to him. That she was more gently bred than a general servant, he could not doubt. Indeed, as he had told his mother, he had more than half made up his mind she was someone's daughter born the wrong side of the blanket. If so, obviously her father, whoever he was, had been a gentleman and had provided for her. Equally obviously, something had made her decide the situation was intolerable and she had run away. Or had her father decided that now that she was a woman her fate was no longer his responsibility? Did it matter? Whatever the answer, it could not lessen the gulf between them. No more than a marriage between a servant and a gentleman would the *ton* countenance a match between someone's illegitimate child and himself. But there was no chance to back out of taking the girl for a drive, for he had already been announced and both Lady Sarah and Phoebe had seen him.

"Ah, there you are, Oliver. Punctual as always," Lady Sarah said, coming forward with a mischievous smile. "Tell me, how do you like the new Phoebe? She pays for dressing, I should say."

"Very nice," Ransford said perfunctorily.

"Why, Oliver, one would think you disapprove," Lady Sarah said with mock surprise.

"What you choose to do with employees in your household is your own affair," Oliver retorted, the corner of his mouth twitching in suppressed irritation.

"Ah, but Phoebe is not an employee," Lady Sarah said, with the same mischievous smile as before. "She is a guest and I mean to present her to some friends of mine at the small party I am giving tonight. I hope you still mean to come?"

Ransford stared at his mother, stunned. When Alvanley had told him of the soirée and the supposedly charming guest, it had never occurred to Ransford that his mother meant to present Phoebe to the *ton*. He had certainly supposed that the young lady in question must be Miss Wetherford.

Ransford was about to retort that under no circumstances would he attend in order to see his mother make a fool of herself when it occurred to him that it might be wise if he did, if only to prevent her from further madness. It was impossible for Oliver to master his voice sufficiently to reply, however, so he merely bowed. He then looked at Phoebe, thinking that it was remarkable how mistaken a person could be in someone. It would never have occurred to him that she would so swiftly worm her way into her mother's confidence and encourage her to take a step so bizarre and so likely to redound to her discredit. A trifle imperiously he said to Phoebe, "Shall we go? I do not like to keep my horses waiting."

Rebecca nodded and reached for her pelisse. She could well guess some of the thoughts that must be running through Ransford's head and she could not blame him for any of them. If, by these tactics, Lady Sarah had hoped to ensure that Rebecca must tell Ransford the truth, she had succeeded. Rebecca could not let Ransford go on thinking that she was taking advantage of his mother. Or, worse, think that his mother had lost her wits. No, whatever Ransford thought of her afterwards, Rebecca would tell him the truth this afternoon. She only wished it did not have to be in an open carriage where the whole world might be privy to Ransford's rage, if it should come to that. A swift glance at Ransford's face served to convince Rebecca that Lady Sarah's belief that he would not berate her in an open carriage was not to be depended upon.

But willy-nilly Rebecca was swept out of the drawing room and downstairs to the waiting carriage. With punctilious courtesy Ransford handed her in and settled the rug about her knees before he went round and climbed up on his side. There was a curt nod from Ransford and a timid wave from Rebecca to Lady Sarah. Ransford told his groom to stand away from the horses' heads and wait here until he returned, and then they were sweeping away down the crowded London street.

The horses were a perfectly matched pair of chestnuts and quite fresh. The drive from Ransford's townhouse to Lady Sarah's had not succeeded in taking the edge off them and it took Ransford's full attention to hold the pair. Rebecca was not surprised, therefore, that he did not speak to her on the way to Hyde Park other than to curtly inform her that that was their destination. When she risked a glance at his rigid profile, however, Rebecca could not deceive herself into believing that his silence was only due to the strain of controlling the horses. Disapproval was evident in the set of his jaw and the line of his shoulders, and Rebecca did not try to tell herself that the forthcoming conversation was going to be an easy one.

Nor was she mistaken. The moment the chestnuts swept through the gate of Hyde Park, Ransford slowed them to a walk. He looked around, satisfied himself that the park was still relatively thin of company, and then lashed out at Rebecca.

"Well, Phoebe," he said scathingly, "you have managed to charm your way into my mother's confidence with a speed I should not have thought possible. And all without the ability of speech. I am amazed. It seems I vastly underrated your talents while you were working for me. I wonder why you did not try such a thing with me. Did you think me too clever? Or perhaps you did not fully credit my wealth until my mother took you out of my house and into hers. Is that it? Or perhaps you did not find me taking enough? My mother has certainly made a pet of you, which I am most unlikely to have done. Is it pleasant to be cosseted? Given clothes and shoes and pretty things? Have a care my mother doesn't tire of you, Phoebe, for then what would you do? I assure you that if you were to apply for a position dressed as you are, you would certainly be taken for Haymarket wares. Which, for all I can guess, you well may be."

The words went on and on, lashing at Rebecca, breaking against her impassive countenance. Her apparent indifference drove Ransford to greater and greater fury. Only to himself would he admit that his rage had its heart in his inexplicable feelings for this girl.

Rebecca was not indifferent to his rage. Her teeth were clenched in an effort to hold back her own rising anger. But over and over she told herself that it was not Rebecca Stanwood he was speaking to, but a servant girl he thought had taken advantage of Lady Sarah. When he knew the truth, he might still be angry with her, but not this way, not for these reasons.

Ransford's tirade continued unabated for several minutes. "I can only guess as to why your former employers dismissed you," he said, near the end. "If you had any former employers, which I am beginning to doubt."

When he paused for breath and looked at her, Rebecca gripped her hands tightly together in her lap and began to speak in a low, clear voice. "I suppose I have no choice but to try to answer your charges. I can understand your anger, but does it not occur to you that perhaps your mother knows very well what she is doing? That far from being a fool whose wits have gone begging, she is better informed as to my circumstances than you are? And that even if I were merely a servant girl your mother had chosen to be kind to, she would have a perfect right to do so? Who are you to criticize Lady Sarah?"

But Rebecca's reasonable words did not mollify Ransford. To the contrary, his lips were pressed together more tightly than ever as he said, "So you lied about that as well. Did you think you would gain more sympathy by pretending to be mute? You were right, of course, and I feel a fool to have been taken in so easily. How many times have you done this? To how many employers? Or did you choose me as your first victim because you had heard how rich I was? I was evidently a fool to think that you came into my garden by accident. Well, I shall not be such a fool again." He paused, but before Rebecca could speak, he went on. "How naive I must have seemed to you. The perfect victim for your schemes. Why did you choose to go with my mother, I wonder? Was it because I did not fall for your charms as you expected? My apologies. I had the absurd notion that it was unfair for one in my position to amuse himself with a servant since it could lead to nothing more than a brief liaison. But evidently you planned otherwise, and when it became evident I did not mean to play your game, you turned to my mother and had better fortune with her."

"Are you finished?" Rebecca asked, her voice cold with rage.

"I am," he agreed. "Why? Do you have a defense? I cannot think it will prove very convincing, but by all means let me hear it. No doubt I shall find it very amusing."

"I did not think you a fool when you took me into your household," Rebecca said, forcing herself to speak as calmly as she could. "I thought you kind and good and I was very grateful to you for giving me the protection of a position in your household. Because I had nowhere else to turn."

"How touching," Ransford sneered. "No doubt you had alienated your previous employer, not having taken the time to employ such delicacy as you have used to further your cause with my mother."

"As you yourself have guessed, I had no previous employer," Rebecca said, trying not to be hurt by his harsh words. "Mrs. Marsh must have told you how singularly unprepared I was for the tasks she set me to do. But I tried my best because you had been kind enough to give me work when I might well have been unable to find it elsewhere. And I needed work. As for taking advantage of your mother, I have told her many times that I find her kindness overwhelming."

"You are very clever," Ransford told her grimly. "I am sure you know just how to do it in such a way that my mother will discount your protests. But what can you hope to gain? Whatever my mother does, however she dresses you, the *ton* will discover that you have been and ought to be a servant, and you will never be accepted. In the long run, you will only be hurt by playing such a role as this one. And I should not like to see that happen," Ransford said, his voice abruptly losing its accusing tone and becoming far more gentle.

Perhaps it was this gentleness that prompted Rebecca to put a hand on his arm in spite of herself, in spite of the anger he had roused in her. Her own voice was also gentle as she said, "Mr. Ransford, you are angry with me and I can well understand that. But listen to me. Listen to my voice. Can you not hear anything there that you did not expect? Can you not hear that my speech is different from that of Mrs. Marsh or Mary, the upstairs maid, or Katie, the scullery maid? That it is even different from yours or your mother's way of speaking? Can you not hear the difference that marks me as coming from Boston?''

Ransford turned to stare down at her. "I hear the difference in your voice, of course," he said slowly, "though I am not certain I would have known you were from America if you had not told me. But how did you get here? And who are you? Are you, as I half suspect, the daughter of some gentleman, conceived out of wedlock?''

A tiny gurgle of laughter escaped Rebecca. "Well, I am the daughter of a gentleman," she acknowledged. "But I was not born the wrong side of the blanket.'' She paused and took a deep breath before she went on. "My name is not Phoebe. I am Rebecca Stanwood and you have entertained my stepbrother, Andrew Pierce, in your house. My father was a Stanwood of Stanwood Hall and my mother a Harcourt. I came to England because it was my father's dying wish that I try to reconcile with both families and my stepbrother offered to accompany me. Your mother knew all this when she took me into her home.'' There was a long silence from Ransford, and when it had gone on longer than she thought she could bear, Rebecca said very quietly, "I was very grateful to you when you took me in and gave me a position as a servant in your household, Mr. Ransford. That may seem preposterous to you, but for me it seemed a far better fate than finding myself in Lord Templeton's clutches, for that was my alternative.''

"Surely your stepbrother could have protected you," Ransford protested impatiently.

Rebecca looked down at her hands. When she spoke, it was with some constraint. "Andrew might have, had he wished to, but he did not. Lord Templeton seemed to him to represent all that he once thought he could have no part of, for he offered Andrew the opportunity to mingle with the *ton*. Lord Templeton also held a number of my stepbrother's gambling vouchers and our funds were at low tide. All I had to do, he said, was to allow Lord Templeton's attentions, and it did not seem to Andrew such a high price to pay. But I could not bear the thought and ran away. I thought it would be easy to find a position somewhere in London until my father's partner, in Boston, could send me enough funds to sail back to America. But I underestimated the vulnerability of a girl alone on the streets and I had to take refuge in your garden. There was, you see, an importunate gentleman who thought to offer me work of a far different sort and who would not accept my refusal.''

It was Ransford's turn to reach out to Rebecca. He placed a hand over hers and said gently, ''Why didn't you tell me the truth, that first night, when I found you in my garden?''

She looked up at him and said simply, ''How could I when my only experience of gentlemen in London had been those who came to drink and gamble at the house my stepbrother hired? Or the ones who followed me on the street when they thought I was a servant? How could I know you were not of Templeton's crowd? What if you betrayed me to him? And, indeed, I have seen him at your house.'' Before he could protest such a charge, Rebecca added, hastily, ''Even supposing you were not of Templeton's sort, what if you felt I belonged with my stepbrother? That I had no right to run off as I had? Or that whatever the evils of my situation, I should not hire out as a servant? If I had told you the truth, would you have hired me to work in your household?'' Rebecca asked sternly.

''No, I would not!'' Ransford agreed vehemently. And when Rebecca tried to pull free her hand, hurt by his adamance, Ransford gripped it all the tighter. ''What I would have done, my girl,'' he said, as though to a child, ''was place you in my mother's care and thrash both Carlisle Templeton and your stepbrother, Andrew Pierce. And perhaps Giles Stanwood as well, for refusing to acknowledge you," he added as an afterthought. "My dear Rebecca, you really ought to have trusted me."

The simple endearment was almost a caress the way Ransford spoke it, and Rebecca felt her color rising. Suddenly shy, she tried again to pull her hand free but Ransford would not let it go. Still, her voice was clear as she said, "I have not been accustomed to finding such kindness in London. I did not know it was possible."

"How does my mother know?" Ransford asked, puzzled. "Did you tell her or did she guess the truth?"

"She gave me no choice but to tell her the truth," Rebecca replied with a smile. "When she first summoned me into the drawing room in your house she told me it was clear to her that there was something havey-cavey about me and that she meant to discover just what it was. She said," and here Rebecca paused, her eyes dancing as she added, "that she was certain I could find a way to communicate the truth to her if I chose to do so. I could not doubt that she would make a formidable enemy and just as formidable an ally. I had no choice but to confess."

"Well, I shall have some choice words to say to my mother over the fact that she did not tell me the truth," Ransford said grimly.

"Please," Rebecca said, "don't be angry with Lady Sarah. I—I asked her to let me tell you myself."

"Why didn't you?" Ransford asked, with some constraint. "You cannot say you have not had the opportunity these past few days."

"I was afraid," Rebecca replied honestly. When he did not at once answer, she added, "I suppose I must seem a terrible coward to you."

"You seem—" Ransford broke off, unable to finish the sentence or to look at Rebecca any longer. Instead he turned his attention to the horses.

He was silent so long that Rebecca hesitantly put a hand on his arm again and said, "Are you very angry with me?"

Now he looked down at her and smiled reassuringly. "I

am angry," he said, "but at Templeton and your stepbrother and Giles Stanwood and the Harcourts, as well."

"I'm sorry I deceived you," she said with some constraint.

Ransford found it difficult to command his own voice as he replied, "I'm only grateful that fate brought you to my door. I cannot bear to think of what might have happened to you if fate had not." He paused, then said, a puzzled frown between his brow, "Where did you come by your manner? It is far more well-bred than your stepbrother's. I cannot believe you lived in a log cabin as some might suspect you of doing."

Rebecca gave another gurgle of laughter. "No, though I was born in one. But by the time I was six, my father had gone a fair way toward making his fortune. He had built a fine house in Boston and I was educated at Mrs. Farthingale's Select Academy for Girls. I made my curtsy to Boston society when I was eighteen and refused several eligible offers, so you needn't think I was considered an antidote at home."

"I didn't," Ransford said dryly.

The corner of her lips twitched, but otherwise Rebecca pretended not to have heard him. "Shortly after that my father had a number of financial reverses. I have always thought that was what caused him to fall ill. He required a great deal of nursing, a task I shared with my stepmother who was truly devoted to him. My father lingered, in pain, several years and it was a relief to us and to him he died a year ago," she said quietly.

"I'm sorry," Ransford said, but did not press her to say more.

She was silent a moment, then said bravely, "I have already told you the rest. My father's deathbed wish. Andrew's offer to escort me to London. My rebuff from both the Stanwoods and the Harcourts. Lord Templeton's attentions. My flight and masquerade as your servant. Not a very edifying tale, I'm afraid."

This last was said a trifle wistfully, and Ransford found himself looking down at Rebecca soberly as he replied, "I collect you expect me to think less of you for your masquerade, but I don't."

Rebecca looked up at him gratefully. "You are kind, but would the *ton* be as understanding if they were to know the truth?"

"Good God, no!" Ransford exclaimed blightingly. "But they won't know. Trust my mother to see to that."

There seemed nothing to say to that, and both were silent a moment. Then Rebecca said hesitantly, "I am glad you will be at Lady Sarah's party tonight. It will be my first venture into society, here in London, for I don't count Lord Temptleton or the gentlemen my brother entertained."

"Well, I shall be there," Ransford assured her. "Though I cannot think you will truly need my support. The *ton* cannot help but find you delightful."

Rebecca only shook her head at him.

An observer, some distance away, spied the couple in the curricle and turned to his companion to say, "Gracefield! Isn't that Ransford?"

"Yes, Alvanley, I believe it is. But who is the lady with him? I don't recognize her. A high flyer, do you think?"

Lord Alvanley shook his head. "Not Ransford. Anyone else, perhaps, but not Ransford. He don't flaunt his high flyers like that. Must be the young lady that Sally Jersey says is staying with Lady Sarah Ransford. No wonder Ransford tried to warn me off from attending Lady Sarah's party. Didn't want any competition. Pity I'm committed to the cock-fighting. Think I'll find a way to arrange an introduction to the charmer, anyway."

"By Jove, that's a splendid notion!" Gracefield exclaimed in approval. "Why don't we hail Ransford and do it now?"

The two gentlemen started in the direction of Ransford's curricle. Unfortunately for their plan, he had spotted them and guessed their intent. Since he did not feel up to intro-ducing Phoebe, or rather Rebecca, to anyone just now, he turned his horses toward the nearest gate and escaped, heading back to Lady Sarah's townhouse. He would have come in with her, but Lady Sarah warned him away, saying, a trifle breathlessly, ''Madame Jeanette has just delivered the dress Rebecca is to wear tonight. She is a day late and it needs certain alterations. You must see, Oliver, that the matter is an urgent one. We shall be occupied for some time so you may as well go home.''

Ransford looked at his mother, his eyes dancing with laughter as he replied, ''A grave situation indeed, Mama. Very well, I shall return Miss Stanwood to you and leave.''

Ransford handed Rebecca down from his carriage as his groom once more held the chestnuts steady. He raised one of her hands to his lips and kissed it before he said, ''I shall see you this evening, Miss Stanwood. And don't worry, I prophesy you will take the *ton* by storm, whatever the current crisis with your dress.''

A moment later he was gone, and a pleased Lady Sarah was leading Rebecca inside past the footman who held the door, agog with interest at what he had seen. Miss Stanwood was already a favorite with the servants, for she never asked for any service without remembering to thank the person who did it for her and all of them wished her well. They would all be delighted to know that Lady Sarah's son was showing such an interest in Miss Stanwood.

15

No more than Ransford did it occur to Templeton that the young lady who was to be present at Lady Sarah's party might be Rebecca. How could it? Lady Sarah might, for her own reasons, have chosen to remove a servant from Ransford's household, but under no circumstances would she dream of introducing such a creature to the *ton*. Even if she had discovered Rebecca's identity, he could scarcely believe she would countenance such a masquerade as the girl had undertaken. And even were she willing to overlook that, surely the refusal of the Stanwoods and the Harcourts to acknowledge Rebecca would stay Lady Sarah's hand from sponsoring the girl. Few ladies of the *ton* would risk the sort of censure that doing so would bring, and Templeton did not count her one of them. He did not know Lady Sarah very well for his tastes ran to younger prey, but she had always seemed to him to be like all the other insipid women who were mothers of his peers. It was, of course, a serious miscalculation. But then, Templeton also knew of Miss Wetherford and, like Ransford, he assumed she was the young lady Lady Sarah was sponsoring.

Indeed, since he had not received an invitation to the event, Templeton had all but put the matter out of his mind. Until, that is, he saw Ransford driving in the park with Rebecca. Like Alvanley, he realized to his chagrin that this must be the young lady to be introduced at the party, not Miss Wetherford, and that he had seriously underestimated Lady Sarah's character. He might, of course, have been mistaken, but it was unlikely. As well as everyone else in London, Templeton knew how impossible it was to suppose that Ransford would be driving his mistress in the park. What affairs he had had were all conducted with exquisite discretion and had never involved flaunting his inamorata to the *ton*. That meant she must still be an innocent and might yet play the role Templeton had envisioned for her. Miss Stanwood must be the young lady Lady Sarah was sponsoring.

Unlike Alvanley, Templeton did not try to approach the carriage. Instead, he stepped back out of sight and thought swiftly. It was not in Templeton's nature to accept defeat lightly and, in this situation, if Miss Stanwood were not Ransford's mistress, he did not intend to accept defeat at all. It was intolerable to know that Miss Stanwood might succeed in taking her place in society and perhaps even marry into the *ton*. Intolerable to know that he had had her all but in his grasp and then seen her slip away. Intolerable to know that she had preferred to seek employment as a drudge than accept his advances. No, Templeton would not accept defeat at the hands of Miss Rebecca Stanwood.

Templeton had not yet decided what course of action to take when he spied Alvanley and his companion, Lord Grace-field watching Ransford's curricle. He watched them start toward the carriage and then halt as it drove out of the park gate. Abruptly Templeton's eyes narrowed and a thin, cold smile crossed his face as he started toward the two men. A few moments later they noticed Templeton and hailed him heartily, saying, "Templeton! Did you see Ransford? And the young lady with him? Who is she? Do you know?"

Templeton hesitated, then he shrugged and said, softly, "As a matter of fact, I do. That is Miss Rebecca Stanwood."

"What? The girl I heard you were after?" Gracefield asked incredulously. "What's she doing with Ransford?"

"That is an excellent question," Templeton said with a grim smile. "I cannot help but wonder."

There was sufficient meaning in his voice to make Gracefield say, with a puzzled frown, "What are you suggesting, Templeton?"

Templeton shrugged. "I suggest nothing. I only think it would be interesting to know where Miss Stanwood has been since she left her stepbrother's roof." He paused, then added reluctantly, "I hesitate to repeat mere gossip, but someone looking excessively like Miss Stanwood was seen in Ransford's household a number of nights ago."

"Good Lord!" Alvanley exclaimed. "Does her stepbrother know?"

Templeton coughed and said, "Surely, without proof, you did not expect me to tell Pierce? What would you say if someone told you such a story about your sister?"

"He's right," Gracefield said with a sigh. "And you can't ask Ransford if it's true, I quite see that."

"Yes, but it don't sound like Ransford to keep a girl in his house," Alvanley said bluntly. "It don't sound like him at all."

"No, it doesn't," Templeton agreed pleasantly. "And that is why I hesitated to mention the matter."

A thought was bothering Lord Gracefield and now he said, "Yes, Alvanley, but recollect how odd Ransford's behavior was at White's last night. And how he tried to hint us away from his mother's party."

"Well, that's proof it couldn't be true," Alvanley objected bluntly. "Lady Sarah would never take the girl in if it were so."

Templeton coughed and said delicately, "Not even if she felt Ransford had taken advantage of the poor girl?"

That silenced the other two men. After a moment Gracefield said to Alvanley, apologetically, "It's possible, deuced possible, you know." He stopped and turned to Templeton to ask, "But if Ransford treated her so badly, why should Miss Stanwood be willing to ride in his carriage?"

"Perhaps she was not an unwilling guest in his house," Templeton replied silkily, "or perhaps she feels she has little choice."

"Absurd," Alvanley insisted again.

"Perhaps," Templeton said with a shrug, "but I should very much like to know the truth before I admitted Miss Stanwood to the *ton.*"

That shaft did not fail of its mark. While allowing that he was by no means convinced, Alvanley hastily reaffirmed his intention to watch the cockfighting instead of attending Lady Sarah's party. Lord Gracefield handsomely offered to accompany Alvanley and give him the benefit of his advice in betting. Templeton merely bowed and said gravely that he would see them there. Then, satisfied with the results of his disclosure, Templeton lazily strolled away.

Back at his townhouse, Templeton had the leisure to think of his next move in this apparent chess game with Miss Stanwood. There was no hurry. He could not act until the full effects of what he had said to Alvanley and Gracefield had a chance to be felt. Then he would strike and Miss Stanwood would, he thought, happily come into his grasp. This time he would not let her go. He considered carefully the hints he had dropped. To be sure, the story was not perfect, but it would do. With an unpleasant smile, Templeton prepared for the evening's cockfight and the chance to spread his tale further.

Rebecca, dressing for the party that evening, had no inkling of trouble. Indeed, her mind was all caught up in the pleasure of preparing for her first appearance in London society. The gown she wore was of pale blue satin and trimmed with blue silk roses. Matching kidskin slippers were on her feet and pale blue gloves were on her hands. The pearls around her neck and the drops in her ears just the sort of pretty bauble to set off her delicate beauty, Lady Sarah pronounced after looking at the complete picture Rebecca presented.

Nor did the color in Rebecca's rosy cheeks detract from her appearance when Lady Sarah made reference to Oliver's expected approval. He was to arrive early and dine with them before most of the other guests arrived. Lady Sarah waited with no little impatience to see his reaction to Rebecca.

Rebecca, herself, felt both trepidation and impatience. This was, in part, what she had come to England for: to take her rightful place in society. To be sure, she had come expecting that she would do so as a Stanwood, with their support and guidance. But if that was not possible, she meant to do so anyway, for she had her father's stubbornness and courage. And if in doing so, a certain Mr. Ransford was also impressed, there was nothing to object to in that.

As for Oliver, he felt no little trepidation at the thought of the evening ahead. Had matters been otherwise, then he would have had no difficulty believing what he had told Miss Stanwood: that she would take the *ton* by storm. She was a beauty and that was always to be admired. But Ransford was shrewd enough to know that beauty alone might not be sufficient if the Stanwoods and Harcourts continued to oppose her admittance to the *ton*. And while he did not think they would take such a step when both he and Lady Sarah were seen to espouse Miss Stanwood's cause, he could not be certain. Nor could he be certain what course the *ton* would take if it became known that she had posed as a servant in his home. The *ton* might choose to be amused and admiring of her courage. It might also choose to be scandalized and give her the cut direct. Much depended upon tonight and how Sally Jersey and the other patronesses of Almack's chose to look upon Miss Stanwood. Oliver Ransford found himself absurdly anxious that they should look kindly upon her. He could not help wishing there had been more time before this party when he had known who Rebecca was, for then he could have, would have, called upon the Stanwoods and asked them to acknowledge her claim upon their name. He would, he thought grimly, have been most persuasive. Had his mother thought of that when she allowed Miss Stanwood to remain anonymous for so long?

Lady Sarah had thought of precisely the same notion, and it was for that reason she had invited the Stanwoods to dinner. She would have invited the Harcourts as well had she not known they were out of town. Giles Stanwood, the current viscount and his grandmother, Clarissa Stanwood, the matriarch of the clan, were to arrive before the rest of the guests. Lady Sarah had not told them why they were invited, but simply sent the invitation. If they chose to believe they would make up part of a larger dinner party, so be it. Once they arrived, Lady Sarah trusted her own persuasive powers as well as Rebecca's charm to keep them there. And to convince them to lend their support to her curtsy to the *ton*.

Giles and Lady Stanwood arrived precisely on time, before, in fact, Oliver. Lord Stanwood was dressed impeccably as always, but it was Lady Stanwood who drew one's eye. A petite lady, scarcely taller than Rebecca herself, she nevertheless projected a forceful image as she stood in the doorway of the drawing room waiting for Lady Sarah to greet her. From the heavy malaca cane she leaned upon to the expensive gray silk of her dress, Lady Stanwood was a presence to be reckoned with. Rebecca was still upstairs, forewarned by Lady Sarah not to make her appearance until summoned. Dressed in a becoming gown of lavender lace and silk, Lady Sarah presented a charming picture and drew a grudging word of approval from the dowager Lady Stanwood. "You always did know how to dress, my dear Sarah," she said. "And how to give a dinner party, which is why Giles and I are here even though I do not often go out these days. But where are your other guests? Are we the first to arrive?"

"The very first, Lady Stanwood," Lady Sarah assured her. "How nice to see you again, Giles. Oliver will be delighted to see you, I am sure."

Lord Stanwood was pleased to bow gracefully and assure Lady Sarah that he was happy to have been invited. There was then a moment of awkward silence before Lady Sarah took her courage in her hands and said, "I must be honest with you, Lady Stanwood, and say that there will only be two other guests for dinner, and they are family. I am giving a party later tonight, but I wished the two of you to come early and give me the benefit of your advice. Particularly yours, Lady Stanwood. I have always had a high regard for your intelligence, and if anyone will know how to advise me, it will be you.''

Surprised but pleased, Lady Stanwood unbent sufficiently to say, ''Of course, I will advise you, my dear Sarah. But what problem could you possibly have?''

Lady Sarah discreetly tugged at the bell pull, the signal that would cause Rebecca to be sent downstairs. ''I have a young lady whom I wish to introduce to the *ton,*'' she said, taking a seat a moment after Lady Stanwood did so. ''She is well bred, intelligent, and quite lovely. Unfortunately, her own family chooses not to acknowledge her.''

Giles Stanwood drew in his breath but before he could speak, Lady Stanwood did so. ''I presume they have good reason not to acknowledge her?'' she said dryly.

''That I give you leave to decide,'' Lady Sarah replied, equally dryly.

A moment later Rebecca entered the drawing room and curtsied to the guests. Giles Stanwood rose to greet her and Lady Stanwood cast a critical glance over the girl before she turned to Lady Sarah and said, ''She is well enough to look at and seems to have proper manners. I think she will do. But I still do not comprehend the mystery, Sarah. Who is she?''

Lady Sarah drew Rebecca forward with a speaking look. Only when the girl stood beside her did she reply, ''I am delighted to hear you say so, Clarissa, for she is your granddaughter, Rebecca.''

''What?'' Lady Stanwood's face was dark with anger as she rose to her feet. ''How dare you play such a trick on me?''

''How dare you refuse to even see your granddaughter before deciding whether or not to acknowledge her?'' Lady Sarah countered gently. ''If there is a fault here, I do not think it is mine. What objection do you have to her? You have said yourself she will do.''

"I?" Lady Stanwood all but shouted. "I did not turn the girl from my door. I turned away an imposter who claimed to be her half-brother. And he did not have the look of my son at all!"

"Andrew is my stepbrother, not my half-brother," Rebecca corrected her grandmother gently. "We share no parent. His mother married my father, your son, when Andrew was ten years old. He came to England at my stepmother's request to help me find my relatives. I came at my father's command to do so. My father's dying command."

"You are obviously a clever liar," Giles Stanwood sneered. "What proof have we of your story? And why did your stepbrother show none when he demanded admittance at our door?"

Gently Rebecca drew a locket from where it had been concealed beneath her dress. "I think you will recognize this picture of my father," she said quietly. "It was painted before he left England, he always said. My mother wore it until she died, then my father gave it to me."

Lady Stanwood came forward to look at the locket, for Rebecca refused to part with it even for a moment. She did not trust these Stanwoods and the locket was all she had left of her father. Lady Stanwood appeared to age visibly as she stared at the tiny portrait. Nor did she argue when Lady Sarah told her, tartly, that she need only look in the mirror to see the resemblance Rebecca bore to her. Finally she said, "You are my granddaughter. But I am still not certain I wish to acknowledge you."

"Why not?" Lady Sarah demanded.

"How can you be so certain?" Giles demanded hotly. "If she is my uncle's daughter, why did we never hear of her before her stepbrother demanded admittance at our door? If my uncle survived his journey to the colonies, why were there never any letters?"

At this Lady Stanwood turned to her grandson and thumped her cane upon the floor. "Your uncle was a proud man," she said. "When your grandfather cast him off and forbade him ever to set foot in England again, you uncle vowed never to acknowledge us. He did so only twice. When he married, just before leaving England, he wrote to tell us of his wife, and the second time was upon the birth of his daughter, Rebecca. Your grandfather burned those letters but I have never forgotten what they said.'' Lady Stanwood turned to Rebecca. ''What do you want of us?'' she demanded.

Rebecca faced her grandmother, uncowed. ''When I first came to England,'' she said in her gentle voice, ''I came hoping to find the family I had never known. My father talked about you often, always with a mixture of bitterness and love in his voice. But I came because my father asked it of me, not because I was unhappy where I was. If you do not choose to acknowledge me, then I shall be content to return home.''

''Why didn't you return home as soon as Giles told your stepbrother we wouldn't see you?'' Lady Stanwood demanded.

''Because my stepbrother felt we should wait and try again,'' Rebecca replied calmly. ''Because my stepbrother fell prey to a number of gentlemen who though it amusing to initiate him into London society and he developed a taste for it. Because by the time I realized your door would never be open to me, my stepbrother had exhausted our funds and I knew I would have to wait until my stepmother or my father's partner could send more.''

''And how did you come to be here, in this house,'' Lady Stanwood asked sharply, ''instead of in your stepbrother's care?''

Now Rebecca looked away. The words caught in her throat and she found herself reluctant to expose to these people the full extent of his folly. But it was impossible to evade the question entirely. ''I was not comfortable with the company Andrew had begun to keep,'' she said at last. ''And Lady Sarah was kind enough to offer me the shelter of her home.''

Lady Stanwood regarded Lady Sarah with raised eyebrows. ''How generous of Sarah,'' she said tartly. ''But she might have spoken with me before she made her offer instead of after doing so. Since you did not, Sarah,'' Lady Stanwood said, turning to Lady Sarah, ''you must accept the consequences of an action I hope you will not live to regret.'' She paused and turned a piercing gaze on Rebecca. ''Where is your mother's family?'' she asked abruptly. ''Why are they not here tonight?''

''The Harcourts do not often come to London,'' Lady Sarah said gently.

Still Lady Stanwood bent her gaze on Rebecca as she demanded, ''Did you apply to them?''

''My stepbrother did so,''·Rebecca replied steadily. ''I can only presume that Andrew offended them as thoroughly as he offended you, for they have refused to see me, as well.''

''I see,'' Clarissa said thoughtfully.

''Do you mean to acknowledge your granddaughter, now that you have seen her?'' Lady Sarah asked gently.

Lady Stanwood hesitated. ''She is better than I expected,'' Lady Stanwood acknowledged reluctantly. ''And I suppose someone must do so if you are bent on introducing her to the *ton.*''

''Grandmama,'' Giles said warningly.

Clarissa Stanwood looked at her grandson and said, tartly, ''You may choose to look like a fool by refusing to acknowledge your cousin, but I do not! Pray, what do you think would be the inevitable end if I did so? The *ton* would say, and rightly so, that I was acting out of spite! Like it or not, we shall acknowledge the girl and do so with apparent complaisance.''

''But it is well known we have refused to do so up until now,'' Giles protested. ''I shall look like a fool.''

''That is simply remedied,'' Lady Stanwood said coolly. ''You need only say that you have met only her stepbrother and that he gave you quite an improper impression.''

''Well, but Templeton advised us not to acknowledge her,'' Giles persisted, ''and he is well acquainted with both this girl and her stepbrother.''

Clarissa Stanwood regarded her grandson with a lifted eyebrow. Her voice was lofty as she replied, "I have never considered Lord Templeton to be an appropriate judge of my behavior. Indeed, if there is anything to be said in this girl's favor it is that Templeton did not wish us to acknowledge her."

Giles gaped at his grandmother. "You never said so before," he retorted.

Again Clarissa thumped her cane upon the floor. "I do not," she said crisply, "defend myself to you. I will acknowledge my granddaughter."

"Well, I will not. I am leaving!" Lord Stanwood said hotly and strode toward the door.

Lady Stanwood watched him leave, impassive in her countenance. When he was gone she turned to Lady Sarah and Rebecca and said calmly, "He will come about. I will see to that. Nor will anyone suppose it odd he chose not to come tonight. I will give it out that he thought the party too insipid. You will not care for that, Sarah, so long as it is seen I acknowledge Rebecca."

Lady Sarah had the sense not to disagree and Rebecca thanked her grandmother prettily for her kindness. Lady Stanwood would have put a number of questions to Rebecca, but before she could do so, Oliver Ransford was announced.

"I collect," he murmured to his mother as he kissed her cheek, "that Giles chose not to come up to scratch?"

"Behave yourself, Oliver!" his mother said sharply into his ear. For the benefit of the rest of the company she said, in a more normal voice, "Oliver, you have met Miss Stanwood and you must know Lady Stanwood."

Ransford bowed in the general direction of the two ladies and Rebecca curtsied while Lady Stanwood inclined her head. "I have been making the acquaintance of my grand-daughter from America," Lady Stanwood said regally. "She ought, of course, to make her comeout from Stanwood Hall, but as Giles is choosing to be difficult, this must do instead.

Tomorrow, however, Rebecca must go for a drive about the park with me in the afternoon, and it is imperative that the Harcourts be brought around to acknowledging her as well, as soon as possible.''

"You're quite right," Lady Sarah said admiringly, a response that drew a sour smile from Lady Stanwood.

The two ladies put their heads together and began to formulate plans for Rebecca's future. Ransford drew Rebecca aside to the window where they could talk softly without fear of being overheard. "My mother seems to have done the trick," he told Rebecca quietly.

"Was there ever any doubt?" she quizzed him wickedly in return.

He looked down at her, warmth in his eyes as he replied, "Not once Lady Stanwood had seen you. Giles is a mutton head! But it won't signify. With both Lady Stanwood's backing and my mother's your acceptance is assured."

Rebecca looked up at Ransford and marveled. "Can it really be so easy? When the Stanwoods were so adamant, before, not to acknowledge me? And the *ton* considered me completely ineligible?"

"Never doubt my mother," Ransford countered, laughter in his fine blue eyes. "You may think her sweet and gentle, but I would have backed her against a thousand Clarissa Stanwoods! Now smile and play the dutiful granddaughter, or my mother and Lady Stanwood will be offended beyond words."

Rebecca did smile at that. A moment later the footman announced that dinner was served and she was able to take her place at the table with composure. If her eyes strayed, once or twice, to Ransford's face or to the empty place left by Lord Stanwood's absence, no one else appeared to notice and the talk was of people and places Rebecca still longed to know. Almost too quickly it was time for the other guests to arrive.

16

The party was a disaster. In one form or another, Templeton's tale was on a dozen lips, whispered in the corners or hinted at to the main participants. Her pleasure destroyed, Rebecca felt the party would never end and, indeed, it was well past midnight when the last of the guests, save for Ransford and Lady Stanwood, left Lady Sarah's party. Rebecca would have fled upstairs had it not been evident to her that the others were given over to outrage and not despair. They stared at one another grimly, trying to find an answer for the disaster that had just occurred. "It will be no better tomorrow," Lady Stanwood said harshly. "The tale will spread even further than it already has."

"I'll swear it was unknown yesterday night," Oliver said with a puzzled frown.

"How can you be so sure?" Lady Sarah asked.

"Because Alvanley asked if he ought to come tonight. He said Lady Jersey had advised him you had a charming young lady to introduce to the *ton*. I said I thought you meant to have Amanda Wetherford here. I did not then know about Rebecca. But, in any event, Alvanley would not have spoken so had he known this story that has so swiftly made the rounds." Oliver paused then said, "I can think of only one person who would have so great a grudge against Rebecca and that is Carlisle Templeton."

"What about Giles Stanwood?" Lady Sarah said thoughtfully. "He was very angry when he left here."

"True. Nor do I think it beyond Giles to do such a thing,"

Oliver agreed, ignoring Lady Stanwood's gasp of outrage. "But recollect that Giles left here only two hours before your other guests arrived. He cannot have had time to spread the story. Nor, I'll swear, did he know that Rebecca had worked as a servant in my house. But Templeton did. I'll swear he is behind all this."

"But how did he know?" Lady Sarah asked, bewildered.

Oliver shrugged, impatient with himself, as he replied. "The night before you took Rebecca away, Templeton was at my house for a card party, as was Rebecca's stepbrother. Templeton ventured into the kitchens to ask my cook for some recipe or other and encountered Rebecca. I remember that he told me I had a singularly clumsy servant and described Phoebe and told me I ought to fire her. I ignored him and then forgot the matter. Last night he mentioned her again. I thought nothing of that, either, but it is evident by tonight's disaster that he must have recognized Rebecca."

"But what can he hope to gain by this?" Lady Sarah asked in protest.

"Revenge. Rebecca's social ruin. Any number of things," Oliver said angrily. "Perhaps he thinks that if her reputation is sullied we will cast her off. And then he means to try once more to force his attentions on her." Oliver paused then added, "I used to think Templeton an amusing, harmless fellow. After what Rebecca has told me, I can think so no longer."

"I hate that man!" Lady Sarah exclaimed, her eyes blazing with fury. "When I think of poor Rebecca and all her happiness dashed by his ill nature, I could cheerfully run the man through with a sword."

"And I should dearly love to oblige you," Ransford said grimly. "But to do so would be to expose Rebecca to even more gossip. When I deal with Templeton, it will be quite privately."

The look in her son's eyes made Lady Sarah shiver, but she could not tell if what she felt was fear or anticipation. Aloud she said, "Pray be careful, Oliver. I do not trust him in the least."

Ransford was amused. "Neither do I," he said. "But I do not fear Templeton. And recollect that it is not only Rebecca's honor that is affected, but mine as well. Even if I did not have any other reason, I must confront him for that."

Lady Sarah did not disagree. How could she? The hints her guests had been at such pains to relate to her, even as they gave Rebecca the cut direct, did indeed impinge on Oliver's honor as much as Rebecca's. And while no one would hold him to the same standards as the girl, there would be those who would believe it and brand him a blackguard of the same stamp as Lord Templeton, and that Lady Sarah could not bear.

Lady Stanwood, who had been listening in patent disbelief now demanded incredulously, "Is the story true, then? Was my granddaughter in your household?"

"Unfortunately, yes," Ransford said curtly.

"I'll have nothing more to do with this," Lady Stanwood vowed austerly.

"To be blunt about the matter," he told Lady Stanwood coldly, "none of this would have occurred if you had acknowledged your granddaughter as you ought to have done in the first place."

"Acknowledge a hoyden so lacking in propriety as to become your mistress?" Lady Stanwood demanded. "How dare you ask such a thing of me?"

Lady Sarah recognized the martial look in Oliver's eyes and made haste to forestall him. Quickly she darted between her son and Lady Stanwood. Her own voice was frosty however as she said, "It was no such thing. You may recollect, Lady Stanwood, that my son has already said she was a servant in his household—a sort of scullery maid, if you will. As soon as we discovered who she was, I brought her here to stay with me. And however rudely Oliver may have said so, it is quite true that Rebecca would never have felt compelled to undertake such a masquerade if she had had the acceptance and protection of the Stanwoods. Protection her stepbrother was not willing to afford her."

"Protection from what?" Lady Stanwood asked skeptically.

"From Lord Templeton's advances," Rebecca replied, feeling that it was time for her to take part in this discussion. "He intended for me just such a position as you imagined I held with respect to Mr. Ransford. Or possibly something far worse. Andrew would not protect me so I ran away, and having nowhere to turn, conceived the notion of seeking a menial post until it should be possible for me to return to America."

"Nonsense," Lady Stanwood said, thumping her cane upon the floor. "A Stanwood would never stoop to such a thing."

"But you would not acknowledge me as a Stanwood," Rebecca pointed out gently. "I had to do what seemed best."

"And now you are all but ruined," Lady Stanwood retorted irritably.

"Perhaps not," Lady Sarah said slowly. "What if I were to claim Rebecca were with me all along? You, none of you, said anything to the contrary tonight, did you?"

"I rather fancy none of us said anything at all to the point," Oliver observed dryly, "and no one dared ask us directly. There were only oblique hints and overheard whispers. But it will not do, Mama. Recollect that Miss Stanwood may be known to have disappeared from her stepbrother's roof before the night you and Miss Wetherford were at the theater. It is not credible that had Rebecca been with you, you would not have brought her as well. Or that you would not have mentioned her until this week."

"A trifling ailment," Lady Sarah suggested, "that kept her home, perhaps? Or the Harcourts? Perhaps they would be willing to say she was with them?"

"No," Lady Stanwood said crisply, "not the Harcourts." Then unbending a trifle, she added, "If we had more time, we might have tried applying to the Harcourts for their support. But we do not. We must know immediately that whomever we name will go along with our scheme. And I have just the person. Sarah, Rebecca was not with you until this week for the very good reason that she was with Cordelia.''

This produced a stunned silence in the room which was broken only when Lady Sarah managed to say, doubtfully, "Cordelia?''

"Yes, my eldest daughter. She was always used to have a kindness for your father, Rebecca,'' Lady Stanwood pronounced grandly.

"She did?'' Rebecca said, blinking in surprrise. "How odd that father never mentioned it. Indeed, Papa was used to say—''

Lady Stanwood ruthlessly cut her granddaughter short. "It was a kindness Cordelia hid because she did not wish to draw down upon her head her father's wrath. Your father did, however, speak of it to you and when you found my door closed to you, you approached Cordelia. She took you in. Quietly, of course, so that I should not hear of it. Or your stepbrother, Andrew, of whom she could not approve.''

Somewhat overawed, Rebecca could not help asking Lady Stanwood, "You do mean to stand by me then?''

"I do,'' Lady Stanwood stated.

"The story might work,'' said Lady Sarah, who had been thinking rapidly, "if Cordelia will go along with the tale.''

"I can vouch that Cordelia will agree to whatever tale we tell,'' Lady Stanwood said with some asperity. "I shall write her directly when I get home and post the letter to her tomorrow. She lives sufficiently removed from society that there is no need to fear that some chance visitor will give the lie to our story.'' Then, a trifle gruffly Lady Stanwood demanded, "But if Rebecca was indeed in your household, Ransford, won't the servants talk?''

"They will not,'' Oliver replied grimly.

"But how does Rebecca come to be in my household now?'' Lady Sarah asked worriedly.

"I fancy I have the answer to that one,'' Ransford said thoughtfully. "If,'' he said to Lady Stanwood, "your daughter is also willing to pretend I visited, on some pretext or other, and met Miss Stanwood there.''

"But what good will that do?'' Lady Sarah asked.

Oliver turned laughing eyes on her and said quizzically, "Can't you guess? I was at once smitten with Miss Stanwood's charms and begged you to invite her to stay with you. Always anxious to see me creditably established, you were perfectly happy to do so.'' He paused, then added with a queer smile, "If, as I believe, Templeton is behind these rumors, that is an advantage. Since word has got about, thanks to Sally Jersey, that he was pursuing Miss Stanwood, these latest rumors will be put down to pique at his discovering that Miss Stanwood and I are betrothed to be married and no one will credit a word of his gossip. At least, they will not if you and my mother and the Harcourts, if it can be managed, are seen to accept the match with complaisance.''

As he spoke, Rebecca stood rooted in disbelief. "You cannot be serious,'' she protested.

"Do you really mean to make my granddaughter an offer?'' Lady Stanwood asked suspiciously.

"Oliver?'' Lady Sarah said in a not altogether steady voice.

Ransford ignored all of them. He possessed himself of Rebecca's hands and led her to the other side of the room. He looked down at her, a humorous gleam in his eyes as he said, kindly, "You are tired and this is not the time for me to be making you an offer. Were the circumstances other than as they are I should certainly have waited for a more opportune moment. As it is, however, I think it best if we announce our betrothal at once. You may always cry off later if you wish.''

Rebecca pulled her hands free and began to pace about. "This is absurd,'' she said in a troubled voice. "You cannot wish to marry me. These rumors—there is no need for you to make such a sacrifice to silence them.''

"I assure you it is no sacrifice,'' Ransford countered, amused.

Rebecca looked at him and said with some asperity, "Oh, no, of course not! I collect you wish for nothing more than to be betrothed to me, your former servant."

"But I do," he replied. Then, outrageously he added, "You were, after all, a most exceptional servant."

"Do give over this nonsense," Rebecca begged him seriously. "I cannot marry you."

All at once the laughter was gone from Ransford's eyes. "Do you mean you cannot bear the thought of being married to me?" he asked quietly.

It wasn't fair, Rebecca told herself, that he should look at her with such anxiety. One might almost believe he meant it when he said he wished to marry her. Quite absurd, of course.

"Why is it absurd?" Ransford asked gently and Rebecca realized she had spoken aloud.

Resolutely she looked at his shoulder as she replied, "You cannot wish to be married to me and I should be at fault if I let you make such a sacrifice."

"I told you it wouldn't be a sacrifice," he pointed out patiently. Ransford was silent for several moments and Rebecca risked a look at his face only to be taken aback by the warmth that blazed out at her. So, too, was the mischief back in Ransford's eyes as he said, "My little goose! Do you really think I am asking you to marry me out of some misplaced sense of chivalry?"

"Aren't you?" Rebecca asked doubtfully.

"No, my little love, I am not," he retorted instantly.

And then, most reprehensibly, he kissed her, and that kiss left no doubt that Ransford felt something far stronger toward Rebecca than mere chivalry. When finally he lifted his lips from hers it was to say, "I am asking you to marry me because I am very sure I do not wish to live without you. And unless you mean to tell me that you do wish to live without me, I do not mean to accept a refusal, my love. So, for the last time, will you marry me, Miss Rebecca Stanwood?"

"Yes!" she said with a sob that was almost lost in the ruthless kiss that followed.

"How affecting." Lady Stanwood's dry voice broke in upon their embrace. "I do think, however, that we had best finish laying our plans. And then you, Ransford, and I had best take our leave so Sarah and Rebecca can get some sleep."

Meekly Oliver did as he was bid and brought Rebecca over to the others so they could, in fact, finish laying their plans.

17

Lord Templeton was in no hurry to close his hand around Miss Stanwood. She would come to him in due time. Not happily, perhaps not even willingly, but she would come. Meanwhile, it was enough to savor the knowledge of her humiliation. It was also, he decided, important that Pierce know what was afoot and what to answer people when asked about Rebecca. Therefore, the morning after Lady Sarah's disastrous party, Templeton paid a call upon Pierce shortly before noon.

Andrew was sober, but a decanter of wine stood at his elbow as he looked over his bills and Templeton thought it would not be long before the bottle was broached.

"What the devil are you doing here so early?" Pierce asked with a look of astonishment as Templeton entered the book room of his hired house.

"I looked for you last night at the cockfighting, but you were not there," he said curtly.

"I had an offer to play cards at a new gaming house, and since the dibs were in tune, thanks to Ransford's card party the other night, I went," Andrew answered testily. "I thought my good luck might continue, but it didn't."

"You have not heard the news then, I collect?" Templeton asked with raised eyebrows.

"Heard what news?" Pierce demanded impatiently. "You know I don't listen to gossip. Always about a pack of people I don't know."

That was, Templeton reflected, probably true. "You've

heard of this person, however," he said smoothly. "The news concerns your stepsister, Rebecca."

Pierce gasped at Templeton. "Look here, Templeton," Andrew began impatiently, "where is she?"

"In Lady Sarah Ransford's care. Oliver Ransford's mother gave a party last night at which she introduced your stepsister to the *ton,*" Templeton said deliberately.

"What?" Pierce demanded incredulously. "Are you certain?"

Templeton bowed. "Absolutely certain," he said bitterly.

"Now what do we do?" Andrew asked, shaken.

"I have already taken the first steps," Templeton replied with a sour smile. "The story is on everyone's lips this morning that your stepsister has been in Ransford's house, presumably for improper purposes. It is believed that his mother must have discovered Miss Stanwood there and taken her into her own house, where Ransford still pursues your stepsister."

"But will anyone believe it? Why should anyone think Ransford did more than give my stepsister shelter, if they even believe that much?" Andrew asked doubtfully.

"If Ransford only wished to give her shelter," Templeton answered silkily, "why would he not have placed Miss Stanwood in his mother's care at once?"

There was no answer to that. Or none, at any rate, that anyone would be able to see. Nevertheless, Pierce continued to play the role of disbeliever. "Perhaps it will be assumed Lady Sarah would not at first accept Rebecca into her household?" he suggested. "After all, if what you propose were true, would she not refuse to take Rebecca into her household now?"

"It is apparent you do not know Lady Sarah," Templeton said with mock sadness. "She is well known to have a kind heart and would never have refused your sister refuge if Ransford had taken her there at the start. But by the same token, if she felt her son had wronged Miss Stanwood, Lady Sarah would take her into her home even after what I had suggested."

It could all have been true. Andrew looked at Templeton and said shrewdly, "Can the story be traced back to you?"

Templeton smiled. "Oh, I said very little, I promise you. A word here, a word there, a hint, a shrug, a suggestion. Really, it took very little. People have such vivid imaginations, you know."

Pierce rose to his feet and laughed. "You are a devil of a fellow," he said admiringly.

Templeton laughed as well. "Oh, I have also suggested to the interested," he said, "that I trust they will not allow themselves to be fobbed off with some improbable tale. A hint that your stepsister might not be entirely indifferent to Ransford and might try to protect him was most efficacious."

Pierce looked at Templeton. "Isn't that risky? If my sister were so fond of Ransford, why should she have fled his house to Lady Sarah's care?"

"Perhaps Lady Sarah gave her no choice," Templeton said mildly. "As much as her ladyship is said to love her son, she would not, I think, countenance him taking to bed your sister without the, er, benefit of matrimony."

Pierce nodded. "That might do the trick. By God, you're a clever fellow, Templeton."

Templeton shrugged. "One can only try."

A moment later, however, Pierce said, puzzled, "But I still don't see the point of all this. If Ransford has compromised my sister, what do we gain by telling this tale? Revenge? Take care Ransford doesn't feel he has to marry her," he added maliciously. "That would put paid to your plans."

Templeton looked at Pierce with raised eyebrows. "But why should Ransford marry her? After all, so far as I know, he hasn't actually compromised her. And he is far too stubborn to be prodded into anything. No, my intent is to drive your stepsister out of Lady Sarah's house and back into our waiting arms."

"I must take your word for that," Pierce said doubtfully. Then, with more excitement, "If Rebecca is the innocent she was when she left here and we do get her back, we could still take her to Medmenham.''

Templeton nodded. ''I knew you would be quick to grasp the possibilities. I suggest you see your stepsister and discover whether she can be persuaded to return to this house,'' he said. ''By now the rumors must be beginning to pinch.''

Templeton did not offer to accompany Pierce to Lady Sarah's house. Instead, he accompanied Andrew outside and waited while a hack was summoned and the driver given Lady Sarah's address. Templeton watched until the carriage was out of sight and then set off for his clubs in excellent spirits.

He would not have been so sanguine had he known that halfway to Lady Sarah's house, Andrew changed his mind and directed the driver to take him to Ransford's house instead.

It was evident Andrew thought, with an unpleasant smile, that it had not occurred to Templeton that he had placed a card worth far more than mere membership in the Hellfire Club and the canceling of his gambling debts in Andrew's hands. What had been a vague notion a few days earlier now became a full-fledged plan. Andrew would see what could be had out of Ransford himself, and he was in a surprisingly cheerful frame of mind as he walked up the steps to Oliver Ransford's townhouse. To his chagrin, however, he discovered that he had missed Ransford by a matter of minutes.

Oliver Ransford, having no notion that Andrew earnestly desired to speak with him, tried without success to call upon Mr. Pierce. He was informed that Mr. Pierce was not at home and his staff did not know when he would return. Nor was he any more fortunate when he called at Templeton's townhouse. His lordship's staff would not even say whether Templeton was in town or not.

Frustrated in his attempts to call to book one or both men, Ransford decided to call upon Rebecca. With the informality

Lady Sarah's staff could not help but deprecate but which they had long since become accustomed to, Oliver did not wait to be announced and said he would go up by himself. He arrived at the top of the stairs to find Rebecca right outside the drawing room door and about to mount the stairs. From the expression of mortification on her face, Ransford concluded that something had happened to upset her. He prevented her from passing him by the simple expedient of taking her hand and pressing it warmly between his own. A certain noise from the room she had just left caused him to draw her toward a small parlor at the back of the house and to close the door once they were inside it. "There," he said with a reassuring smile. "Now we may be perfectly private, and you may tell me what has happened to overset you, without fear that we shall be overheard." When she did not at once answer, he went on, "You've been having a hard time of it, I fear. What has happened to vex you this time, my dear?"

Rebecca tried to smile in return but could not. Instead she looked up at him and found herself almost undone by the kindness she saw in his eyes. "It is your mother who has been treated unkindly," she said, trying to control the tremor in her voice.

Ransford frowned at that and Rebecca found herself wanting to smooth away the crease on his forehead. Already she regretted the words and wished them unspoken. And yet, he ought to be warned. Troubled, she looked at Oliver Ransford. "Should I go?" she asked. "Should I leave this house before I cause your mother further trouble?"

Ransford's grip tightened on her hand. "No," he said instantly. Then, regretting the harshness in his voice, he went on, more gently, "This is not your fault. And besides, if you fled now, the rumors might only grow worse." He smiled at her and said reassuringly, "We shall come about, you know. Can you doubt my mother so shockingly?"

Rebecca shook her head. "No, nor Lady Stanwood. She is here as well and has faced down your mother's critics.

For today, at any rate. She has even brought my cousin, Lord Stanwood, and he grudgingly agrees to acknowledge me. But I would feel better if I knew Lord Templeton and my step-brother would cease their efforts to ruin me.''

"I have not yet seen your stepbrother or Templeton," Ransford told her gravely, "but I shall and I promise you they will cease to bother you. Come, will you go for a drive with me?"

"I wish I could," Rebecca replied, shyly, "but Grand-mama has invited me to go for a drive with her, and I cannot help but think she is right in saying it will help my position. I was just on my way upstairs to change."

"To be sure, her credit is far greater than mine," Oliver said with a twinkle in his eyes.

It was impossible not to smile up at him in return, and Rebecca did so willingly. Nor did she object when he took her in his arms and kissed her. If this was a dream she did not wish to wake up from it. Let tomorrow bring what it would, today she knew she was loved. All too soon, however, Ransford released her and opened the door of the parlor.

Rebecca went upstairs to change her dress and Oliver went on into the drawing room. He greeted his mother, Lord and Lady Stanwood, and the three ladies who were about to leave. When they were gone, Oliver turned to his mother and asked, "Do you mean to tell me what those jealous tabbies said? Or am I to conjecture the worst on my own?"

Lady Sarah laughed. "Oh, dear," she said, "I was hoping you wouldn't guess."

"He was bound to find out soon enough, anyway," Lady Stanwood said tartly. "You must know, Ransford, they were here to see my granddaughter and to tell your mother that the latest *on-dit* is that not only will Rebecca be refused vouchers to Almack's, but if your mother does not cease her sponsorship of Rebecca, her own welcome there will be in doubt."

Lady Sarah broke in to say, "Oh, Oliver, I am, if you please, a feather wit, sadly shatterbrained, and far too easily taken in for my own good. You, moreover, are an unprincipled blackguard whom no mother ought to allow near an unprotected daughter. I vow, I don't know which of all the absurd charges vexes me the most!''

"I do," Ransford retorted, his eyes dancing in spite of the gravity of the situation. "It is the charge that you, my dearest, wisest mother, are a shatterbrain. If anything were needed to prove the absurdity of all this, that would surely be sufficient to do so. As anyone who knows you will attest.''

Lady Sarah gave her son a grateful smile. "I wish I could think so," she said with a sigh. "But I used to count Lydia Callendish my friend, and even she thought it necessary to warn me that I have all but brought myself to ruin by countenancing Miss Stanwood. Rebecca, Lady Stanwood, and I contrived, as you suggested, to tell the story we concocted last night but it is too soon to know if it will answer.''

She paused and Lady Stanwood spoke. "I fancy,'' she said, not without a note of satisfaction in her voice, "they were not expecting me to see me here. Between us, we managed to rout them.''

Ransford cocked a knowing eye at Lady Stanwood. "Came all top lofty over them did you? I wish I might have been here to see it.''

Lady Stanwood laughed, not at all displeased by the tribute, then said comfortably, "Giles's presence didn't hurt matters either.''

Ransford turned to Lord Stanwood with a friendly smile and said, "No, I suppose it would not. How are you Giles? Reconciled to your cousin and to having me enter the family as her husband?''

"Well, as to that," Giles said uncomfortably, "your betrothal to Rebecca is the one thing that does reconcile me to my cousin. I cannot like matters as they stand. This sort of scandal is abhorrent to me. But if she is my cousin, I suppose I must support her.''

"You are too kind," Ransford murmured. He hesitated then turned back to his mother and said, "I must suppose this has all been very distressing for Rebecca."

"The poor child offered this morning to leave here because she did not want me to suffer for supporting her, but of course I told her I wouldn't hear of such a thing," Lady Sarah replied warmly. "As though it were her fault! How I should like to have revenge on whoever started this absurd rumor. It must have been Templeton."

"So I think, also," Ransford said grimly. "And I mean to do my best to find out."

"I have already written to Cordelia, and as soon as Rebecca is ready, I shall take my granddaughter out for a drive," Lady Stanwood said decisively. "The news that I have at last acknowledged my granddaughter has not got about as fast as the news of her supposed ruin."

Ransford glanced at his watch and said, "Well, I suppose I must do my part. I shall try again, later today, to speak with Miss Stanwood's stepbrother. And with Lord Templeton. I cannot help but believe he is behind much of this. You will excuse me now, I know."

Ransford took his leave of both ladies and Lord Stanwood, and went back out into the hall just as Rebecca came down the stairs. To her delight, he waited for her.

When she came up to him, Oliver took Rebecca's hand and kissed it. There was a pronounced twinkle in his eyes as he said, "I must not detain you from your grandmother or we shall both be in the suds. But I wanted to tell you again not to let any of this worry you, my love. Between my mother and Lady Stanwood, you will come about with the *ton,* and I shall see to Templeton and your stepbrother."

18

Ransford returned home to discover Andrew Pierce waiting for him. Eames, recognizing at a glance the young man who had attended a party there a week or so earlier, had shown him into the drawing room when he expressed an urgent need to speak with Mr. Ransford. At the same time, Eames was quick to realize that Andrew Pierce was not of the *ton* and only a perfunctory offer of liquid refreshment had been made. One which Andrew was quick to refuse. He could, he certainly felt, use some fortification, but an innate shrewdness informed him that it would be wisest to face Oliver Ransford entirely sober.

In this, Andrew Pierce was not mistaken. When Ransford returned home, Eames informed him that Mr. Pierce was waiting to see him in the drawing room. "Is he sober?" Ransford asked bluntly.

"I believe so," Eames replied austerely. Then, after a moment's pause, he added, "Mr. Pierce asked about Phoebe, sir."

"I trust you told him nothing?" Oliver said sharply, cursing himself for not having spoken of it to Eames earlier.

Eames bowed. "It is not my place to speak to such a person about any of your staff, sir. Particularly when it is Lady Sarah's wish that we not do so."

"My mother warned you, did she?" Oliver said with some surprise. "When was that?"

"When she took Phoebe with her, she asked Mrs. Marsh to speak to the staff," Eames replied, even more surprised that his employer did not know this.

A slight laugh escaped Ransford. "Excellent," he said. "You will continue to follow her wishes." He paused, then added, "I am betrothed, Eames. You may wish me happy."

"I am very happy for you, sir," Eames replied. "May I ask who the fortunate young lady is?"

A smile twitched at the corners of Ransford's mouth as he said, "I am betrothed to Miss Rebecca Stanwood. When I bring her to this house as my bride, Eames, I fancy some of the staff will think they have met her before. They will contrive to forget it."

If Ransford expected Eames to be surprised, he was disappointed. Instead, Eames coughed and said, "That would account, no doubt, for the groom thinking he recognized Phoebe in your curricle, sir."

Ransford frowned. "The devil!" he said. "How many people did he tell?"

"Only myself and Mrs. Marsh, sir. We ventured to give him the hint that there must be something more to the matter than he could see and that you would not approve of him gossiping," Eames replied.

"What an excellent fellow you are," Ransford said approvingly. "Well, if you know that, then I suppose I may as well tell you that Miss Stanwood pretended to be a servant in order to hide from Lord Templeton and her stepbrother, Mr. Pierce. Only the direst need could have prevailed upon her to do so."

"Lord Templeton and Mr. Pierce, sir? In that event, it is perfectly understandable," Eames said with a bow. He paused, then said delicately, "Might I venture to share that information with Mrs. Marsh, sir? She will know just how to handle the junior staff."

Ransford was amused. "Yes, of course. I must have told her something, in any event. Miss Stanwood's grandmother, Lady Stanwood, and my mother have arranged between them a story that will inform the *ton* that Miss Stanwood was staying at an aunt's house during the time she was here. Naturally I shall not want any of my household to contradict that story. But you have already assured me of the discretion of my staff. And now I suppose I had best go in and see Mr. Pierce."

"Yes, sir."

Ransford opened the door of the drawing room softly and found Pierce pacing about the room impatiently. "There you are," he thundered as Ransford came into the room.

"Yes, I am and so are you here," Ransford replied mildly. "May I ask why?"

Pierce looked taken aback. "You know why," he said, recovering swiftly. "I have come about my stepsister."

"Your stepsister," Ransford said, with raised eyebrows, "is with my mother. Unless, of course, she is still out driving with her grandmother, Lady Stanwood. May I offer you some sherry?"

"No," Pierce answered, resolutely refusing to be diverted. "I know Rebecca is staying with Lady Sarah. But it is you I wish to see."

"Oh, why?" Ransford asked laconically.

"Because you have ruined my stepsister!" Pierce said in outraged accents.

For a moment, silence hung in the air, then Ransford's voice answered sharply, "Nonsense!"

Pierce gaped at him. "But all of London knows Rebecca was in this house, unchaperoned, for days!" he said.

Ransford regarded Pierce with raised eyebrows. "Indeed?" he said coldly. "I think you will find that very soon all of London will know that your sister was with her Aunt Cordelia. Unless, of course, she came to stay with my mother."

Pierce began to shake with anger as he saw the ground being cut out from under his feet. "Liar! I know she was in this house. As a servant!"

"Dear me," Ransford said mildly. "Are you angry with me for supposedly seducing her or for hiring her at appalling wages? Either way I think you will find the story is incredible."

"This is not a joke," Pierce retorted swiftly. "My Lord Templeton saw her here, carrying coal scuttles. He will swear to it, if need be."

"Will he?" Ransford said skeptically. He looked at his

well-polished hand before he went on, "But, you see, even
if Templeton were willing to swear to such a thing, I doubt
he would be believed."

"Why shouldn't he be believed?" Pierce asked angrily.

Ransford smiled. "Because, my dear sir, it would be put
down to pique. Pique that Miss Stanwood is going to marry
me instead of succumbing to his attentions."

"You're going to marry my stepsister?" Pierce gasped
at Ransford. Swiftly, however, he recovered. "That's
marvelous," he said. "Why, that was the reason I came here
today. To ask you to marry Rebecca. But if you're going
to do so anyway, there isn't the least need for us to quarrel.
Let me shake your hand, sir. I meant to suggest that if you
didn't wish to marry Rebecca we could come to terms, but
if you've already decided upon marriage that's even better."

Pierce started toward Ransford, delight written upon his
face, but Oliver held him off with an upraised hand. "Just
a moment," Ransford said coldly. "I am not marrying your
stepsister because you or anyone else believes I may have
compromised her. I am marrying Miss Stanwood because
I very much wish to do so. I'm curious, however, as to what
price you would have put on relinquishing your demand that
I marry her."

Andrew shrugged impatiently. "Whatever your reasons,
I don't care. Just so long as you do marry her. I am anxious
to discuss what settlement you intend to make on her. I was
going to suggest ten thousand pounds if you didn't want to
marry her, but of course you will want to be even more
generous if you do. As her nearest relative, here in London,
you may make all the arrangements with me. In fact if you
should care to advance me some money so that she could
properly be outfitted with her bridal clothes—"

Ransford cut him short with a well-bred murmur. "Now
where, I wonder, did you get the notion I was a fool? If I
discuss settlements with anyone, it will be with Lady Stanwood or some other member of Miss Stanwood's family.
Nor, since she is currently in my mother's care, need I

advance you any funds for her clothes or any other purpose, either. My mother will see to all that.''

Pierce's face darkened with anger at these words. ''Really, Ransford? I think you might do well to reconsider. There are a great many things I might tell the *ton,* if I chose. If you do not pay me well for my silence I shall scream to the rooftops how you brought my sister to this house in the guise of a servant and then seduced her. How will you like that?''

Ransford regarded him with contempt. ''Will you be believed? And if you are believed that your sister was in my house as a servant, will you like it when it is said that she undertook such a masquerade because she could not turn to you for protection from unwelcome advances? Who will he hurt more then? For do not doubt that my mother and Lady Stanwood between them could contrive to turn Rebecca into a heroine and you the villain.''

Pierce regarded Ransford with loathing. ''Very well,'' he said, ''I won't tell that tale. Instead I shall tell the tale of how my stepsister went willingly to the revels of the Hellfire Club and how she entrapped you—''

He got no further before Oliver's right hand flew out and struck him forcefully on the chin, knocking him to the floor. Then, very deliberately Ransford said, ''If you say one word against your stepsister, I will have you kidnapped and taken aboard the first ship I can find willing to sail anywhere. And if in sinks in a storm, you will have no more than you deserve.'' When he was certain that Pierce did not mean to fight, he said more mildly, ''Tell me about the Hellfire Club. I thought it had disbanded fifty years ago.''

Pierce eyed Ransford malevolently but only said, ''It must have been resurrected. Ask Templeton. He said that if I brought Rebecca to a meeting of the Hellfire Club, he would see I was made a member.''

''And you agreed?'' Ransford demanded incredulously. Then, answering his own question he said, ''Yes, of course you did. That was what prompted Miss Stanwood to fly from your house, wasn't it?'' He didn't wait for a reply but went on, "Where does the Hellfire Club meet? And when?"

When Pierce did not immediately reply, Ransford stepped forward as though to hit him again and Andrew said quickly, "In Medmenham. I don't know when for certain."

Ransford stood back as Pierce got to his feet. "I shouldn't tell Templeton we've had this conversation if I were you," he said coolly.

"You'd be well served if I did!" Andrew said hotly.

"I meant what I said before," Oliver replied deliberately. "I won't let you throw a rub in my way." He paused, then added, "I would advise you to let me know at once, however, if you should get word that Templeton means to go to Medmenham, though I wouldn't go there myself."

"Don't worry," Andrew retorted sullenly. "Without Rebecca I'm not welcome."

"Yes, I've no doubt you feel yourself ill-used," Oliver said, with faint amusement in his voice. "But I assure you, you are not. And if you throw no rub in my way, I shall pay your current bills and arrange passage for you back to America as soon as possible."

A hopeful gleam sprang into Andrew's eyes. "I could be very helpful to you," he said.

"Oh, no," Oliver replied, shaking his head. "I'm not a fool to be bled by you. I'll pay your current bills and give you something besides to tide you over but I'll not be bled. No, nor frank your gambling, either."

Once again Andrew turned sullen as he said, "How am I to come about if you won't pay my gambling debts? You have no notion the amount of blunt I owe Lord Templeton."

"Does he hold all your gambling vowels?" Oliver asked, curious.

"Most of 'em," Andrew agreed. "He bought them up from other gentlemen who were not so willing to wait to be paid."

"And so that he might give you all the more reason to cooperate in handing your stepsister over to him?" Oliver suggested gently. Andrew did not disagree, and after a moment Ransford went on. "You need not worry about the gambling debts you owe Templeton. I think I can guarantee you that he will not be dunning you for them."

"They are a debt of honor. They must be paid," Andrew said hotly.

"A debt of honor?" Oliver said ironically. "Ordinarily, I would agree. But in this case I should rather call it a debt of dishonor. But you must do as you please. Arrange to pay him a little at a time or write home for the amount or arrange something else. Perhaps, if I am feeling very generous, I may help you discharge them, though I doubt it. But I strongly suggest you incur no more of them." He waited but it appeared Andrew had nothing more to say. "I shall give you some funds now, enough to tide you over for a bit. You will send the rest of your bills round to me and I shall arrange to have them paid. I shall see about arranging passage for you back to America and you will go as soon as I am able to do so," he added curtly.

"What if I don't want to go?" Andrew asked sullenly.

Ransford looked at him and his voice was steady as he replied, "You have caused your stepsister enough distress. You will go when I tell you. Otherwise you will find that England has become extremely unhealthy for you. You will also refrain from doing anything further to trouble her. Do I make myself clear?"

"Perfectly."

Oliver then rang for a footman, and when he appeared told the fellow, "You will escort Mr. Pierce out."

Andrew went.

For some time after Pierce left, Ransford stood deep in thought by the fireplace, staring at the flames as they leapt about. He was recalled to a sense of the present only by the knock on the door by his butler Eames, who wished to know if he would be dining in that evening. Ransford looked up sharply and took a moment to reply. "No," he said slowly, "no, I won't. I shall dine at one of my clubs."

"Very good, sir." Eames hesitated, then added, "I have taken the liberty of putting Mrs. Marsh in possession of the facts. I regret to say that she is not entirely pleased. I ventured to tell her that you would speak with her, yourself, about the matter.''

"Yes, thank you, Eames," Oliver said with a grimace. "I suppose it had better be sooner than later. Send Mrs. Marsh in to me, will you?"

"Certainly, sir."

Ransford had not long to wait. It was only a few minutes later that Mrs. Marsh knocked on the drawing room door and then entered. "You wished to see me, Mr. Ransford?" she said, a mutinous expression on her face.

"Yes, Mrs. Marsh, pray come in," he replied, with his most engaging smile. He directed her to a comfortable chair by the fire and then asked, his eyes dancing, "Am I in disgrace with you? I should quite understand, I promise you, if that were the case."

Mrs. Marsh, who had come in to the drawing room prepared to explain to Mr. Ransford in plain terms why she would find it very difficult to welcome to this house as mistress a person who so recently was a servant in it, now found herself unbending sufficiently to say, "Well, it's not you, precisely, I disapprove of, Mr. Ransford."

His eyes were reassuring as was his voice was he replied, "Tell me what is troubling you, Mrs. Marsh."

"It's that Phoebe, sir!" Mrs. Marsh exclaimed, unable to restrain herself any longer. "The notion of that chit of a girl to be married to you, sir! When you might have looked as high as you wished for a bride. It fair tears my heart, sir, nor will the others like it either."

"But I shall expect you to help them like it," Ransford said, gently but implacably.

"Well, I can't," she retorted. "Bedazzled, that's what you are. Taken in by a—a shameless hussy! And one with no voice, besides. How will you get on with a wife who can't speak?"

A tremor at the corner of Ransford's mouth betrayed his amusement, but his voice was solemn as he said, "Phoebe, that is to say, Miss Stanwood, Miss Rebecca Stanwood, can speak quite well. She chose not to while she was here, for fear you would discover she was a gentlewoman. A gentlewoman from America. Yes, yes, I know you had reason to distrust her. How could you not? You told me yourself that you could not believe she had been in service before. You were quite right. She is, however, of excellent birth. She is a Stanwood and her grandmother is Lady Stanwood of Stanwood Hall.''

''If that's so, sir, then what was she doing carrying coal scuttles in this house?'' Mrs. Marsh demanded belligerently.

Ransford smiled wryly and took a moment to answer. ''Picture yourself, Mrs. Marsh, in another country with no way to return home. The fellow in charge of your care has gambled away all the funds and now proposes to hand you over to a hardened libertine to use as he wishes. What would you do? Submit tamely, or run away? But where would you run to, if there were no one willing to help you? How would you support yourself? Suppose someone proposed that you disguise yourself and take an inferior post. Would you agree? How would you ensure that no one guessed you were from foreign parts, as they surely would if they heard you speak?''

''But if that were so,'' Mrs. Marsh said, genuinely shocked, ''why didn't she confide in you? Or in me?''

''Perhaps there have been so many people in her life upon whom she dared not depend, that she dared not trust us either,'' he said sadly.

Mrs. Marsh could not help but be touched by this affecting portrait. ''Well, if it's as you say, Mr. Ransford,'' she said with a gusty sigh, ''the poor thing has had a hard time of it.''

''It is as I say,'' Ransford replied curtly. ''I spoke with her stepbrother, in this very room, not half an hour ago and he confirmed everything. Indeed, what he showed of himself was worse than anything Miss Stanwood could bring herself to tell me,'' he added grimly. Then his face softened as he said to Mrs. Marsh, coaxingly, ''That is why I depend upon you to help me make Rebecca feel at home when I bring her here as my wife.''

Mrs. Marsh sighed again. For all her faults, she was a sentimental woman and could not help feeling sorry for anyone caught in such a predicament as this girl had been.

"Well, I'll do so," she said at last. "Mind, I don't like being hoaxed as I was, but I suppose I might have done the same had I been in her shoes."

"Thank you, Mrs. Marsh," Oliver said gravely. "I shan't keep you from your duties any longer, but I hoped I might count on you."

Correctly interpreting this as a dismissal, Mrs. Marsh rose to her feet and curtsied to her employer. She paused in the doorway, and Ransford asked gently, "Is something still troubling you, Mrs. Marsh?"

She hesitated and the words tumbled out. "It's just that we're all so wishful to see you happy, sir!"

Ransford smiled then, and Mrs. Marsh found her own heart in a flutter as he said, "I shall be happy, Mrs. Marsh. It is a love match, you know, whatever else may be said."

And that, thought Mrs. Marsh as she finally left the room, counted for more than anything else Mr. Ransford had told her. She began to form plans in her mind as to how she should tell the rest of the staff what she wished them to know. Mrs. Marsh was determined that Mr. Ransford should have nothing to blush for in the way in which his staff greeted their new mistress.

For some time after she was gone, Ransford again stood lost in thought. Finally he rang for Eames and gave his major-domo certain orders that startled the fellow. "I shall be in the library. Let me know at once when they arrive," he said.

Eames was too well trained to betray his astonishment at his orders, however, and by the time Oliver had dealt with his correspondence and certain other matters on his desk, he was informed that the persons he had asked for were waiting in the hall. He directed Eames to show them into the library where he gave them a number of orders, paid them handsomely, and sent them out again. Shortly after that, Ransford went out himself. He had an errand to run in Bow Street and it could not wait.

19

Andrew's first impulse when he left Ransford's house was to see Rebecca and discover what he could get out of her. He did not do so, however, for his instincts told him that nothing would be more certain to draw Ransford's wrath down about his head. Still, he had told Templeton he was going to talk with Rebecca, and it occurred to him that it would be best not to see his lordship until he had decided what story he would tell.

The more Andrew Pierce thought about the matter, the angrier he grew. So Oliver Ransford promised to settle his debts and advance him funds to live on? Paltry! Particularly when he would not frank him at gambling. How else was he to acquire the means to live as he deserved? And to be ordering him to leave England as soon as Ransford had arranged passage for him was beyond bearing. Andrew had soon worked himself into a state in which he saw not Ransford's generosity but Ransford's thwarting of his dreams of being a member of the *ton*.

There was room enough for anger at Rebecca as well. So she was to be a fine lady, was she? While he returned to America no better than before? No, he could not bear the thought. It was not for this that he had accompanied his step-sister to England.

There was even room for anger at Templeton, for it was plainly unthinkable that Pierce should blame himself for his current situation. Andrew had a guilty notion that Templeton would not be pleased to learn he had told Ransford of the

Hellfire Club, and he took refuge in defiance. From having been a great gun, a prince of a fellow, the best of companions, Templeton quickly became the source of all Andrew's troubles. He was the one who had been so cowhanded with Rebecca that she fled her stepbrother's house. He was the one who would thrust a spoke in the most brilliant marriage Andrew could have imagined for her. From there it was but a short step to the conclusion that had it not been for Carlisle Templeton, Rebecca might have become eligibly betrothed at any time these past two months. Aye, and on better terms than he now stood with his prospective brother-in-law. Had it not been for Templeton, he'd have gotten a great deal more out of the betrothal than this. That, combined with heavy inroads into a bottle of sherry, shortly after he reached home, served to work Andrew Pierce into a strong sense of injustice.

Templeton, when he called to discover the effect of Andrew's visit to his stepsister, found him in just this mood. "I collect you were unsuccessful in persuading Miss Stanwood to return to your roof?" he said curtly.

Pierce regarded Templeton fixedly, his eyes glittering. "I haven't seen her," he said at last. "I saw Ransford instead, and he's warned me away from her. He means to marry her, you know. He's persuaded his mother and Lady Stanwood to lend her countenance."

"You've bungled it," Templeton said sharply. "Now what are we to do? You were to see your stepsister and persuade her to come back into our hands, not allow Ransford to bamboozle you. Now I, I have taken great care not to be at home when Ransford has called, or to encounter him anywhere where he might be private with me." Templeton paused then considered. He knew Andrew very well and when he spoke it was to say, spitefully, "So your stepsister is to marry Oliver Ransford and lord it over you. How that must make you happy! And you? Are you to be welcomed into the Ransford family as well?"

"Curse you, no," Andrew all but shouted in reply. "I'm

to go back to America, my bills paid but my pockets to let, for Ransford won't pay my gambling debts.''

Templeton smiled thinly. ''And you accepted this decree? My but you've grown tame,'' he marveled.

''I've not gone tame.'' Andrew denied the charge hotly. ''But what else am I to do? You won't pay my bills without Rebecca and we don't have her.''

''Tell me,'' Templeton said softly, ''is she still an innocent?''

A cross look settled on Andrew's face as he replied, ''How the devil should I know?'' Then, more temperately, he added, ''From Ransford's manner, I should think she is.''

''Excellent,'' Templeton said decisively. ''We may yet come about.''

''How?'' Andrew asked suspiciously. ''By telling more fairy tales? You'll catch cold at that with Lady Stanwood and Ransford's mother supporting her.'' A thought occurred to him and he added, ''And don't look to me for help with that. I don't choose to be knocked down again by Ransford's fist. Which is what he says will happen if he finds out I've been traducing her character. Worse, he said he would have me kidnapped and shipped out of the country on the first boat he could find. I don't choose to face that, thank you.''

''No,'' Templeton said with some asperity, ''I am not going to tell more tales. I am going to take action.''

''What sort of action?'' Andrew asked doubtfully.

Templeton eyes Pierce meditatively before he said, ''Give me a moment to think.''

Ignoring Pierce, Lord Templeton spent some time planning his strategy. He might have taken any of a number of courses of action, but the circumstance that the next day would be Sunday had a powerful effect upon him. The more he considered, the more appropriate it seemed to him that Miss Stanwood should form a part of the next meeting of the Hellfire Club, and it seemed a perfect irony if that meeting should take place on Sunday night.

The discovery that Ransford meant to marry Miss Stanwood and that her grandmother had been persuaded to acknowledge her was a severe blow. Templeton did not have to be told that anything he might say against Miss Stanwood would be put down to pique that she preferred Ransford's suit to his own. Soon Miss Stanwood would be out of his power entirely, and Templeton was determined that should not happen. On the other hand, whatever step he took would require care, for Oliver Ransford would make a formidable enemy. If he suspected Templeton of harming his bride-to-be, no power on earth would protect Templeton from him. Either it must look as if Miss Stanwood went with him on her own accord and temperament and Oliver Ransford must be convinced that he was mistaken in the character of his fiancée, or there must appear to be no connection between Templeton and her disappearance whatsoever. Precisely how to accomplish that ticklish goal was the dilemma which occupied Templeton. Briefly he toyed with the notion of abducting her in broad daylight, in an open carriage, and making it look as if he were doing so with her approval, for that would not only accomplish her ruin but ensure Ransford's humiliation as well. And Templeton felt he owed Oliver something for the way he had thrust a remarkably effective spoke in Templeton's plans. The only difficulty with this plan was that Templeton could not imagine any circumstance in which Miss Stanwood would willingly get into a carriage with him.

The other question which excerised Templeton's mind was that of what to do with Andrew Pierce. Templeton had not missed the gleam of resentment in Pierce's eyes. He had clearly been cowed by Ransford and Templeton did not place any dependence upon his continued silence on the subject of the Hellfire Club or certain of Templeton's other activities. Of course, if Pierce had a hand in Miss Stanwood's ruin he would not dare to betray Templeton, for in doing so, he would be betraying himself. Better yet, let Pierce assist in her ruin and then be disposed of. Then Templeton need not worry about any betrayal at all.

Abruptly it occurred to Templeton how he might deal with both Rebecca Stanwood and her stepbrother in one bold step. A little laugh escaped him, then he frowned, considering the scheme from every angle. It was a gamble, of course, but anything he did would be a gamble. This solution, at least, appealed to his sense of humor.

His decision made, Templeton wasted no time. "I shall need your assistance, Andrew," he said briskly. "I have a way to both reclaim your stepsister and have our revenge upon Ransford."

"How?" Pierce asked eagerly.

"I shall need you to write a letter to Miss Stanwood. I will tell you what to write and see that it is delivered into her hand tomorrow morning. With luck, tomorrow night we shall all three be participants at the Hellfire Club in Medmenham," Templeton explained swiftly.

Pierce hesitated for barely a moment before he agreed. To the devil with Ransford's threats! Revenge sounded very sweet.

Sometime later the letter was written and Templeton left the house with it in his breast pocket. He did not even notice the man who shadowed him as he hurried along the street, for he was too deep in thought. There was so much to be done. Messages must be sent and he must change to evening wear. Whatever was to take place tomorrow, he must be seen, tonight, to be following his usual course. If he did not wish to have Miss Stanwood's disappearance laid at his door, he must also set the stage for his own absence from town, beginning tomorrow. There would be those who were shocked, of course, that he meant to travel on a Sunday, but not greatly so. A friend in the country, an invitation to meet a young lady, a hint, a wink, a smile, and the trick was done. He would even, he thought with a grim smile, listen to reports of Ransford's betrothal with patience and few words of good wishes for the couple's future happiness. Why not, when he knew he would win out in the end?

Templeton smiled. This time Miss Stanwood would have

no forewarning and this time he meant to be certain that she did not escape him. He still wore that smile when he spoke with his tiger, giving him instructions that seemed, on the face of it, innocuous. But Templeton's tiger had been with his lordship some time and knew that smile. It portended lively doings that his conscience would disapprove of, however innocent his own orders might appear to be.

But if William recognized the look on Templeton's face, so too did Templeton recognize the look on his diminutive tiger's face, and a generous helping of gold coin passed from his palm to the tiger's hand. "We are going," Templeton said impassively, "to have something of an adventure, William. I trust you have no difficulty with that?"

If William did, he was not about to say so. And, indeed, given what he had already countenanced since taking this extraordinarily lucrative post, it was ludicrous to think that he would actually protest now, whatever the dictates of his easily suppressed conscience. The tiger merely moved closer to the door as he bowed his agreement. Templeton smiled coldly to himself. He had not really expected an answer and was pleased to find his judgment had not been mistaken. The day that it was, William would have to go, his body probably never to be found, and it was the tiger's instinctive understanding of that fact that accounted, at least in part, for his acquiescence now and in the past. It accounted for the virtually instantaneous obedience Templeton received from all those he had hired over the years, for the special tasks his regular servants knew nothing about. Templeton had had a surprisingly low number of failures among his special staff, considering the nature of some of the tasks they had been asked to perform. It did not displease him to know that one reason was the nickname they used among themselves for him: the Devil's son.

Ransford stopped in at the Countess Lieven's rout party later that evening, hoping to see his mother there and, if not, to do what he could to cajole the patroness of Almack's to consider approving Rebecca. He soon found his mother seated on a sofa in one of the salons. Lady Sarah was with Lady Jersey. Ransford greeted both ladies with a bow, and not by the slightest twitch of his lips did he betray his impatience at finding his mother so occupied. For several minutes the three conversed politely and then Lady Jersey rose to her feet. She tapped Oliver on the shoulder, saying playfully, "I shall expect an invitation to dance at your wedding, Ransford!" She turned to Oliver's mother and added kindly, "I shall do what I can, Sarah. I liked what I saw of Miss Stanwood at your party; she seemed a very prettily behaved young girl. And if you and Lady Stanwood vouch for her, then that is all that is wanted from me."

When Lady Jersey was safely gone, Ransford cocked an enquiring eye and asked, "Marshaling your forces, Mother?"

Lady Sarah was amused. "Of course," she replied. "You are not the only one who can do something about the matter. Sally is a foolish woman but no one can deny her influence. And if she and a few others accept Rebecca, the *ton* will follow."

Oliver hastily seated himself beside his mother before anyone else could come along. "How is Rebecca?" he asked quietly. "I do not see her here tonight."

Lady Sarah smiled at an acquaintance and then told her son in mild reproof, "Surely you did not think I should be so brass faced as to bring her to a party to which she had not been invited? Recollect that the countess sent out her invitations before Rebecca came to stay with me."

"True. I beg pardon," he replied with a rueful smile. "How do you find the company tonight? Still inclined to censure you for supporting her?"

"A little," Lady Sarah agreed. "But very few dare say so to my face."

"What did you tell Sally Jersey?" Oliver asked.

"The story we concocted between us. In strictest confidence, of course," Lady Sarah said calmly.

He frowned. "Will it serve? Was she convinced?"

"I think so. She pomised to help. Of course all depends upon Lady Stanwood convincing her daughter Cordelia to support our story. I only wish we had had her reply before being obliged to tell Sally Jersey it was so," Lady Sarah replied worriedly.

"It's a risk," Ransford agreed.

"Yes, and one I would prefer not to have taken," Lady Sarah said briskly, "but recollect that Clarissa was certain Cordelia would agree, and I could not fob off Sally and tell her to wait for an explanation." She saw that Ransford was still frowning and she leaned forward to place a hand on his knee. There was a distinct twinkle in her eyes as she said, "I could see she put you out of countenance by demanding an invitation to your wedding. I hope you are not angry, dearest, that we have had to tell everyone about your betrothal to Rebecca. Sally was delighted with the news, I promise you." She paused and the twinkle went out of her eyes as she added, "The only thing is, Oliver, that if you should decide you don't wish to marry Rebecca, after all, it will be excessively difficult for you to cry off."

Oliver looked at his mother with some amusement. "I do mean to marry her," he replied undaunted. "And not because anyone may say I have compromised her either, Mama. I mean to marry Rebecca because I am very sure I do not want to live without her."

"Famous!" Lady Sarah exclaimed. "I knew it would do you good to fall in love and it has."

Ransford rose to his feet and, looking down at his mother, laughter in his eyes, "Yes, well, I suppose it has. And I have no doubt you will greatly enjoy planning my wedding, but now I must be going. Will you tell Rebecca that I have spoken with her stepbrother, Andrew, and that she had nothing more to fear from him?"

"Of course I shall," Lady Sarah answered at once. "Will you come by tomorrow?"

Ransford's own eyes were dancing as he replied, "I shall escort you to church. How is that, Mama?"

"What a dutiful son you are," Lady Sarah retorted with a laugh, not in the least deceived. "Well, Rebecca and I will both be happy to have your company. And now I shan't keep you any longer. I collect you want to go to one of your horrid clubs or something."

"Or something," he agreed mischievously and was gone.

20

Rebecca sat for a long time at her dressing table staring at the note one of the maids had given her. It was Andrew's handwriting, and when she had received it her first impulse had been to consign it to the fire. But she could not. It was brief and requested that she meet Andrew this morning in Green Park. He said that it was very important that he talk to her about Oliver Ransford. She must, he said, speak with him before she married the man. If she would not come to him, he would come to her, but she might find, he warned, that she would greatly regret his doing so. There was much, he wrote, that she must know but which he dared not put down on paper. There was even an oblique reference to Lord Templeton, Ransford and the Hellfire Club.

As Rebecca read the note, her hand crept up to her mouth, as though to stifle whatever sounds might come out. That Andrew meant to make trouble, she could not doubt. Lady Sarah had told her, last night when she came in, that Oliver had seen Andrew and she was not to worry. Did that mean that Andrew had tried and failed to extract money from him and now meant to try if he could obtain some from her? Or the promise of some, once she were married? That would be like him. It would also be like him if the warning meant that he would make mischief if she did not buy him off. But once begun there would be no end to that, and it was one of the reasons Rebecca was tempted to consign the letter to the fire. Unfortunately, she believed Andrew when he wrote that he would force his way in here if she did not go to meet him, and Rebecca had no wish for him to distress Lady Sarah.

Rebecca read the note again and a second meaning occurred to her. Lord Templeton and the Hellfire Club. Did Andrew write to warn her not of mischief on his part, but about Oliver? Impossible! What had her betrothed to do with either? And yet bits of memory, of how Ransford's staff had talked of Templeton being a frequent visitor to the house, intruded. Was he one of them? Was that what Andrew wanted to tell her? And if he did, would she believe him? Oliver Ransford was too kind and gentle to be a member of the Hellfire Club. And yet Rebecca could not help remembering how kind and generous Templeton had seemed when she had first met him. He, too, had told her to trust him and promised to look after her interests.

Surely this was different, Rebecca tried to tell herself, pacing about the room in agitation. But she had no proof. And if Andrew did indeed have proof that Ransford was a member of the Hellfire Club, then however painful it was to be told, she must know that. If it were true then there could be no question of her marrying him. Nor of staying in Lady Sarah's household. Where she would go, whether to Lady Stanwood or somewhere else, was something Rebecca could only decide after she heard what Andrew had to say. Reluctantly, she decided she must meet Andrew as he asked. After all, what harm could he do her in a public park? It would mean missing church, but if Andrew did indeed have an important warning to give her, it would not do to cavil. Thus, when Lady Sarah appeared at her door to ask if she were ready to leave for church, Rebecca pleaded a headache and said that she would lie down on her bed, instead. Lady Sarah kissed her on the forehead and bade her do so at once, then departed.

As soon as she was gone, Rebecca rose again, dressed quickly, and pulled the small traveling bag out from under the bed. In it was the pistol she had brought from Andrew's house, and she placed it in the pocket of her cloak. Rebecca had not worn the cloak since coming to this house, for it was not as fashionable as the pelisses Lady Sarah had bought for her. But it was the only one with a pocket deep enough to conceal a pistol and she did not intend to go to meet Andrew without some measure of protection.

It was not to be expected that Rebecca would be able to leave the house unseen, and she did not. A startled porter held the door for her and she told him, "I shall be back directly. I have the headache and I thought a walk might help set it to rights."

"Yes, Miss," he replied, unconvinced, but it was no part of his duties to stop her.

Within twenty minutes of brisk walking, Rebecca reached the appointed spot, never having noticed the figure who followed behind her at a safe distance. She was a trifle early and had a few minutes to wait until Andrew appeared. She was surprised to see that he was driving a curricle, but reflected that he might have thought they would be less likely to be overheard driving than if they walked and encountered others strolling through the park for, despite the hour, there were still quite a few people about. He drew to a halt beside her and said, "Quickly! Into my carriage. We must not be seen lingering here!"

Pale but collected, Rebecca stood where she was as she said, "What do you want of me, Andrew?"

"I shall tell you directly," he replied impatiently, "but I do not wish to make a present of what I have to say to the entire park. In my curricle we may be more private."

Rebecca hesitated but then shrugged. What harm, after all, could he do her in an open carriage? She climbed into the curricle and waited as Andrew set the horses going. Neither she nor Andrew noticed the person who stood watching them, muttering to himself. Or the second who just joined the first and conferred with him. A moment later, one of them headed back in the direction of Lady Sarah's townhouse and the other followed Andrew's curricle as best he could. As soon as the edge of the park had been reached, he tried to hire a hackney to follow Pierce's carriage, but found himself at point non plus for there were none about. Still, he consoled himself with the knowledge that he would be able to tell Mr. Ransford that the pair had taken the Bath to Bristol road and the gentleman had appeared to have had a number of trunks strapped on back.

As for Andrew, he seemed to have become afflicted with a severe case of stammering. "It—it is not s-something I c-can easily e-explain. It—it will b-be far easier t-to show you," he said when she once again demanded to know what he had to tell her.

Rebecca was not alarmed though she was wary. "How far must we go for you to show me?" she asked coldly.

"Just t-to the outskirts of L-london,." Andrew replied quickly, "j-just past H-Hounslow Heath." Then, gaining courage he added, "I thought you'd want to know the sort of man you're marrying. Of course, if you do not trust me or don't wish to know, I can leave you off here."

"No, I'll come with you," Rebecca replied steadily, grateful for the pistol in her pocket.

"Good."

Andrew did not speak again for some time, for it took all his skill to control the horses as they drove through the streets of London. When they were clear of the worst of it, Rebecca ventured to say, mildly, "It seems a little odd to have you, of all people, warning me about Mr. Ransford. Why should you care who I marry?"

Andrew flushed. His voice was sullen as he replied, "I know I haven't taken very good care of you since we've come to England. All the more reason I should make a push to warn you now."

"What is there to warn me about?" Rebecca asked, pale but composed. "And why could you not have told me before?"

Pierce hesitated. Then, obedient to his instructions, he said, more sullenly than before, "I didn't know. How was I supposed to know when I've never been to a meeting of the

Hellfire Club? Lord Templeton never mentioned he was a member. But when I spoke with him yesterday, Mr. Ransford told me I need not try, any longer, to coax you into going there. He said he would take you himself, for you had come to trust him, even believe that he meant to marry you.''

For a moment Rebecca felt as though she could neither speak nor breathe. Finally she managed to say, "And you have decided to save me from this fate? How honorable of you!''

Andrew flushed. "Yes, I know I would have taken you there, myself, but I'd have got something out of it. Now, between them, Ransford and Templeton mean to bring you as their prize and I shall get nothing.''

Rebecca placed her hand over her pocket as she said, "And do you mean to take me there yourself? Is this the road to Medmenham?''

It was not yet the road to Medmenham. It was, instead, part of Hounslow Heath and they had reached a deserted portion of the road. Before Andrew could answer, a distant shot rang out and he slumped forward. The horses bolted and it took all of Rebecca's attention and skill to regain control. The sound of hooves pounding the road behind her did not reassure Rebecca, and she could only think that it was the most absurd time for highwaymen to choose to try to hold her up.

But it was not highwaymen. It was a phaeton driven by Lord Templeton with his diminutive tiger standing up behind. He dextrously pulled ahead, then forced her to draw to a halt or risk overturning in the ditch by the side of the road. "My dear Miss Stanwood," Templeton said unctuously, "you appear to have had an accident. William! Go to the horses' heads and hold them while Miss Stanwood climbs down and then up into my carriage.''

"I am not going anywhere with you, Lord Templeton," Rebecca said calmly, though her heart beat wildly in her breast. "My stepbrother has been hurt and I must try to get him to a surgeon.''

"It won't be of the least use," Templeton said kindly. "Either your stepbrother has shot his bolt, or he will very soon. William, check Mr. Pierce."

The tiger let go of Rebecca's team and did as he was bid. A moment later he said darkly, "Aye, dead 'e is, m'lord."

"Then I must take his body to the nearest constable," Rebecca replied resolutely.

Templeton laughed softly. "I think not," he said. "We shall leave the body here to be found as testament to an attack by highwaymen. I repeat, Miss Stanwood, you will come with me."

Rebecca did not move and the tiger took it upon himself to say, a note of desperation in his voice, "Please, Miss, do as 'e says! You won't like it, what will 'appen, if you don't. I won't like what I 'as to do!"

Rebecca looked down at him, never doubting that he meant what he said. Even so, had it not been for the pistol in her pocket, she would have refused. But it was there and while she did not think she could draw it out and fire, at precisely this moment, nevertheless, it was ready for a better opportunity. An opportunity that would not come if she were to be rendered unconscious as she half suspected the tiger was threatening. Therefore, after staring down into his face for some moments, she said, with apparent defeat, "Very well. Since you give me no choice, I shall come with you, Lord Templeton."

"William, holdl her horses!" Templeton said peremptorily.

Templeton held out one hand to help her mount into his phaëton, the other controlling the horses easily. "Hurry," he said. "I should not like another carriage to come along until we are on our way. William?"

The tiger did not waste time in useless answers but let go the horses of the other curricle and scrambled up behind Templeton. A moment later they were bowling down the deserted road with Rebecca huddled into her cloak, hands thrust in her pockets, in apparent dejection. In truth, however, her hand was on her pistol and her mind running rapidly over her choices. She might, of course, draw out the pistol and shoot Templeton at once. But she had no reason to believe his tiger would not extract revenge or, at the very least, continue to convey her to Medmenham, for she had no doubt that that was where they were bound. On the whole, she thought she would be better waiting until they came to a posting house, for she was certain she remembered one on Hounslow Heath from her journey on this road when she and Andrew had first arrived in England. There, she might call for assistance. Before they reached the posting house, however, Templeton had turned northward on the first road that offered. Rebecca steeled herself to wait for a village. The first shot she fired must bring people out of their homes and surely one of them would help her.

Rebecca had not long to wait. She was forewarned by Templeton himself who told her, ''I shouldn't scream, if I were you, as we pass through this village. William can render you unconscious in a flash and I shall simply say you fainted.''

''I shan't scream,'' Rebecca answered grimly, in a low voice.

And she did not. Instead, when they were halfway through the village, without drawing the gun out of her pocket, she pointed it at Lord Templeton and fired. He clutched his side and, for the second time that morning, the horses of the carriage she was riding in bolted. Templeton swayed in his seat but did not fall, though the reins slipped out of his grasp. Rebecca seized them and managed to halt the horses. ''I always thought you had spirit, my dear,'' Templeton managed to murmur. A moment later he slipped from the seat of the phaeton and onto the ground.

Templeton's tiger was instantly out of his post at the back of the carriage and beside his master as Rebecca fought to hold the horses who had taken exception to this new indignity. As soon as she had them under control she said to the tiger, ''Is he dead?''

"Not 'im, not by a long chalk," William answered feelingly, "but I don't doubt 'e'll come along poorly for many a day."

"Good," Rebecca said coolly. "You'd best fetch a doctor for him."

But unexpectedly the tiger replied, "Must we, Miss? Maybe if we waits long enough, 'e will go off."

Rebecca was torn between amusement and impatience. "Yes, but I don't wish to have to stand trial for murder," she retorted.

"I'd be willing to swear as 'ow it was self-defense," the tiger offered.

"I daresay, but—" Rebecca broke off for the sound of her pistol firing had brought half a dozen persons out of the village church. Now they were running toward the carriage and Lord Templeton. "Here, take the reins," she said, thrusting them toward the tiger and starting to climb down.

"Now what's a going on?" the first person to reach them, an older, official-looking sort of fellow demanded.

"This person was trying to abduct me and I shot him," Rebecca answered quietly.

There was a gasp from the people who had reached the scene. The man looked from Rebecca to Templeton and back. It was an incredible notion, and yet Lord Templeton was not unknown along this road. The man rubbed his chin. "We'll have to sort this out later. Best we'd get this man to a doctor first," he said, indicating Templeton. "What about him?" he added, looking at the tiger. "Did he help his lordship try to abduct you?"

The tiger cast such a look of pleading toward Rebecca that she said gravely, "I'm not entirely certain. He is certainly afraid of Lord Templeton."

"P'rhaps we'd best lock 'im up until we're sure," one of the crowd suggested.

Rebecca took pity on the tiger who had a look of terror on his face. "Let me try to discover the truth of the matter. Is there an inn where I might rest a bit and talk to him?"

"Aye, there is and all. This way, if you please," a woman said, bobbing a curtsy to Rebecca.

"Thank you," she told the woman in her soft voice. Then, over her shoulder, Rebecca said to the tiger, "You'd best come with me."

The tiger made haste to obey her. He much misliked the looks on the faces about him, and in any event, he did not want to be around when Lord Templeton regained consciousness and began to demand why his tiger had not defended him or taken revenge. If he'd known she didn't mean to shoot to kill, he might have done so. But how could he have guessed that a female intrepid enough to sport a pistol would be too squeamish to make the matter final? And by the time he had realized it, there were too many people about and it would have been too risky. Nevertheless, now his future appeared dependent, to some degree at any rate, upon her good will and he was not about to throw it away, so he hurried to keep up with her. When they were in the private parlor Rebecca had requested, the tiger said, "Why'd you go and shoot 'im 'ere?"

Rebecca answered promptly, "Because I wasn't certain if you would be a problem, and if you were, I didn't think you'd let me reload my pistol. This way, whatever your inclination, people would hear and come running." She paused, then asked, "Why did you want Lord Templeton to die?"

"Because if 'e lives, 'e'll like as not blame me for letting you shoot 'im," the tiger grumbled. "Asides, I don't want to work for 'im no more."

"Then why don't you simply leave his employment?" Rebecca asked, puzzled.

"It's plain you don't know Lord Templeton," the tiger retorted. "There's them as knows nothing and them as knows too much of 'is lordship's business, and they ain't allowed to quit. The last fellow 'oo tried weren't never seen again."

"I see," Rebecca said, and thought she did. "What will you do when Lord Templeton recovers?"

"I don't know," the tiger said honestly. "Maybe go to America. I can't stay in Lunnon. Unless," he added hopefully, "I could come work for you?"

"I wish you could," Rebecca replied, "but I haven't any money. I'm dependent upon the kindness of Mr. Ransford and his mother, Lady Sarah."

The tiger nodded gloomily. It was, he reflected, just his sort of luck to be in this position. Silently he debated the relative merits of running away and hiding somewhere versus going to Lord Templeton's side and pretending he had never considered doing otherwise. When he awoke, his lordship would be in a foul temper, but he had weathered such bouts before.

Rebecca interrupted his thoughts, however, to demand his opinion as to whether he thought it permissible to take Templeton's rig back to town or whether she ought to try to hire a post chaise by promising that the charges would be paid when she reached Lady Sarah's house. Assuming the constable allowed her to leave town. The tiger gave it as his opinion that she would be very unlikely to find anyone willing to hire her a carriage under those circumstances, and yet he was not willing to advise her to use his master's rig. Not, leastwise, before he figured out where he would disappear to if she did.

As they stood discussing the matter, a carriage driven at a spanking pace could be heard bowling down the main street of the village. It pulled up outside the inn and someone could be heard asking questions. A few minutes later, footsteps were heard outside the private parlor, the door was flung open, and Oliver Ransford stood there, staring at Rebecca and the tiger.

21

Lady Sarah and her son returned from church to discover two unsavory looking fellows on the doorstep, one of them patently out of breath. Far from being angry, however, Oliver took a step toward them and said, "Quick man, what is it?"

"It's the young lady, sir. She got in a carriage with a young gentleman, with luggage strapped on the back. By the time I knew what she meant to do, I couldn't stop her, sir."

"It was the gentleman you set me to watch," the second fellow said, trying to catch his breath. "I tried to follow but couldn't. They looked to be taking the Bath road, p'rhaps as far as Bristol. Leastwise, that's what I heard the gentleman tell his porter he was to say, if anyone asked."

"Bristol?" Lady Sarah exclaimed in disbelief. "Why would Rebecca be going there? And who is this gentleman you keep talking about?"

"Rebecca's stepbrother," Oliver answered curtly. "I was afraid he might try to cause trouble and it seems I was right." Then, to the man he said, "When did they meet?"

"No more than half an hour ago," the first fellow said.

"Good." Ransford turned to the second man and said, "You know where my stables are. Go round there and tell them I shall want my curricle and grays, at once. Have them brought here."

"Yes, sir."

When he was gone, Lady Sarah said to her son, bewildered, "But why would Rebecca go to meet her stepbrother? I don't understand why she would trust him."

"Neither do I," Oliver said brusquely. "Perhaps you'd better go inside and discover if anyone delivered a message to her this morning or last night. I shall wait outside, for I mean to be off as soon as my carriage arrives."

"Yes, of course," Lady Sarah said with quick sympathy.

Ransford did not have long to wait before a third husky character arrived. "Guv'nor!" he said, as out of breath as the earlier fellow. "I went to your house, sir, and they sent me here. I was watching his lordship's house, like you told me, and I saw him come out and get in his carriage. He told his porter to tell callers he was away in the country. But I heard him say that if there was an emergency, the man was to send to him in Medmenham."

The word acted with powerful effect upon Ransford, who straightened and said swiftly, "I shall need both of you to carry a number of messages for me. They shall need to be delivered at once and it is imperative that you not fail me."

Since both men had been more than once the recipient of considerable largess from Oliver Ransford, neither hesitated to assure him they would carry out his wishes without delay.

"Good," he said curtly. "Wait here while I write out the messages you are to deliver."

Ransford went inside and was shown to his mother's writing desk where he quickly scrawled a number of brief messages and wrote their direction on the outside. That is where Lady Sarah found him. "Oliver," she said, "I have found this on Rebecca's dressing table."

Ransford set down his pen and took the note she held out to him, reading it at a glance. "So that is how her stepbrother drew her there," he said derisively. "I might have guessed."

"What will you do?" Lady Sarah demanded. "Has Rebecca decided to leave England with him? Have they gone to Bristol to find a ship?"

Oliver had turned back to address the last of the messages he had written and now he gave a slight, sharp laugh. "No, Mother, they are not gone to Bristol, though I have no doubt that is what I am meant to believe. Another of my men, however, has discovered that Templeton is on his way to Medmenham.''

"Medmenham?" Lady Sarah echoed, more bewildered than before. "But what is at Medmenham? And what has Templeton to do with Rebecca driving off with her step-brother to Bristol?''

"That, I fancy, is a move to throw dust in my eyes,'' Oliver replied dryly. "I should very much doubt they are going there. I have more reason to believe Andrew Pierce means to take Rebecca to Medmenham where he and Templeton will make a present of her to the Hellfire Club.''

"The Hellfire Club?" Lady Sarah said blankly. "But Oliver, the Hellfire Club was disbanded more than fifty years ago!''

"So it was,'' he agreed soberly. "But it appears that certain gentlemen, Templeton among them, have revived the tradition.''

"Good Lord!'' Lady Sarah exclaimed. "Oliver, you must stop them, but how? There will be too many of them at Medmenham for you to deal with yourself.''

"Oh, I mean to overtake Pierce long before he reaches Medmenham,'' Oliver replied, a muscle twitching in his cheek. "I am driving my grays, you know. And I shall take one of those men you saw with me. All of them have fought in the ring. Furthermore, these messages I have just written will bring me reinforcements. One is for Bow Street and the others will go to certain gentlemen I know who will be bound to help. Recollect, Mother, that there are families who have good cause to remember and hate the Hellfire Club and wish to help see it destroyed.''

So grim was his expression that Lady Sarah laid a hand on his arm and said, "You will be careful, Oliver, won't you?''

He placed a hand over hers and smiled at her reassuringly. "Be sure that I shall,'' he said. "And I shall bring Rebecca back to you safe, by tonight, however late that might be.

But now I must be on my way. My carriage ought to be here by now.''

Ransford was right. When he reached the front door, he found a groom walking his grays in front of the house and his three hired men waiting as well. Swiftly Oliver gave the notes he had written to two of the men. ''Deliver them as quickly as you are able,'' he said. ''And make sure the first is the one to the Runners in Bow Street. They will be expecting it. You, Hawkins,'' he said to the third man, ''are to come with me.''

Five minutes later, Ransford was bowling down the street toward the Bath road, the powerfully built fellow beside him. Once they were out of the city, they had the road all to themselves for it was Sunday and there were very few carriages about. Hawkins clung to his seat for dear life, for it seemed that a madness had possessed Ransford. He urged his cattle to a shocking pace and the curricle swayed with every jolt in the road. Nor did Ransford check until they were already on Hounslow Heath and they saw a curricle at the side of the road. Then, with a haste that nearly threw Hawkins from his seat, Ransford halted the horses and curtly told Hawkins to hold them. He sprang down without looking to see if he was obeyed and strode to the abandoned curricle. Hawkins recognized it at once and the unmoving person in it. He ought to, after having tried to follow both earlier this morning.

As Hawkins watched, Ransford checked Pierce's body for signs of life. He grimly noted the luggage strapped to the back of the curricle as well. ''Pierce is dead,'' Oliver said curtly. ''But where the devil is Miss Stanwood?''

''P'rhaps she got down and walked?'' Hawkins suggested doubtfully.

''That or she was taken up in another carriage,'' Oliver agreed.

''P'rhaps she's on her way back into town,'' Hawkins suggested hopefully.

Ransford shook his head decisively. ''No, we passed no carriages going the other way nor did we pass Miss Stanwood. And if she were walking, I should think that is the direction she would have taken.''

Hawkins could find no reason to disagree. "Where should we be looking for her, then?" he asked. "Further along this road?''

"No," Oliver said, climbing back into his curricle and taking the reins from Hawkins. "We'll go to Medmenham by the first road north that we come to. Whatever route Lord Templeton or his henchmen have taken, that is their destination. I mean to be there either hard on his heels or before him.''

Hawkins made no dispute, and within moments they were again traveling at breakneck speed, checking only to turn onto the first road north, as Ransford had promised. They were still traveling at this speed, though the horses were beginning to labor, when they reached the first village. Hawkins begged Ransford to slow, saying, "If you don't, sir, there's no telling who you might run over.''

Ransford laughed queerly, but he did so. A moment later he was grateful, for he spied a phaeton abandoned at the side of the road. It, too, had luggage strapped to the back and a pool of blood stained the dirt road beside it. Instantly he pulled up and tossed a coin to one of the children gaping at him. "Hold my horses, will you?" he asked briskly.

The awed child nodded and Ransford turned to another and asked, "Who was in this carriage and where are they now?''

One of the girls managed to find her voice to say, "In the inn, sir. A lord and a young lady and a—a tiger!''

In spite of himself, Ransford laughed at the awe in her voice, but his own was strained as he asked. "Who was hurt?''

"The gentleman, sir," the same girl answered.

Ransford's expression lightened perceptibly and he started toward the inn. Over his shoulder he said, "Come along, Hawkins. I may need you.''

"Coming, sir.''

At the doorway of the inn, Ransford checked at the sight of a great number of people just inside. Many of them began to speak at once, wanting to tell him what had occurred. Ransford's voice cut through them as he said, loudly but gently, "Yes, yes, I shall help you sort it out in due time. For the moment, I wish to see the young lady."

The innkeeper bowed and offered to show Ransford to the private parlor where the young lady and the gentleman's tiger were closeted. Ransford agreed. To Hawkins he said, "Wait here for me."

"Yes, sir," Hawkins replied, but he misdoubted that his employer even heard him.

Ransford hesitated at the door of the parlor, and then wrenched it open to find Rebecca and Templeton's tiger staring at the doorway.

Very pale, Ransford came several steps into the room and demanded, ignoring the tiger, "Are you all right, my love?"

Rebecca came forward into his arms as though it were the most natural thing in the world and, at the moment, it was. "Perfectly all right," she said, lifting her face to his. "But I've shot Lord Templeton."

That startled Ransford so much that he almost let go of her. "Shot him?" he asked blankly.

"Yes, sir, but not fatally," the tiger hastened to explain. Then, with a touch of contempt to his voice, he added, "I doubt me she 'ad the stomach for that!"

That surprised Ransford into a laugh. "Yes, well, perhaps. But I'll admit I'd rather it wasn't such a serious matter. Where is Templeton?"

"Some of the villagers took him to the doctor," Rebecca said. "One of them is to come and let me know how he goes on."

"I shall check for myself, presently," Ransford assured her.

"Er, guv'nor, you wouldn't be wanting a tiger, would you?" Lord Templeton's tiger interrupted to ask.

"I would not," Ransford said, his voice tinged with amusement.

"Of course not," the tiger said gloomily. "It'll 'ave to be America, after all."

"America?" Ransford asked, quirking an eyebrow at Rebecca.

"He's afraid that Lord Templeton will be angry with him for not stopping me from shooting him, and he's afraid to simply quit his post," Rebecca explained.

"You needn't worry," Ransford assured the tiger grimly. "Lord Templeton will have too much on his mind to worry about you. Indeed, if he isn't clapped up into prison over today's work, I expect he'll be taking a sudden trip to the continent when he recovers."

"With things as unsettled there as they are?" Rebecca asked doubtfully.

"I think Templeton will discover things are even more unsettled here," Ransford told her. "By tomorrow I expect a Bow Street Runner will be here to ask him questions about the Hellfire Club and certain persons who have disappeared."

At these words, the tiger, who had begun to look upon Rebecca as his benefactress, now changed his mind and began edging toward the door. Ransford stopped him with the stern admonition, "I shouldn't run away, if I were you. The Bow Street Runner will also be wishing to speak with Lord Templeton's servants and former servants who might be able to shed light on matters."

"How do you know?" Rebecca asked earnestly.

"Because I have reason to believe that by now a number of sturdy fellows are on their way to Medmenham where they mean to catch the Hellfire Club in session tonight. Two Bow Street Runners should be with them."

"But how do you know the Hellfire Club will meet tonight?" Rebecca asked, bewildered.

"Your stepbrother, Andrew, and Lord Templeton made a valiant attempt to hoax me into believing that you meant to leave England. I suspect that tonight a vessel will sail from Bristol and were I to ask, I would be told you were on it. But I have had men watching them, for I was afraid they might try something of the sort, and I know enough to believe

you were meant to be taken to Medmenham tonight,''
Ransford explained dryly.

At the reminder of her stepbrother, Rebecca buried her
face against Ransford's chest. "Oh, Oliver," she said.
"Andrew's dead!"

"Yes, I know," Ransford said grimly. "I passed his
curricle on the road and stopped to see if he were still alive.
Did you shoot him as well as Templeton?"

"No." Rebecca looked up at him now and explained, "At
the time, I thought it was highwaymen. But then Lord
Templeton and his tiger came up beside me and Lord
Templeton forced me to mount into his carriage and
accompany him."

Ransford's arm tightened around Rebecca. A moment later
he said gently, "I read the letter Andrew sent you, my love,
but I still don't understand why you were in his curricle."

That caused Rebecca to hesitate. After a moment she
replied, "Andrew threatened to make trouble and I knew
that he meant to do so. And I had to find out what he meant
about you and Lord Templeton and the Hellfire Club. I did
not see what harm he could do me in an open curricle.
Particularly since I had brought my pistol with me."

"Your pistol?" Ransford said with some surprise. "What
do you mean, your pistol? I realize you must have gotten
hold of one to shoot Templeton with, but—" He broke off
in confusion.

"I bought it when I first realized the sort of company
Andrew meant to invite to the house he had hired," Rebecca
explained quietly. "And I took it with me when I left his
house and became a servant in yours. It seemed a good idea
to bring it with me this morning, as well."

"You were right, of course," Oliver agreed. Then, returning to the rest of what she had said, he asked sternly, "But
what did you mean about needing to see Andrew because
he linked my name with the Hellfire Club? Did you think
I was part of that abomination?"

Ransford's voice frightened her, but Rebecca met his eyes

steadily as she replied, "I thought that you might be." His eyes narrowed in anger and she went on in her quiet way. "You see, when I first met Lord Templeton I liked him. And while Andrew and I have never been close, I thought we had been friends. Until we came to England. I have not felt I could trust my own judgment for some time now. It didn't seem possible that you were one of them, but what if I were wrong? You were friends with Lord Templeton."

"I see. And do you still think I may be a member of the Hellfire Club?" Ransford asked coolly.

Before Rebecca could answer, the tiger spoke. His voice was scornful as he said, "Of course, 'e ain't!"

Ransford's voice was amused as he asked, "And how do you know that?"

"Setting aside as 'ow I knows every gent as shows up at the meetings," the tiger explained confidentially, "you ain't wearing the sign."

"The sign?" Ransford echoed, considerably startled.

"It's a little pin, it is, with a devil's 'ead and rubies for eyes." The tiger described the object with relish. "Not so big as you'd be likely to notice it, particular, unless you was looking for it."

"Good God!" Ransford said blankly. "Then the Earl of Andover—"

Before Rebecca could ask what he meant, there was a rap at the parlor door and Ransford moved to open it. The innkeeper stood there, an anxious look about his face. "Sir, ma'am, the gentleman what was wounded, he's asking for the lady."

"We'll both come," Ransford said at once. "And you'd better wait here," he warned the tiger.

"Oh, I shall, guv'nor, I shall," William replied fervently.

"See that you do," Ransford told him sternly. Then, more gently he added, "I shall make certain the Bow Street Runners know how helpful you've been." To the innkeeper he added, "Tell my man Hawkins to come in here and guard him."

The tiger did not look altogether gratified by this piece of information, but since he did not doubt that if he did slip out, this gentleman would pursue him and lay him by the heels, he settled into a chair to wait.

Rebecca and Ransford followed the innkeeper up the stairs and into the room where Lord Templeton was being attended to by the village's doctor. The surgeon looked up as they entered and continued to put away his things as he told them briskly, "You may have ten minutes, no more. His lordship's wound is a serious one though not, I am certain, fatal. Did I not think it would be more dangerous to thwart his lordship than to grant this wish of his to speak with you, I would bar you from the room altogether."

Ransford nodded. "We shan't stay any longer than necessary," he promised.

"Good," the doctor said approvingly. Then he turned to Templeton and said curtly, "You'll do, but not if you exert yourself. I'll send someone to come look after you until you recover."

Templeton hurled a curse at the doctor's departing head, shocking the innkeeper's wife. At her gasp, he turned to her and said, with some asperity, "I'll thank you to wait outside until we're done."

"But what if she—" the woman broke off in confusion.

Templeton looked sardonically at Rebecca then said, "Miss Stanwood has no need to harm me further, or so I think."

"I do not," Rebecca agreed.

Reluctantly the woman left the room and Templeton turned his painful gaze on Ransford. "So you're here as well," he said in an aggrieved voice. "How did you find us?"

"It was not difficult," Ransford told him. "I only needed to follow the road to Bath until I found Pierce's curricle and then take the first road north toward Medmenham." He paused then added quietly, "Was it really so needful to resurrect the Hellfire Club, Templeton?"

Templeton would have risen but his wound would not allow him to do so. Instead he cursed and said, "So you know about that! I never meant you to know. You were supposed to think that Andrew persuaded her to take a ship back to America.''

''Was it necessary to kill Pierce?'' Oliver countered quietly.

''You'll never prove that one,'' Templeton sneered. ''My tiger will swear I never fired a shot. And I didn't.''

''No, but I'll vow you gave the orders,'' Oliver replied coolly. ''Why?''

Templeton leaned back against the pillows and it was a moment before he could speak. ''I thought he was growing unreliable. He was drinking too much, gambling too much, and I didn't trust what he might do.''

''It was a risk,'' Oliver pointed out dryly. ''Your man might have missed. Or perhaps even hit Miss Stanwood by mistake.''

Templeton smiled weakly. ''One has to gamble sometimes,'' he said. ''And I choose my tools well. And my day. On a Sunday morning I knew I might find the road all but deserted.'' He paused, then added reluctantly, ''What will you do about the Hellfire Club, Oliver?''

''The Bow Street Runners will be in Medmenham by evening, along with a number of gentlemen who will be delighted to lend their hands to ending your club. When I leave this room I'll give orders to hide your rig so that it won't give anyone warning who comes along this road. I should think England will be an uncomfortable place, for some time to come, for anyone connected with the Hellfire Club.''

''And what happens to me?'' Templeton demanded. ''Do I leave England as well, or am I to be brought up on charges?''

''There was a time when I thought you would be allowed to leave England,'' Oliver said, his face grim. ''But after today I can only tell you that it must depend on what is found in Medmenham.''

Templeton turned his head away from them. When it became clear that he would not speak to them again, Ransford led Rebecca out of the room. They had not gone far when a shot rang out. Oliver spun around and ran back into the room to discover Templeton with a smoking pistol in his hand and half his head blown away.

The doctor reached the room in the same moment. Appalled at the sight before him, he said to Ransford, "I had no notion! He asked to be allowed to keep his pistol in case the young lady attacked him again. There seemed no reason to refuse since it could always be taken from him when he slept, if need be, and it seemed to ease his mind. I had no notion he would kill himself. What did you say to him?"

This last question was spoken sternly and Ransford replied in kind. "I told him that his sins in resurrecting the Hellfire Club had come home to haunt him. And he chose this way out."

Still clucking, the doctor chased Ransford from the room and Oliver went to join Rebecca in the passageway.

22

Oliver and Rebecca went quietly down the stairs and into the private parlor once again. "Hawkins," Ransford said curtly, "take Lord Templeton's tiger into the coffee room. Then go out and hide his rig. I don't want anyone traveling along this road to tonight's meeting of the Hellfire Club to know what has occurred here today."

"Yes, sir." Then, a trifle doubtfully Hawkins said, "Was that a gunshot I heard, sir?"

"Yes, Lord Templeton has shot himself and this time he is dead," Oliver replied quietly.

Far from showing any signs of grief, the tiger gave a pronounced sigh of relief and went with Hawkins out of the room. When they were gone, Rebecca asked, "What will become of Lord Templeton's tiger?"

"I suspect the tiger will manage well enough, for himself," Oliver said dryly. "There is nothing to trouble you anymore," he added gently.

Rebecca smiled but shook her head. "You are forgetting the mischief Lord Templeton has already done. All the gossip."

Now it was Ransford's turn to smile. "Mama and Lady Stanwood will, between them, turn you into a heroine. I quite expect to find that the *ton* will try hard to make amends for its shabby treatment of you the other night. I predict that even the Harcourts will dance at our wedding. Sally Jersey has already told me she expects an invitation to do so."

Abruptly Rebecca stepped away from him, her eyebrows

drawn into a frown. "Are you quite certain you wish to marry me?" she asked doubtfully.

Ransford drew Rebecca into his arms again. He smiled down at her quizzically and said, "I thought we had settled all that two nights ago. But if you need further reassurance then let me tell you that yes, my sweet goose, I am quite certain I wish to marry you. Nor can you delude me into thinking you are entirely indifferent to me."

Rebecca could not bring herself to look at him but instead fixed her gaze on the top button of his coat. "N-not entirely," she agreed.

"Wretch!" he said with fond exasperation. When she still did not look up at him, Oliver tilted up her chin so that she was forced to do so, but his voice was kindly as he asked, "If you are not entirely indifferent to me, then what is the trouble, my love?"

Treacherously a tear welled up in each eye and Rebecca tried to blink them away as she said, "What if your mother and Lady Stanwood can't retrieve my reputation?"

"Is that all that's troubling you, my love?" Ransford asked gently, his eyes beginning to dance. "If so, then I must tell you that in that event, it is even more imperative that you marry me."

"Why?" Rebecca asked suspiciously.

He grinned down at her as he replied. "Because otherwise I can see no way to retrieve my own reputation. Having ruined me, you must marry me to make amends. Surely you can see that? Besides, you've already agreed."

Rebecca's own eyes began to sparkle now as she countered, "But you told me I might cry off if I changed my mind later."

"That was before I saw how pronounced would be the effect of our betrothal," he said. "You could not cry off now without creating the scandal all anew."

"Ah, but I might run away back to America and leave you to face the music alone," she pointed out primly.

Oliver's arm tightened about her waist as he said, anxiously, "You would not go, would you?" Rebecca did not at once answer and he dropped the bantering tone from his voice as he said, seriously, "My love, I do not think I could bear it if you ran away and I lost you."

Rebecca lifted a hand and gently stroked his cheek as she answered softly, "No, I shan't run away from you." She hesitated, then made herself go on. "The other night, when you said you would marry me, I thought it was only because of circumstances. Sometimes I'm still afraid that is so."

Ransford caught the hand against his cheek with his own free one and kissed it. Then he kissed her full upon the mouth, and Rebecca discovered that there was nothing the least proper or detached about his embrace. He was as lover-like as any girl could wish, and far more so than any mother or chaperone would approve. When, some time later, her bonnet had been set upon the table and she was seated on his lap in a chair by the window, Ransford told her severely, "Now you must marry me, my love, or I shall think you the most shocking flirt imaginable. Will you marry me, Rebecca, with no more goosish objections or put offs?"

With a tiny sigh of contentment, Rebecca nestled her cheek against his shoulder and said, "Yes, my love, I will."